THE DREAMS OF DEHME

THE THIRD BOOK OF LOST CARCOSA

JOSEPH SALE

Copyright © 2024 by Joseph Sale

First Edition

All rights reserved

ISBN: 978-1-940250-66-3

Cover Art by Mushfiq A.K.

Interior Layout by Lori Michelle
www.TheAuthorsAlley.com

Printed in the United States of America

Visit us on the web at:
www.bloodboundbooks.net
https://www.bloodgutsandstory.com/

"For the dusk-rayed edge of Sleep is the border of Thy lidded orb
And the Night-without-End is the Field of Thy Secret Pleasure."
—*The Dragon Book of Essex,* Andrew D. Chumbley

"To realize that all your life—you know, all your love, all your
hate, all your memories, all your pain—it was all the same thing.
It was all the same dream, a dream that you had inside a locked
room, a dream about being a person."
—*True Detective,* Nic Pizzolatto

PROLOGUE

THE PAST IS a treacherous kingdom. Its ways sprawl labyrinthine beyond the doorway of the mind's eye. Many get lost in this kingdom. Some never return. Alan Chambers knew this, but still could not stop himself from opening the door upon a memory he'd almost forgotten, one that returned to him as though upon the singing winds of the desert.

Fourteen-year-old Alan sat in the back of a taxi, drunk and trying not to show it. He had a good hour-long journey in which to sober up before his parents questioned him on every microscopic detail of the party. The smell of weed clung to his clothes, though he hadn't partaken. It wasn't that he morally objected, simply that its promises seemed so sundry next to the exotic visions of his imagination. Alcohol, on the other hand, was attractive because it numbed and quieted said overactive imagination, which at times bubbled up so strongly within him he felt he might explode—in all senses of the word.

The party had been so-so. His friends always promised so much. Alan's mind would be filled with fantastical dreams of social ascension and euphoric release in the build up, but in actuality the parties were often awkward, sometimes a little dreary, and only seemed to emphasise his loneliness rather than dissipate it. Perhaps that was just him? He'd always known he was a weirdo. Maybe he should give up the whole social thing altogether? Become a hermit in a far off land . . .

It didn't help his social standing that his mother *insisted* on ordering him a damn taxi back at eleven o'clock, when everyone else was crashing. It both exiled him from the intimate boy-talk conversations that inevitably occurred just before bed and made him seem like a posh twat. His parents were richer perhaps than the average family in Alan's school, but not outrageously so.

1

THE DREAMS OF DEMHE

Forking out for a taxi every time Alan went out however made them seem like the very embodiment of the out-of-touch moneyed elite.

Perhaps *because* Alan was slightly wasted, he couldn't help but fixate on some of the odd details of the taxi and its driver. The car was ancient, hailing from the '70s at least. The driver was a gruff-looking man. Not exactly scary, but not pleasant either. It seemed most of him was draped in shadow, as though the darkness embraced him for comfort from the light. Even when they passed streetlights, the shadows remained. They churned and turned and warped, but they never left him. Thus, only a few odd details ever really jumped out: a bristly chin, suggesting he hadn't shaved in some time; black sunglasses that made his eyes a mystery; and large, spidery hands that scuttled across the steering wheel with light dexterity. They were the kind of hands Alan expected to belong to a pianist.

The driver sensed Alan's inspection, and his dark sunglasses turned towards the rearview. A grin of pearlescent teeth ruptured the darkness.

"Mind if I smoke, kid?"

"Be my guest."

Alan was never one to come between someone and their pleasure.

The driver took one hand off the wheel, fished in his jacket for the packet, and brought it to his lips. He bit down on a cigarette and pulled. He returned the packet to his inner pocket. Next, he fished out a lighter. A beautiful silver thing, its engravings impenetrably intricate—or perhaps Alan was just too drunk to work it out. A little flame cast momentary relief on the driver's features: dark, leathern, the face of a man who'd endured blistering sunlight, and perhaps harsh cold too. Still no eyes behind the dark shades. The cigarette began to emit smoke like an ireful dragon. He wound down the driver-side window, and the smoke coiled out. Even so, the smell was pungent and thick in the cloister of the car. Alan quite liked it. Tobacco had a strangely uplifting aroma; the bitterness pricked the senses into life.

"Thanks," the driver said.

"No problem, Mr . . . " Alan looked for a name-tag. The driver's license pinned to the dashboard was partially obscured in shadow, but Alan could make out the first two letters of his name: UB. *Ub,*

Alan thought to himself, stifling a laugh. *That's the kind of name that would feature in an '80s fantasy flick. A goblin or ghoul.*

"Something funny?"

"No." Alan forced his expression into one of sobriety.

"Yeah it is. But it's okay. You don't have to tell me. I believe everyone should be allowed their own secret world."

There was a pregnant pause after this, as though the driver were gauging Alan's reaction. The boy's curiosity was certainly piqued. Imagination was something of a taboo topic in his home. Partly because Alan tended to want to enact the fantasies in his head, not merely content to let them play out in his mind.

"What do you mean?"

The driver puffed on his cigarette. Reflections of fire played in the dark lenses of his glasses. Why would anyone wear sunglasses at night? Alan's mother said people who wore sunglasses all the time were usually drinkers or druggies, hiding their drooping eyelids. Alan, however, thought it far more exciting to imagine his taxi-driver was a vampire, sensitive to light.

"The mind is a secret palace. We can choose to fill it with wonders. Or we can choose to fill it with horrors. We can try to control the inhabitants of the palace, like a tyrannical king, in which case things get very miserable indeed. Or we can let the freaks play where they will. Everyone is entitled to their palace, their way. Though of course there are consequences."

"Consequences?"

"A great woman once wrote, 'Unbridled license leads to degradation; but unbridled idealism leads to psychopathology.' You'd do well to remember that, kid. Balance is everything."

"I'm all out of balance . . . " Alan muttered. He hadn't meant to be confessional, or to sound so mopey, but the truth of it left his lips like a bird eager to escape its cage—before he could seal the gilded door.

"You're having a hard time adjusting is all." The driver spoke like he knew Alan, and that raised the hackles at the back of Alan's neck, made his heart hammer in his chest. He was wary now. He knew there were men—and sometimes women, too, but it was most often men—who preyed upon children. Alan was fourteen, a teenager not a boy, but he knew he wouldn't stand a chance against a fully grown adult, especially one like the driver, who looked so solid as to have been sculpted from the hardened enamel of the earth's deepest core.

THE DREAMS OF DEMHE

"I didn't mean to alarm you, kid, but I've got a bit of a sense about me. I can feel when people are different. When they're going through something. You strike me as the kind of kid who's felt like an outsider his whole life."

"Can we talk about something else?"

"Fair enough." The driver lapsed into silence and, no sooner than he stopped talking, Alan wished he would start again. He had never felt understood, and here he was, for the first time talking with someone who seemed to know his struggle, and he'd told them to be quiet. Alan lacked the courage to start up the conversation again, however, so instead he looked outside at the world streaming by.

Residential houses, each a redbrick copy of its neighbour, rushed past in a crimson blur. As they slowed due to late night traffic, no doubt many other souls wending their way back from parties like Alan, he saw a group of kids in grey hoodies on the pavement. They were throwing eggs against the windows of a house, shouting and screaming. The eggs made a resounding *thud* as they struck the glass and shattered, so loud it could be heard over the sound of the taxi's engines and the groan of car-wheels on tarmac. The eggs left smeared yellow yokes in their wake, like melting citrine eyes.

But Alan was more fascinated by the scattered eggshell. Some clung to the exploded yokes. Some lay at the foot of the house. These little pieces resembled fine china or pottery, something infinitely precious shattered. And he found something within himself rearing like a serpent. A vague image—or perhaps it was a memory—of a cave, dark and glittering and deep. There was eggshell all over the floor, but the pieces were huge pink-white slabs, as though an urn the size of Alan's head had been cracked open, and he was crawling through those massive pieces of shell.

Weird, even for your imagination, Alan thought. He shivered and shook off the vision. The taxi soon sped up and they left the egging kids behind. Alan was glad. The memories—or dreams—or whatever they were of the cave had unsettled him. It had felt momentarily so real, as though the taxi drive were just a videogame, a simulation, and he had temporarily been yanked back into sensate reality. The cave's shiny crystalline walls had been so perfectly clear in his mind's eye. He could feel the porcelain texture of the giant shell beneath his inquisitive hands.

"You ever wondered what came first . . . the chicken or the egg?"

Alan looked up sharply. Using the rearview mirror, he searched the taxi driver's face for some hint of dark humour. But there was none. *Was he reading my thoughts?* Alan believed in pretty much everything supernatural: telepathy, telekinesis, psychic phenomenon. He'd yet to evidence-base his findings, but he was sure there had been a few unexplainable instances in his life. *Relax, he simply saw the kids too, and his brain followed a train of thought, like yours.* Maybe that was true. Strangely, Alan wanted to believe it wasn't.

"Well I guess it depends."

"On what?"

"If you're a creationist or not."

The taxi driver roared with laughter, so much so that his cigarette flew from his mouth. He scooped it out of his lap and hurled it out of the window. In a few seconds, he'd replaced it with another.

"Something funny?" Alan parroted.

The taxi driver's manic hilarity subsided in an instant.

"Oh? So he gives as good as he gets, does he? Interesting. Well, you certainly strike to the heart of things, kid. Am I a creationist? Well, I'd have to say I am. All things come into existence as a result of intelligence. This universe is probably no different." The driver flexed his fingers. Alan knew it was some kind of tic, an unconscious habit connected to familiar runnels of thought. Something clicked.

"You're an artist."

The driver showed his pearl-white teeth again.

"My, you are sharp. A chip off the old block."

Alan frowned.

"You know my dad?"

"Depends what you mean by your dad."

Alan felt cold again. He shivered. The driver interpreted the gesture literally and wound his window up. The car began to fill with grey, bitter-smelling smog.

"What're you saying?"

"What do you think I'm saying?"

"You're . . . I don't know . . . you're making weird comments about my dad."

"I did no such thing. I just said, 'Depends what you mean by your dad'."

Alan gritted his teeth.

"You're trying to say my dad's not my dad. Why the fuck would you do that, man?"

Alan rarely swore—he was introverted by nature, and his obsessions rarely led him to anger, only to absorption—but this guy was asking for it.

The taxi driver's stupid fucking grin remained plastered across his shadowy face. Alan had never felt a stronger desire to knock someone's teeth out.

"Relax, kid. I'm only messing with you. Although, to be fair, if you're getting so hot under the collar, it probably means you've thought about it before, right? Something not quite adding up . . . Something disjointed . . . "

"Shut up." Alan hated how weak he sounded, but the taxi driver hit a nerve. He *had* thought he might be adopted. He looked nothing like his mother, who was the quintessential pale English Rose, nor like his father, who was a black-haired gallant; Alan was short where his father was tall, brown-haired where his mother and father were blonde and black, brown-eyed where they were blue, angular where they were soft, dark skinned where they were fair, just about different in every conceivable way.

"Don't worry about it, kid," the taxi-driver said, as though they had been discussing something no more personal than passing one's driving test. "All things are revealed in the fullness of time. Nothing can remain secret, nor static. The nature of the universe is ever-changing, transformative, and knowing the patterns of that transformation is the essence of magic."

Alan's heart thudded in his chest, his breathing shallowed. *Magic!* Now there was a word he loved and didn't hear nearly often enough. His peers thought of magic as silly playground tricks, and his parents laughed at it. But Alan believed and longed to discover the real thing. And if ever he had met someone who gave off the energy of a real sorcerer, it was this mysterious driver.

"Tell me!"

The taxi driver took a drag on his cigarette.

"Never stop believing the world's magic. There are gunna be times when you don't. Hard times. Times when you think the world and everything in it—especially the people—is just shite flowing out of some giant, cosmic orifice. But keep the faith. Keep it deep in your heart, where no one can find it. The world's magical, and so are you."

The car came to a slow stop. Alan had been so wrapped up in their conversation he hadn't noticed they had arrived just outside his house. A light shining through the window on the bottom floor told him his mum was waiting up for him. He dreaded the interview. And what's more, he dreaded returning to normalcy, when the taxi-driver, Ub, or whatever his full name was, had offered him a glimpse of paradisical mystery.

"I'm sorry, kid. I can't hang around. I would have liked to talk more." Strangely Alan heard sincere regret in the driver's voice, even a crack of deeper emotion. "It's just the way it is. Got places to be. Times to be too. But all things spin upon the dragon-wheel. That which is lost returns to us in glory. I look forward to that day."

Alan stared at the driver. There was a secret hidden in these words, but he could not grasp it. He yearned to ask so many questions, but ultimately his voice failed him, and with a mantle of abject failure he climbed out of the car and stood on the pavement.

For a second, a brief second, Alan caught sight of the driver's eyes, glimpsing what lay behind the thick sunglasses.

They were bright yellow, like strange stars.

But the glimpse was only momentary, for the driver was suddenly speeding off, at illegal speeds in fact, his wheels screeching upon the tarmac. He rounded a corner and vanished into the night, leaving Alan shellshocked and questioning whether he had truly seen the yellow eyes, eyes that promised an answer to the mystery of his aberrant soul.

With dragging footsteps, he walked up to the door of his house and knocked. It swung wide and his mother stood framed in yellow light, but it seemed a false light to Alan, a garish simulacrum of the shining secret in the driver's eyes.

"Finally!" She ushered Alan inside, practically with force, slamming the door shut. She behaved as if murderers could, at any time, rush down the street to take Alan's life. But no sooner was he safely inside the house than he became the suspect.

She bid him sit on the sofa; she sat opposite in an armchair. The living room was the very model of a middle-class abode: TV, coffee-tables, languid décor, beige everything. Alan much preferred the more garish, '90s designs that he'd seen round friends' houses, including the one he'd just been to, but his mother and father were painfully modern.

His mother had bags around her eyes and worry lines that distorted her otherwise elfin features. Alan loved his mother best when she allowed her inner pixie to emerge, but as she got older, it seemed anxiety, and all the fears that accompanied slavish devotion to the games of society, were catching up with her, weathering the cliff-face of her beauty into increasingly jagged formations.

She asked about the party, tersely. He answered vaguely. He didn't really care about it, anymore. What he wanted to ask about was what the driver had insinuated, and he was so tired, and still a little drunk, that he blurted it out without a shred of decorum.

"Am I adopted?"

His mother looked as though he'd slapped her. But behind the rage, did he see a note—a sliver—of fear? And why would there be fear, unless there was something to hide, unless Alan really was adopted.

"Nonsense!" she said. "What on earth brought this on? Are you drunk?"

"I only had a few beers." This was a lie, but he sincerely wasn't drunk. Couldn't be with the flame of truth burning at his core. "Mum, it's okay if I am, but I really need to know."

"What's brought this on?" his mother said, ignoring his question. "Was someone saying this to you at the party? Who?"

Alan rolled his eyes. His father was the lawyer, but over time his mother had developed a lawyer's mindset, perhaps by a process of osmosis, and in every slight she saw an opportunity to sue.

"It's not like that mum. I was just thinking in the taxi ride home." He added sheepishly, "Thanks for that, by the way."

"Thinking about what?" The anger had returned, an undertow beneath the waves of her words.

"About how different I am from you and dad."

Alyssa Chambers relaxed, sitting back in her armchair.

"Alan, *I* was so different from my mother. Or so I thought at my age. When I got older, I realised we were actually very similar. I think every person goes through a phase where they feel different and alienated from their parents. But ultimately, we're family, and more alike than you might care to admit. I was like you at fourteen—I just wanted to live in a fantasy world. And I hated social events. God, your father used to drag me to networking events even when we were young, and I hated it." Alan smiled at this. "But when I grew up, things changed. And they'll change for you too."

"Thanks, Mum." Alan stood up, walked across the room, and kissed his mother on the cheek. She smiled warmly at him in return.

"You stink of beer and cigarettes," she said.

Alan grinned sheepishly.

"Have a shower before you go to bed."

"I will."

"Okay, off you go."

Alan went to the stairs. He felt reassured, and the taxi ride—with all its ominous yet enticing mystery—was already beginning to fade like a dream. He felt he had woken up as he stepped inside the house, and all the strange coincidences and phrases that had seemed so loaded with significance now seemed a load of nonsense and gibberish. *I was probably drunker than I realised,* he thought. *Luckily, mum has taken the whole thing pretty well.* Even so, he couldn't help but think about the look of fear in his mother's eyes when he asked whether he was adopted: the look of a woman who'd long feared the day would come when her changeling came to know his own strangeness. When that day came, the darkness of things not understood, that had always dwelt on the periphery of their lives, would finally spill in.

CHAPTER 1
APPROACHING DREAMLAND

ALAN AWOKE UPON the edge of the desert, the bittersweet nectar of memory still burning his tongue. The dream had disorientated him. He'd become so accustomed to Carcosa's weird and wild landscape, to its aberrant stars, that dreaming of Earth and modernity had thrown his senses and expectations out of whack. It was as though the last few months of his life had been a vivid fantasy, nothing more. The thought constricted his heart with such anxiety he could scarcely breathe.

For the first time in his life, he felt purpose, that he had arrived at the place of his destiny, though that destiny was still somewhat hidden from him. He also felt, for the first time, acceptance and love. He reached over and touched Cassilda, who still slept beside him. She was a princess, yet she shared a humble mattress with him, only a tattered blanket to shield them from the gulf of the night sky and the whispering winds. He smiled.

By Cassilda's side lay the black, ruby-crowned staff. Even as the princess slept, it emitted a dark and dangerous glow, an invitation to probe the secrets of life and death. Alan wondered if the staff was not having a similar effect on Cassilda as The Claw was on him. With it, she had attained a godlike power. But at what cost? No power was free . . .

Across from them lay LeBarron, the servant of The Stranger, handsome features and long limbs wrapped in a dirty cloak of seemingly infinite depths. Petruccio slept nearby the actor on a thin, ascetic rug that suited the dwarf's monk-like personality. The final member of their party was Roland, the great warrior of Carcosa, who had chosen to accompany them at least to the edge of Demhe, if not farther. He was already awake, crouched by their bright yellow fire, which had smouldered through the long night. Alan knew what he saw in the fire: Cali. The desire for vengeance burned in Roland's eyes. It was a desire Alan knew well, one perhaps that they all shared.

They were making for the village of Al Shujah, where they would be able to stock up on their final provisions before setting off across the Dreaming Desert. Alan thought they would also be able to question the locals about Cali, though he doubted any had seen her. She would move like a shadow, swift as thought and hidden by night. Still, travelling at such speed might well mean she had made one or two mistakes, mistakes they would be able to track. There was no doubt in Alan's mind, from everything Cali had said and all that the others had advised, that she was heading to the land of Blue Light, to Pe'kar, the Demon King. But why, he did not know.

Roland had eschewed his bulky eurypterid platemail in favour of leather armour and a desert cloak. He carried the tattered banner of Uboth at his belt, rolled up and contained inside a bronze cylinder. A spear rested across his lap. Alan envied Roland, for he could no more detach The Claw, his own dreaded weapon, than he could detach his own head from his shoulders.

Of late, he felt the talons of The Claw biting ever more deeply. He heard voices, voices that sounded as though they came from real throats, just a few steps away, a single doorway out of sight. At times he awoke in the night with The Claw reaching for something, trying to throttle an invisible assailant. He always collapsed back upon his mattress, as though he'd run miles.

As afraid as he was of how much The Claw was taking hold, he loved the feeling of power. The great Siege Ender itself had fallen beneath him, along with the demon Tal'agron. And what had the necromancer Scarleth said? He had only just begun to tap the Claw's immense reservoir of power . . .

He shook the thoughts from his head. That way madness lay.

Alan rose gently, so as not to wake Cassilda. The first of the twin suns peaked its head over the horizon. They ought to get going soon, for the days were growing hotter as they moved westward. But Alan had not spoken much with Roland and felt this was an opportune moment. He sat beside the warrior at the fire.

"I know that look. The same desire burns in my heart," Alan said.

THE DREAMS OF DEMHE

Roland nodded.

"I feel I have glimpsed madness," Roland said. "My mind revolves around her and only her. I cannot clear it. No prayer cleanses her disease. She has infected me."

"Betrayal is the deepest sin. That is why the traitors are in the lowest rung of Dante's hell."

Roland smiled.

"Hell? Now that is a word few men know the true meaning of. I should have known—all of us should have known—that Cali spent too long there. No one may endure hell for long without being changed, although of course the nature of that change is ironically a form of stasis. She has been fixed in her transgressive patterns. Nothing will break the cycle except death . . . " Roland smiled grimly. "We should keep and eye on your mummer friend, there." He nodded to LeBarron. "I overheard him saying that he, too, had spent time in the lands of Blue Light."

"What is it about Pe'kar's domain that is so . . . influential?"

"Corrupting, more like," Roland growled. "Imagine it not as a landscape . . . " Roland took up a handful of sand and let it run through his fingers. "But as a state of being. All places are states of mind, and vice-versa, if truth be told. For all things issue from mind."

Alan was reminded of distant words, spoken long ago, a dark taxi ride home . . . But he could not quite summon the memory.

"Carcosa is a state of mind," Roland said. "A hideous glory. An awful beauty. Yhtill is a state of mind, albeit a decayed one. And Demhe, where we shall follow Cali, that too is a state of mind. More than all the rest, perhaps."

"Is it true the desert dreams?"

"All things are true, to a degree."

Alan smiled.

"I didn't know you were a philosopher as well as a warrior."

Roland smiled, this time more warmly.

"War is poetry; poetry is war. Or at least, that is what I tell myself on the dark days. Come, we shall see if Al Shujah still stands after Pe'kar's march."

After waking and eating a meagre breakfast, the five set off, riding black-furred quinels—strange camels with five legs—over the undulating dunes. Carcosa still sparkled in the far-distant east, like a bright jewel, tormenting them with promises of splendour.

Alan didn't wonder why Pe'kar coveted the city so. Seen far off, it seemed a glittering crown for one worthy enough to wear it.

But their road wound westward, where there was nothing to see except more desert, the horizon eternally obscured by dunes rising to the height of small hills. Both Roland and LeBarron knew the way, and so rode slightly ahead of Alan, Petruccio, and Cassilda. Roland gave no indication of his suspicions about LeBarron, as far as Alan could see; the two even laughed upon occasion, remarking upon some comical feature of the landscape, sharing war-stories about women in the way braggadocios men did. Perhaps Roland had learned a bitter lesson from Cali about playing one's cards closer to the chest? He was a rival actor in their troop if this was the case.

"You look nervous," Cassilda said, speaking to Petruccio.

It was true that the stoic dwarf was sheened with sweat. In normal circumstances, Alan might have put it down to the heat, but Alan had seen Petruccio endure far worse conditions and never break a sweat. Not only this, but his eyes were heavily shadowed, as though his sleep had not been restorative in the slightest. Alan had endured a few such nights in his lifetime, where he had blacked out for a good twelve hours yet risen the next morning in agony as though he'd lain awake all night.

Petruccio swallowed.

"I suppose I am," he admitted. "They say the dreaming dredges up your past, your memories. While we were in Alar, I fought to forget everything I had done in Cali's name. But in the desert, it will be harder to forget."

"You are ashamed," Alan said. Again, it was an emotion he knew well.

Petruccio nodded.

"Yes."

"There's no shame in being deceived," Cassilda said, softly. Her golden-bright eyes fixed Petruccio, and the dwarf could not help but smile.

"I thank you for your kind words, but what the head knows the heart can find difficult to accept."

"It will take time," Alan said. "For all of us to move on. Only when she's dead . . . " The word seemed horribly final. Alan hated Cali. He could only imagine what Cassilda felt, Cali having seemingly slain their father—though Alan did wonder whether the

THE DREAMS OF DEMHE

King In Yellow was truly dead. Be that as it may, Cali had certainly tried to kill the Lord of Carcosa. And yet even so, to pronounce death on anyone seemed wrong to Alan. He had killed in self-defence as they fought to save Carcosa from Pe'kar's legion, but that did not feel the same as killing someone in cold-blood. In battle, reason and intellect fled, unable to stay one's killing hand. But what if they found Cali in such a way that reason and intellect stood present at the judgement? It would be harder to take her life then. Especially as Alan had known her so . . . intimately. Not as intimately as Cassilda, that was true, and his heart was infinitely bound up with the golden-haired princess. But still, Cali had initiated him, she had shown him Carcosa, they had shared something divine and profane and secret.

When Cali first betrayed them, Alan had reviewed all of his interactions with Cali as necessarily false. But now he saw that Cali had not entirely been untruthful, and some of her actions even pointed towards a genuine favouritism. Hadn't she extended the hand of peace to him? Hadn't she given him The Claw?

No, you claimed The Claw for yourself—to save Cassilda. Cali is a villain.

But it was hard for Alan not to pity her, for Cali was wretched beneath her beauty, and Alan felt he had been wretched his whole life.

"And *you* are becoming increasing thoughtful," Cassilda said.

It still made Alan smile whenever Cassilda spoke in common parlance, dropping her excessively formal dialect. And she was right. He found it harder and harder to get outside of his own head, especially as there seemed to be a war going on inside. The Claw on one side, the stranger, more mysterious voice on the other side, and his own infant mind stuck in the middle.

"The emptiness of the desert begs to be filled with reflection," Alan said.

Cassilda smiled.

"Here that truth may become literal."

Alan saw the pain on her face, the fleeting shadow of dark memories. Though everything in Carcosa was old, ancient even, he knew that the people here did not feel time the way they did on Earth. Therefore, old grievances and feuds felt like yesterday's deeds, and scars took far longer to forget.

"Do you fear anything?" he asked, not quite sure how to broach the subject.

14

Cassilda nodded, looking downward. They had spoken only twice about her encounter with The Stranger on her wedding night, a night so awful it was perversely immortalised in the play, *The King In Yellow*. As if having one's deepest trauma performed upon a stage for all to see were not a painful enough reminder—no wonder she had isolated herself in the palace for so long— LeBarron, who played the part of The Stranger in the bleak drama, rode with them. Alan wondered at Cassilda's strength of character that she did not break down, curse them all, or else leave them to their fate, returning to her fortress, both physical and metaphorical. Maybe what she'd said was true: Alan had instigated a change in Carcosa, and now the pieces would move whether they willed to or no.

"I fear he'll be there, in the dreaming," she said. Alan did not need to ask who "he" referred to.

"If he is, I'll kill him."

Cassilda smiled at that. He loved how the innocence of her features could twist so wickedly. Beneath her veneer of celestial purity was a darker mistress, and he found himself intoxicated by both women equally. He knew, too, it was his own perverse nature that partially attracted her, as much as any supposed nobilities within him.

"Then you will be killing a mirage."

"That may be so, in the dreaming desert. But if he were to appear before us, enfleshed. I would kill him for you. You have my word."

Cassilda looked grave at that, which surprised Alan. He'd thought his show of bravado might at least win amusement, if not admiration.

"Be careful what thou wishest for, Alan Chambers."

With that formality bestowed, she drove her heels into the flanks of her quinel and rode to the crown of a dune to see where the town of Al Shujah lay.

CHAPTER 2
A NEW MASTER

CALI RODE LIKE a storm through the black of night. The *Hand of the Empress* was slung across her back, and her last deadly bolt, an arrow capable of slaying a god, was secured at her belt.

Her steed was a mighty gorgonopsid, a disgustingly large predator favoured by Pe'kar. It had been no surprise to find one lurking outside the walls of Carcosa, for Pe'kar's second legion—which the Demon King had hurled full-force at the wall—was predominantly a cavalry force. The riders, combined with these savage, feline reptiles, made for a potent combination. Still, for all their might and numbers they had failed to take Carcosa.

Because of him . . .

The thought was a black sun burning at the centre of her being. *Alan Chambers.* Once again he had humiliated her. Once again he had defeated her plans. The shame had almost been beyond endurance, and, as she had burned at the bottom of the Screaming Pit, her very soul torn asunder and then reforged by the agonising screeches of her own Shadow, she had considered suicide. For how could she live with this bitterness, with this alloyed taste upon her tongue? Cassilda had won. Her father had won. She was exposed, her wretchedness laid bare. What was there left to do but die?

But within herself she had found some deep and dark reservoir of power. The despair and hatred had been coalesced by the action of suffering. As each scream tore through her being, ripping not at the flesh but at the etheric and energetic body, at the very soul, this mercurial element within her had been hardened into a coal as unbreakable as diamond.

And so, she had decided to rise.

No common spell could have affected her escape from the Screaming Pit. She'd had to reach deep within her psyche, into the bowels of memory, there to dredge the forbidden arts taught to her by the Demon King himself. The spell was called *shimen'nehah,* and it was a spell forbidden, for it allowed the sorcerer to circumvent the binds of curses and wards by the flaying of their own flesh from the bones.

In other words, she had quite literally screamed her own skin off.

Then, tying the fleshy rags about her waist, she'd clambered as a glistening, fleshless creature up the Pit's interminable shaft. When she reached the light, she had cast another spell, donning her own flesh again. The sensation was uncanny, and still she felt her own skin was not perfectly sealed to the muscle, that it was somehow loose about her, the discarded clothes of some giant she had made her own. Nausea rose in her whenever she dwelt too long upon the sensations. But she was free, and that is what mattered.

The things she had allowed Pe'kar to do in order to pay for such wisdom had been . . . wondrous. Monstrous, yes. But wondrous too. What a being he was! It had taken all of Cali's strength, all of her Will, to leave the Six-Ringed City in the first place. It took all of her strength now not to bow down in awe and supplication even to the mere memory of the Demon King, such was his splendour, radiating from his six-fold form . . .

But she had terrifying strength within her. Perhaps, she had to bitterly acknowledge, it was her father's blood in her that allowed her to resist, to forge her own destiny. *And to forge His undoing* . . . But was the King In Yellow truly dead? The arrow had passed through Him and left only a cloak upon the ground, like some grand magician's disappearing act, the flourish of a black cape that left an empty stage in its wake. Cali snarled. No matter if He had found some way of cheating death. He would have to come out of hiding eventually, and by the time He did, she would have amassed enough power to destroy Him once and for all, and to claim Carcosa as her own.

But first, Pe'kar.

It was a risk, a terrible risk, but one she had to chance for the ultimate victory. She had to return to the Six-Ringed City, enter the Court of the Demon-King, stare into eyes that had hypnotised the greatest of gods, demons, and men, and then kill him. A dark smile came to her lips. Yes. She was on her way to kill the Demon King, to take his power as her own. And no one—especially not Alan Chambers—would stop her.

She rode across the dunes towards the lands of Blue Light. Little did she know the hulking alpha she straddled was the same beast that had once borne Haercus upon its back. No ordinary gorgonopsid, it stood at the apex of its species in both strength and cunning. This former aspect she had noted, for the creature had raced for two days without rest over the wastes and showed no signs of tiring or resenting how hard she drove it.

For now, the creature seemed all too content to serve a new master, perhaps realising with its uncanny intelligence that Haercus had become more beast than the gorgonopsid itself.

Her mind alive with dreams of the future she would claim, Cali rode deeper into the desert, where such dreams could become nightmarish realities.

CHAPTER 3
BORDER TOWN

BELOW THEM, the village of Al Shujah shimmered in the sandbowl created by a circle of rocky mounds. At the westward and eastern points of this circle, the stone had been cleared away, or else naturally parted, forming gateways which gave the village a grandness above its station. As the last outpost of fixed reality, Al Shujah possessed the strangely contrary qualities of gritty solidity and ephemeral ghostliness. The public and private houses seemed simply to have been hollowed out from pre-existing boulders rather than raised brick by brick. Like black moles on skin, they looked immovable save by some vicious act. Yet, the village seemed to Alan to rest on a slant, as though looking at it from the wrong angle would cause the whole mirage to disappear. When in conversation with one of the others, he thought the town moved in his periphery, crawling across the dunes like a nest of telluric scorpions.

He began to understand the fear taking hold of the others.

They descended the eastward slope of the bowl towards the town's gate. There were watchmen seated on the great, dilapidated standing stones, though they seemed little interested in the fearsome party approaching their town—more interested in the card-game they had just begun. They were strange men: orange-fleshed, rusted almost. Silver swords hung at their sides. Their clothes were loose and leathern. They might have been cut from the skin of animals, but what animal, Alan could not determine.

The guard on the right begrudgingly set down his colourful cards and turned to the newcomers, one leg dangling over the ledge.

"Halt! No farther."

THE DREAMS OF DEMHE

Alan and the party pulled the reins of their quinels and brought them to a standstill. The guard slowly stood up. One hand rested on his sword.

"What business in Al Shujah?"

Alan noted his eyes lingered on Cassilda's jewelled staff. Whereas he could partly conceal his Claw beneath the folds of his robes, there was no hiding the necromantic staff. Its power was evident, if not its purpose.

"Respite," Roland answered. "And supplies. Then, onward across Demhe. You would do well not to impede our mission, for it comes at the behest of the King In Yellow himself!"

If that last statement had any impact on the guard, he did not show it, turning instead to his mate.

"More dreamers!" the guard said disparagingly. "Well, if you wish to throw your lives away, I shan't prevent you. Cause no trouble in the town, and it will cause no trouble to you. If you're looking for beds for the night, there's *The Bloody Graal*. Careful on the westward side of town. The dreaming's stronger there."

Clearly bored, and unwilling to devote more time to them, the guard sat back down and picked up his cards. His opponent grinned and nodded, eager to continue their game. Perhaps there was money at stake.

"Have you seen a woman come through here?" Cassilda asked, undeterred by their apparent lack of interest. "She could have been mounted or on foot. Serpent eyed. She would have been armed with a strange bow."

The guard gave her a cursory glance, then shook his head.

"Sounds like a demon to me. I didn't see no demon. Except that army, of course. They marched by here not too long ago. But they was heading eastward, towards Carcosa. I assume you don't mean them?"

"Answer directly!" Roland snapped.

"I didn't see no demon-whore."

"Art thou sure?" Cassilda hissed. "For if we discover thou hast been hiding a criminal . . . "

The first guard threw his cards down.

"I ain't seen your demon!" Then, under his breath: "Royal cunt . . . "

"Me 'neither," the other guard grunted. "But you're welcome to ask around the town. There are eyes open here all hours of the day."

With that last cryptic remark, he went back to the game. Cassilda opened her mouth again to argue, but Petruccio touched her arm and shook his head. The artist was right, there was no point. If they *had* seen Cali and been bought off by her, they were more likely to feed them misinformation than simply deny having seen her. It seemed unlikely the guards were stationed here at all hours of the day and night. Cali could easily have slipped through. Perhaps she had even circumnavigated the town entirely.

"Let's go to that inn he mentioned," LeBarron said. "I could use a drink. And he's right, there's likely to be someone there who knows something useful, whether about Cali or the dreaming."

Cassilda let out a long sigh.

"You're right. Let's move on."

The five rode into the town. The roads were little more than flattened tracks of sand. The buildings squatted like furtive crustaceans. Alan felt unseen watchers gazing on their party. Even though he had wrapped some of his new robe about his Claw to conceal it, he sensed that the dwellers of Al Shujah knew already of the talisman he bore, and its dreadful significance.

"Show them The Claw. Bid them bow down before you, a living god."

Alan closed his eyes. He knew none of the other four had spoken those words. It came from The Claw itself, perhaps. Or rather what The Claw had awoken within him. Always it was pushing and prodding in directions he found disturbing, begging him to succumb to forms of atavism. At first, its promptings had been primitive, asking him merely to shed blood. But now, its requirements were more involved—worship seemed to be the gist of what it sought, identifying within Alan a primal hubris that had long lain dormant.

He shook himself. Cassilda noted the gesture, and her brow creased with concern. He forced a smile. She reached out and gently stroked his arm, the same arm connected to The Claw. He felt a dangerous spark of energy, a quickening current, as though a serpent slithered through his body, using his flesh as a suit. He pulled away from her. Her eyes caught the darkness in his face, and she bowed her head, saddened.

LeBarron and Roland led the way forward, eventually stopping their quinels by a larger building. It was three storeys, capped with a mosque-like dome. Ugly square windows stared out from its walls like eyes. A large doorway welcomed them inside, a blood-red curtain hanging down, concealing what lay within. There was no name written anywhere to signal what the place was, but on the upper beam over the doorway, a spidery series of letters were carved, forming the words, "*It is the blood that dreams (x.viii).*"

"What do the numbers mean?" Alan asked.

"Act and scene, Alan," LeBarron replied. "It's a quote from *The King In Yellow*. I'm surprised you don't remember it."

"It's a long play, with many lines. I only saw it once."

LeBarron grinned. He'd regained something of his roguish charm in the days since their departure from Carcosa, though still shadows lurked in the very depths of his eyes, and he'd lost his chameleon-like ability to change his skin, where once he'd been able to transmutate his very essence. Alan hoped the actor would one day be able to metamorphose as he once did. For now, death seemed to have fixed him in place, nailing him to one fixed flesh.

"The only good play is a long play," Le Barron said. "My own epic, *The Queen in Black,* shall be the longest epic ever written! I swear it."

"You still plan on writing that?" Cassilda snarled. "After everything she did?"

"I admit it has needed heavy revising," LeBarron said. "The play is not really about Cali, anymore. The New Queen has become her own tragic figure—perhaps born out of my shadowed unconscious. I really am quite moved by my own writing."

Alan laughed.

"You say you've revised the play, but I've yet to see you pick up a parchment and quill even once!"

LeBarron looked at Alan as though he were crazy.

"The play is written in my mind, Alan. And that is likewise where I revise it."

LeBarron dismounted from his quinel and tied the creature's reins to a post jutting out of the ground near *The Bloody Graal*. Roland and the others followed suit, with Alan tying his steed off last, deep in thought, pondering on what LeBarron said. All creativity began in the mind, he knew that well, but to retain such vast creative expanses without setting them down . . . Either LeBarron was a genius, or modern man had lost a portion of its greatness with the innovation of tabula and pen.

"Be on your guard," Roland said. "Border towns are laws unto themselves." The soldier's distaste was clear.

They filed into the tavern, passing through the red curtain. Once inside, Alan nearly gasped out loud, for the interior seemed the antithesis of the rugged, primitive dwellings they had seen outside. The exquisitely fine tables, the long bar, and the chairs were made of ebony wood, shiningly black. A black staircase wound upward to further floors, its bannisters sculpted with entwining serpents around their girth. Red lanterns sat on the tables. Red draperies hung from the walls. The inhabitants were a curious mixture of humanoid beings. The majority were orange-fleshed like the guards, but two women sat near the entrance were as lilly-white as Cassilda, as though Al Shujah—ironically bordering a desert—had never seen the sun. The lilly-white women wore silver robes, near-translucent, and talked in ghostly, soft voices.

"The shades . . . " Cassilda whispered. "Here, they become visible . . . " The princess, who had seen and knew so much, sounded awed by this revelation.

The ghostly patrons turned to Cassilda briefly, nodding as though she were an old, familiar acquaintance. Alan did not know if it was his imagination, but their eyes lingered on him for a while. He contemplated what a strange existence it must be, to live in an earthly realm but without a body with which to enjoy it. *Surly, a type of Hell?* But perhaps it was not. Perhaps being bereft of body freed the mind and spirit? H could not imagine such a fate.

At last, the pair of shades returned to their whispered conversation.

In one corner of the bar sat a patron unlike the others. He wore purple robes, tattered and bulky, with a pointed hood. Two blood-red eyes shone out of the darkness of his cowl with no evidence of a face—the lusting eyes of a dream-spectre, composed from the ashes of voyeurism. His belt was adorned with a plethora of differently sized glass vials, each containing a violently coloured substance that seemed neither liquid, gas, nor solid, but an intermixture of all three. Though he sat at a table, with a drink before him that lived up to the tavern's name, his left hand gripped a stave ending in a cruel-looking sickle. If Alan had to guess his profession, he would have said a farmer, but what one could farm out here in the desert was anyone's guess.

THE DREAMS OF DEMHE

"Well, hello there."

The sultry voice drew them with the potency of a siren's song. Alan turned and beheld a woman at the top of the stairs who could only be the mistress of the tavern. She descended the stairs with an effortless fluidity only possible to one whose lower half was entirely serpentine. At the waist, the supple flesh of her upper body—bare-breasted and pale as milk—gave way to viridian scaling. *A lamia,* Alan thought. *Is that the right word?*

Despite the voluptuousness of her upper half, the captivating darkness of her eyes, the way her black ringlets framed her delicate collarbones, it was the serpent-half of her that suddenly enflamed Alan. He almost turned away in shame, embarrassed to be suddenly aroused, and by a woman half-beast, no less.

What is wrong with you? Get a grip!

But then the still, quiet voice within him—the one who opposed the violence of The Claw—spoke: *Nothing that is natural can be against God. Only ask why you feel such things.*

Alan searched his mind for answers, feeling as though he were trying to wring a dry sponge of moisture, but to no avail. Whatever deeper truth his inner voice—what he thought of as the voice of Carcosa itself—hinted at, it was beyond him for the moment. He could only do his best to distract his mind from the arousing vision of loveliness now slithering toward him, and push down the evidences of his shame.

"My name is Liliya," the serpent-woman said. "I am the owner of this establishment. What brings such royal folk out to the border? I trust you are not chasing foolish dreams?" She giggled coquettishly, looking at each of them in turn. As her eyes met Alan's, he sensed that she was sucking his secret fantasies from him—as a vampire sucks blood. But he was not the sole recipient of her attentions, and to each person, even Cassilda, she gifted her piercing gaze. He suspected they each likewise felt their deepest desire surface, woken by her inspection. She lingered on Cassilda longest, perhaps because the princess was most difficult to read, or perhaps because her desire burned brightest and deepest.

"We come seeking a traitor and murderess," Petruccio said, shaking off the spell. As ever, he remained the grounded one. "We therefore must follow her, even into Demhe if need be. We will also need supplies."

Liliya turned her eyes on the dwarf.

"My, my, the great Petruccio! I have one of your pieces hung upon my wall. 'The Crimson Sea', I believe it's called. You have such a fine eye, and a feeling for the unknown."

Petruccio bowed in gratitude for the compliment, and perhaps a little embarrassment.

"I thank you. It was a hard piece to part with. They all are. But that one especially."

Liliya smiled.

"It is funny, isn't it? That which we covet most is often what we must give up to achieve our aim. Thus, the artist sells their most precious creations." She looked at LeBarron. "The actor must give up his personality in order to become known throughout the world." LeBarron smiled his rogue's smile, though Alan could tell he was unnerved. Her eyes shifted to Roland. "The soldier lays down his life to save the selfsame kingdom he would enjoy in the days of peace." Roland scowled, giving away no outward indication the words had reached him. "The lover must give up their virginity to become chaste." Liliya laughed as Cassilda clenched her fists and gritted her teeth. Lastly, Liliya returned her gaze to Alan. "And the wanderer must become lost in order to find himself."

"You riddle prettily," Cassilda said, not bothering to conceal her disdain. Alan wondered if she'd sensed his immediate attraction to the serpent-woman. His shame doubled. "But we are not here for auguries or vague suggestions—"

"Then you have come to the wrong place," Liliya snapped, something of the serpent's hiss in her voice as she cut across Cassilda. "This is Al Shujah, bordering Demhe, the desert that dreams. Here, distinctions are dissolved. Truths become lies. And certainty becomes mere memory. You are a sorceress, royal highness." Liliya nodded at Cassilda's staff. "And a good thing too, for you will need magic where you intend to go." Liliya sighed, cooling her anger. "But if you are seeking more concrete answers, you might wish to speak to the Harvester over there." She pointed to the purple-robed spectre. "He is out in dreamland every day. If anyone has seen your quarry, it's him. Now, I shall fetch you our finest graals of wine."

"Desire?" LeBarron said hopefully. "It surely must be, given the loveliness of the hostess?" He flashed a cocky smile and winked at the serpent-woman. Liliya laughed.

"It is the wine of Obsession, my friend. A richer vintage, though too much for some to handle. And I would not tempt me with carnal delights, for to lie with me is to lie with your own death. Such is the fate of all men who take pleasure in my bed." With a parting smile, in which great fangs flashed like two white pillars, she left them, snaking towards the bar to prepare drinks.

LeBarron looked longingly after her, as did Alan and Petruccio. Roland and Cassilda wore expressions of repulsion instead.

"I almost think it would be worth it," LeBarron said, with a sigh.

Alan held his tongue.

CHAPTER 4
REBIRTH

A GONY GRIPPED HIM like the black hand of a vengeful god.

At first, there had been no pain, only a monstrous unfurling of that which lay dormant within him, awoken by the dark god Pe'kar. But soon, as the transformations had become more frequent—more extreme—as the wounds had become the breeding ground of new flesh, of new ideas—new forms and species that should never have been given life—he had known pain like never before, pain that made the tortures of Pe'kar's dungeons seem a mere splinter.

He trudged westward, a behemoth of roving appendages, gifted with eyes where there should not be eyes, mouths where there should not be mouths, orifices vomiting liquids that sluiced along the ground, carving rivulets in the sand, and there planting—though there was no soil—a fecundity of quixotic life. Blind worms birthed in the excrement of his passage. His mouth was a nest of chittering scorpions. A thousand tongues licked the air, tasting its alchemical properties, guiding him onward into the desert. The one limb he possessed that still looked vaguely human clutched a black sword, forged in the fires of a dying planet, hooked with lamprey serrations and gleaming with Pe'kar's choicest bile. It was aptly named *Hope's Devourer*; that is what Haercus had become.

His body was transformation itself, a constant gyre of forms pushing out of whatever previously existed. Like a serpent continually shedding his skin, he left the rags of his old self behind, though these discarded raiments were not purely dead flesh, but fertile with the instinct of becoming. Thus, he was not just *one*, anymore. He was many, an army. Like the Beast of Revelations he slouched into the heart of the desert, and behind him, his children followed.

CHAPTER 5
DEEPER DREAMING

THE DREAMS BEGAN as minor deceptions. These, Cali had swept by without a second thought, easily seeing through the illusions and phantoms of her past. A young girl with her throat torn open begged Cali to shoot the reptilian beast that ravaged her. Cali had persuaded the girl, Alikya, to go adventuring with her in the swamps of Yhtill outside the city walls. A foolish venture for anyone, let alone a child. But Cali could be persuasive, even as a young girl, that was one of her many gifts. And so she and Alikya had gone out to the swamps, and there Alikya had died, torn apart by a dimetrodon. A needless death, her father had said. But Cali didn't think Alikya died needlessly. Her death taught Cali a valuable lesson—that the only person she could truly rely on was herself.

These apparitions were familiar to Cali. She had ridden across Demhe many times. They were distracting to the weak-willed, luring like a mermaid's beautiful face beneath the ocean's waters. But for someone like her, possessed of great cunning and power, they were no more unsettling than mist.

But that was changing. Every mile Cali travelled west upon the great gorgonopsid, which still showed no signs of tiring, the dreams were getting *stronger*.

First, her father loomed out of the swirling sands, raising His hideously deformed hand, bidding her stop, turn back.

"I killed you, Father," she said, though in truth she was not sure. She'd hoped to rip off His cloak, to see His true face, to finally watch the life leave His cursed eyes. But no, He had denied her even that.

The horrid, grey-cloaked figure cocked His head at her words.

THE DREAMS OF DEMHE

That which dreams shall never die . . .

Cali spat, cursing. The words were not her father's; they belonged to Alan Chambers. Even here, in a place of infinite possibilities, Alan mocked her. She lashed the reins and her gorgonopsid rushed on, as eager to leave the illusion behind as she.

The spectre was so real-seeming that she almost thought she felt the filthy sleeve of his cloak brush her cheek as she rode past Him.

The phantom called after her.

Thou shalt die like little Alikya! I tried to save you, daughter!

Cali gritted her teeth and rode on.

Next, she met her mother—or rather, Queen Camilla. The last time Cali had seen the queen, she had been brought forth naked, broken, and humiliated before the gates of Carcosa. *And Father did nothing to save her . . .* The sight had almost deranged Cali's mind from its purpose, caused her to regret what she had done in instructing Pe'kar's assassins in her capture. Cali had nearly thrown herself over the battlements and charged towards Pe'kar's second legion. *I could have saved her . . .* Perhaps that was true, though more than likely she would have been slain by the six true demons, Pe'kar's generals, and that would have been the end of Cali's tale.

She suspected Camilla had been brought back to the lands of Blue Light by those same generals, or what was left of them, for at least two had been slain. *Another reason to journey to the Six-Ringed City. Perhaps she is there. Perhaps she can be brought back from the brink of madness . . .*

Though Camilla had every reason to hate Cali, for she was a reminder of Hastur's indiscretion, the queen had been the one to show Cali boundless love. When Cali demonstrated an aptitude for the ecg'tar, Camilla taught her, the two spending long evenings together strumming its twenty-two strings, sometime giggling and playing about with the curious sounds it could make, sometimes deep in concentration upon its mysteries. Camilla even gifted Cali her own humble ecg'tar, forged from hali-tree wood, for her sixteenth birthday.

Now Camilla stood in the desert before her, clad not in her royal robes, but in a simple gown of yellow. Her raven hair hung about her shoulders, lustrous curls that sickeningly reminded her of Cassilda despite the different colouration.

"Cali . . . " Camilla said, a terrible note of sadness in her voice. As Cali drew closer, she saw bleeding lacerations across her mother's once nymph-like face. She had been beaten black and blue. Her eyes gleamed with a haunted intensity.

Cali pulled hard on the gorgonopsid's reins and the massive creature begrudgingly slowed its ferocious pace, almost disquieted by a pause. The beast was more relentless and restless than Cali herself. *But this could really be her,* Cali thought. It was unlikely, but what if the queen had managed to elude her captors and flee after the battle? What if Camilla truly stood before her?

"Mother?"

Camilla nodded, tears welling in her eyes. She reached out both hands to Cali, a gesture of almost idolatrous supplication.

"Cali! Oh, my dear daughter! I am so glad to see thee! I have suffered so long in the desert! Demhe has been cruel to me, tormenting me with visions of the Demon King." Camilla fell to her knees, shrieking her next words. *"I can still feel my limbs stretched upon his rack, feel his delight . . . "* She buried her face in her hands and sobbed.

Cali dismounted. The gorgonopsid snorted at her disconsolately, but she ignored it.

"Mother . . . I am sorry . . . " And Cali meant it. She had wanted revenge on Camilla because her step-mother never prevented the King In Yellow abusing Cali, never stood up for her no matter how much she professed to love her, but Cali saw now her vengeful actions were misplaced, mere perverse energy. She should have devoted all her attentions to undoing her father, not wasting time taking revenge upon Camilla, who had, despite her flaws, been one of the few to give Cali anything approaching love.

Camilla continued to sob and wail. For a second, Cali had the harsh thought that it was typical of her mother to weep like a dramaturge, even in the midst of a desert, with no audience to see. But then, she banished her harsh judgement. Camilla was self-righteous and dramatic, but she was not evil, not like Hastur, not like her father . . .

Cali took a single step forward, intent on consoling her mother, maybe even taking her to some safe place until Cali's plan had been enacted.

Her mother screamed. Pieces of her were torn asunder in a violent explosion. Cali shrieked and lurched backward, raising her hands to shield against the shower of gore. It was as though Camilla's limbs had been tied to four rebellious horses who pulled until her arms were torn from the shoulder-sockets, and her legs dismembered from the hip, leaving gory cavities that stared like bleeding eyes.

"Oh gods!" Cali whimpered, lowering her arm, seeing blood and bone smeared in incomprehensible patterns upon the sand. A twisted ruination of human form lay where her mother had once been, the mangled cartilage covered by a crude yellow shroud.

Cali fell to her knees.

"Mother . . . I'm . . . "

Something nudged Cali's back and she turned sharply, reaching for a blade that wasn't there. She hadn't had time to recover her sword when she fled Carcosa.

But staring at her was the gorgonopsid, its malicious features curled into what she could only identify as a sneer.

"A dream?" Cali said.

The beast's xanthous eyes gleamed with terrifying intelligence.

She looked back and saw there was nothing there. Sand, dunes, and the emptiness of her own heart—all her secret desires unfulfilled.

"I thank thee," Cali said, momentarily slipping into the formal dialect she so hated, but the incursion of the past and future simultaneously had deranged her sense of self.

"I should name you . . . You have been more useful than any steed I ever rode. You must be one of Pe'kar's finest?"

She wondered if she didn't catch a slightly mocking look upon its face before she clambered onto the beast's back and kicked her heels. But the gorgonopsid was already galloping, taking her deeper into the dreaming.

She shook herself, blinked rapidly, whispering a few incantations for clear-sight. The dreaming had never so fooled her before. She must not be caught again. There were stories of men and women who'd wandered aeons in the desert's invisible runnels. Though it looked open and barren, in truth it was a labyrinth, a psychic maze. At its heart: the mountain of Al Qaf Saba and the Cave of Wonders, a place Cali would never dare return to. In times past, Cali'd had no trouble navigating Demhe's idiosyncrasies, but all things were changing, as she had told Alan Chambers. She spat at the bitter thought of him.

The dream-world fell quiet for a time, which was more unnerving than the materialisation of a host of spectres. During that time, he gorgonopsid showed it did not know the meaning of tiredness.

"I'll call you Satan," she said, at last. "For you run like the Black Stallion himself." A grin split her features.

A cry broke across the dunes.

"Your highness!"

Cali could not stop herself from looking around, so urgent and familiar was the voice. A strong wind blew, sending sand and grit into her face, limiting visibility. Her steed galloped on, yet the winds increased their fury, howling, blowing great waves of sharp sand that raked the skin and eyes like merciless claws. Satan slowed, and Cali shielded her face once again. Still, a voice called in the desert. "Your highness! Your highness! Over here!"

"Curse it all!" Cali snarled. "Curse Demhe! Curse the fucking pigment!"

Suddenly they were through the storm; the loss of oppositional force was disorientating and she nearly fell from Satan's back. The gorgonopsid sensed her imbalance and thus rebelled, jerking and bucking. Perhaps Satan hated the desert as much as she did.

"Whoa there! Whoa!" She pulled Satan's reins, steadying the thrashing beast. It let out a hiss that was at once feline and reptilian, the murderous language of a predator. But it was not *her* Satan hissed at . . .

Cali searched the dunes before her and saw what irked the gorgonopsid. There, in the garb of a motley archimime, was Eric the Courtier. Eric the Foolish.

Eric the Brave.

Cali felt as though Haercus's cursed Claw had closed about her heart. She fought back tears and told herself it was the stinging grit in her supersensitive eyes.

"Stand aside!" She did not care if Erik was a phantom—surely he had to be, given she had watched him die—for whether living or dead he barred her path.

He turned sad eyes up at her.

"O Cali, you have gone too far."

"Not far enough!" she cried, and her heart slipped from the claw's grip, replaced by the embrace of black flame. "I've so much yet to be done, and your memory cannot drag me down!"

THE DREAMS OF DEMHE

"Drag you, Cali? As *I* was dragged to the ground, pierced by the blades of Carcosa's enemies?" Erik took a step towards them, and Satan once more hissed, hairs bristling, eyes gleaming dangerously. But as in life, Erik was more fearless than his fool's garb let on. "Think what you could have been had you not taken the traitor's path!"

"I would have been nothing, so long as my father lived," Cali spat. "And He lives an eternity." A sneer curled her lips, and she added with dripping sarcasm, "You can see my conundrum."

Erik stared her down. She hated that she found it difficult to meet his eyes.

"You are lost, Cali. That is why you cannot tell dreams from reality. You have strayed from your purpose, and hence from your power."

"Enough!" Cali snarled. "Be ye phantom or no, I shall slay you!"

Eric grinned, a shit-eating smile.

"You are welcome to waste your deadly bolt, one you spent so long forging in the Fires of Manifestation. I should have realised that you were not making such a weapon for any useful or good purpose."

"That is your problem," Cali sneered. "You spent your life subjected to the word 'should', never questioning His authority, and never seizing what could have been yours!"

Cali spurred her steed, and Satan all too gladly pounced forward. His huge jaws widened and closed, slamming shut around Erik's waist.

The phantom flashed out of existence—and Cali was bitterly reminded of her father's vanishing trick. She screamed in frustration. Satan growled, throwing back his head and hissing at the sky. So enraged was the beast he reared up on his hind legs; Cali fell, tumbling to the sand. She let out a pained grunt, but quickly clambered to her feet.

Satan did not flee from her, but continued to hiss and growl, sweeping his great head about.

Where Erik had stood, there was now a shimmering silver pool. Its surface was almost painfully bright, reflecting the light of Carcosa's twin suns.

Satan approached the body of water, sniffed once, then recoiled. Cali crept forward hesitantly. The pool was not water, that much was certain. Her reflection stared back at her, perfect as

34

though she gazed into a silver mirror. The argent glow looked faintly poisonous.

Mercury, she realised.

She could not help but admire her reflection, despite the mar of yellow scars, reminders of Alan's victory over her, reminders of failure.

She was about to look for a way out when something in the pool's mirror caught her eye.

Her reflection was sobbing.

Cali swallowed, her heart pounding. All her instincts told her to look away, that to look deeper into the pool could only lead her off the true path, and into the maze of madness. Yet, she could not tear her eyes away from her weeping reflection. Did this represent some hidden part of herself? A shadow she was concealing?

Slowly, with a trembling hand, she reached out toward the pool.

No sooner than her fingers made contact, the pain began.

CHAPTER 6
THE HARVESTER

ALAN, LEBARRON, ROLAND, Cassilda, and Petruccio approached the purple-garbed shade sitting in the corner of *The Bloody Graal*—not without some trepidation. As they drew nearer his crimson eyes rose and fixed upon them unblinkingly. Alan was reminded of a sleep-paralysis demon, a shadow conjured by the brain's half-dreaming state. If anyone belonged to the dreaming, it was this strange figure. No doubt he did have useful information, but whether he could be trusted was another matter.

"Greetings," Alan said.

The figure inclined his cowled head. With grave-slow movements, he reached for the phylacteries at his belt and drew them up to eye-level. They jingled and tinkled like keys upon a jailor's ring. Alan could have sworn he saw a tiny nude woman trapped in one of the glass vials. His skin crawled.

"You have come to inspect my wares?" The Harvester's voice was gravel in a cement mixer.

Alan shook his head.

"No. My apologies. We have come for information."

"Information?" The shade chuckled; the dissonant sound sent a horrid tingle down the nape of Alan's neck. *"The most valuable asset of all. Come, sit."*

Returning the phylacteries to his belt, the shade motioned with a grand sweep of his hand to the empty chairs before his table. The party of five all took seats, Roland and LeBarron grabbing two more chairs from empty tables.

"We seek—" Cassilda began, but the shadowy merchant held up a hand, indicating she should be silent. Alan saw Cassilda's eyes

36

flash dangerously, her flesh and the ruby atop her staff momentarily glowing, magical powers kindled by anger. Then she regained control of her temperament, forcing a smile. Roland hadn't been wrong: out here, royal authority seemed meaningless.

"*Pleasantries first,*" the shade said, inclining his head slightly in gratitude to the princess. "*That is the way we do things out here. Pleasantries before business. A ritual, yes? Like your magic.*" Though there was no nose visible in the shadow of the cloaked hood, Alan heard the merchant *sniff*.

Could he smell Cassilda's magical essence?

"Very well," Cassilda said. "I am Nala." Alan forced his face to remain neutral, though within his mind whirled with surprise. It took him a moment to realise she was, wisely, concealing her identity from the strange spirit. "This is Alan Chambers, a warrior from the realm of Urth. LeBarron, a famous mummer. Roland, a decorated soldier of the Great City. And Petruccio, He—"

"A wandering artist," Petruccio said, hastily cutting in. "In search of inspiration, more than anything else."

Alan and Petruccio's eyes met for a brief second. Alan saw the sense in concealing Petruccio's new role as Head Courtier; no doubt there were many willing to capture such a dignitary in the hope of obtaining ransom from the city. Cassilda had already revealed much about their group, perhaps a little too much, though at last she had left out her own royal heritage. There was no harm in a little deceptive modesty.

"Yes," Cassilda said, cottoning on. "For what are heroic deeds if none are there to record and remember them?"

The merchant's blood-red eyes scanned their party. Alan heard the same dog-like sniffing noises emerge from the hood.

"*Memory is the only hope of futurity,*" the merchant said, the words like thick porridge in his unseen mouth. "*A strange group, to be sure . . . A ragged assortment . . . I wonder what purpose could bring you together? Intriguing!*" Again, horrid laughter issued from the seemingly cavernous hole of his face. The merchant placed a hand on his chest and performed a half-bow. "*I am Mazael, the Harvester. Dreams are my business.*" He jingled the little vials on his belt again. "*Capturing them. Selling them to those who need them. Some seek alleviation of pain . . .*" With this, his red eyes flashed to Roland. "*Others seek the fulfilment of dark fantasies.*" His eyes—to Alan's surprise—rested on Cassilda. "*For *others it is about knowledge . . . "* The red orbs shifted to Petruccio. *"But it is not my place to question the reasons why, merely to supply Seekers with what they most desire."*

"But how does one capture a dream?" Alan asked. His curiosity momentarily overcame the urgency of their mission, and the true purpose of questioning Mazael.

Mazael laughed. Alan wished he would stop, but the strange spirit seemed in grand humour.

"We border the dreaming itself, warrior of Urth. Dreams abound here, ready to be reaped." Mazael fingered the strange scythe-like implement Alan spotted earlier. *"Though of late they have waned. The dreaming is not as it once was."*

"We seek a woman," Cassilda said, steering their conversation back onto track. "Half-demon, though also with royal Carcosan blood in her veins. A powerful sorceress. Has anyone like that come through Al Shujah?"

Mazael's eyes glinted like rubies.

"Yes. After that great host marched by here—indeed, many thought doom had come upon our town—a little while later I saw a woman riding one of Pe'kar's beasts. She rode like the Demon God himself came after her! Oh, a fell beauty she was, and mad too: she rode right into the heart of Demhe without rest. The dreaming may be diminished of late, but only a fool would contend with its illusions so directly. There are safer roads . . . "

At that moment, the Harvester's story was broken off by the arrival of Liliya. As before, her serpent's tail meant she moved with subtle, silent elegance. She carried a silver tray, laden with five graals, each filled to the brim with blood-red liquid, the so-called Wine of Obsession. Alan had become enamoured of Desire-wine and so was eager to try this stranger—and no doubt stronger—vintage.

"For my valorous guests," the hostess said, smiling sweetly. Cassilda eyed her warily, sensing an unspoken sentiment, and perhaps sensing, too, how Alan's eyes lingered on Liliya's luscious, serpentine coils.

Liliya leaned over and whispered in Cassilda's ear. "Might we discuss payment?"

"A moment," Cassilda said, not bothering to conceal her sourness.

The princess left them and spoke in quiet tones with Liliya for a moment. Cassilda produced a satchel, which had been secretly strapped to her upper thigh. Unknotting the bag's drawstring, she drew out three large jewels. Liliya smiled, seemingly satisfied. She took them and bowed humbly, then left the party to their interview with Mazael. Cassilda returned, muttering under her breath.

"We have board for the night," she explained. "Enjoy it, for it cost Carcosa dearly."

Mazael laughed.

"*Value is always in the heart of the desirer. The greater the desire, the greater the value. And what could be more desirable than a dream?*"

"You were saying . . . " Petruccio said.

"*Ah, yes. Your quarry . . . the woman in black! Ha! She rode through Al Shujah and out into the dreaming. All the town was asleep, save for I. Mazael never sleeps. I sell dreams, I do not consume them!*"

Alan was reminded of the crude phrase he'd heard dealers spouting when he'd moved in less savoury circles: *Never get high on your own supply*. Mazael was adhering to that principle, albeit in an extreme form.

"You said she went into the dreaming. Which direction? West?" Cassilda pressed.

"*Direction? You think compass points matter in the heart of Demhe? No, there is only one fixed point, the mountain Al Qaf Saba! That is halfway . . .*"

"Halfway to where?" Roland said, not fully grasping Mazael's metaphysics.

"*To where you want to go.*" Though without a mouth, Alan sensed Mazael was grinning, enjoying stringing them along. To compound the mystery of his mouthless face, he picked up his graal and loudly glugged down liquid. Red stained the black canvas of his featureless visage. He wiped away the bloodstains with the back of his hand.

Alan lifted his own graal to his lips and sniffed, aware of how he was aping the weird merchant. The graal at least didn't smell of blood. The rich perfume of sweet wine filled his nostrils. He knew there was risk, still. They did not know Liliya's intentions, and for all he knew, she could be working with Cali. Then again, The Claw had saved him from infection before, in the depths of Alar. He had faith it would prevent poisoning. He knew he wasn't immortal—a sword through his heart or skull would kill him, sure enough. But he wanted to enjoy his increased constitution while he had it.

He drank deeply from the cup.

Immediately, a fire started in his belly. He opened his mouth and let out a breath that was almost a dragon's hiss. His eyes felt like they rolled around in his sockets. A moment later, he felt the arms of every woman he had ever desired upon him, stroking him, caressing him. They whispered to him too, begging him to perform perverse sexual acts. *I don't need any more voices in my head,* Alan thought, pushing aside his graal. He would not drink any more. He was mad enough without the dead beckoning him to bed.

"Strong stuff, isn't it?" LeBarron said, licking his lips. Neither Cassilda nor Roland touched their graals. Petruccio was already taking a second deep draught. Alan wondered what those two saw, whether their obsessions were carnal like his or perhaps more refined.

"So, what you are saying . . . " Cassilda said, baring her teeth slightly. "Is that if we know where Cali is going, then we shall be able to follow her there?"

"*In a sense, yes.*"

Cassilda looked at the others.

"She will be heading to Pe'kar's lands. It is the only possible explanation."

"*Indeed . . . *" Mazael said. "*That is where most people head when they seek to cross the desert: the land of Blue Light. What a place it is.*" His eyes bored into each of theirs in turn. "*Should it be your dream to reach those lands, I can take you. For I am the fulfiller of dreams, and a reliable guide.*"

"Your opportunism is admirable," LeBarron said, with a slight smirk. "But I have been to the lands of Blue Light and crossed the desert of Demhe. If a guide is needed, I will be your man."

Cassilda smiled with poisonous sweetness at Mazael.

"Thou hast been most helpful, Harvester. I thank thee." She rose, and the others followed suite. "Good fortune be upon thy trade. And let the blessings of the King—*Deathless Be He*—go with thee."

They had all turned away when the merchant spoke once more, a hook in his words, as ensnaring as the sickle-blade of his harvesting tool.

"*What road would you take them by, noble mummer?*"

LeBarron fixed the Harvester with a hard stare. It was easy to forget, with LeBarron's joviality and wit, that he was also a deadly warrior. He had fought in many battles alongside Alan now, and his blade-work was worthy of its own poem.

"What is it to you?"

"*I care about the safety of those who pass through Al Shujah . . . I cannot sell dreams to the dead!*" At this, Mazael let out more warped laughter, which Alan endured with gritted teeth.

"Do away with the riddles and speak plainly," LeBarron snapped.

"*Well, a common road taken by those in pilgrimage to the Six-Ringed City is the Crooked Path to the Emerald Mountain. Would, perchance, you be considering that road?*"

"You know that I am," LeBarron said, his impatience causing his nostrils to flare. "Speak plainly."

Mazael drank of his graal, forcing them to wait as he guzzled the dark nectar down. Alan had been curious what Petruccio and LeBarron experienced in their cups, but he dreaded to imagine what such a creature might find in the wine of Obsession.

"*The Crooked Path has become dangerous of late. A great beast stalks that path, along with its children. It moved in recently. I would not recommend that way. You will be killed.*"

"What manner of beast is it?" Roland said. Alan could tell the soldier fancied their chances against any opponent. With Cassilda now bearing the black staff, Alan was inclined to agree. It took great restraint not to show The Claw to Mazael, though in truth, Alan suspected the Harvester, with his wretched nose for magic, already knew of Alan's prize, and for whatever sinister reason had decided not to draw attention to it at this time.

"*Not a beast of the field or the sky,*" Mazael answered. "*Nor a beast of the dreaming. Something altogether . . . strange. Two hunters from this town went out to fight it and were killed. Their magic was naught, for the chaos of its form welcomed the touch of spell and blade alike. I watched them torn limb from limb. Then the children feasted upon the innards!*" Mazael giggled. "*Yes, the Crooked Path is closed for now, at least until that beast moves off. But there is another way . . .*"

"What way?" LeBarron said.

"*Ah, but if I tell you, I shall no longer be of use to you. Haha! No, better that I show you. Besides, it is not a straightforward route, more Crooked than the Crooked Path by far! But it still leads to the Emerald Mountain of Al Qaf Saba. From there, the road to Pe'kar's lands is easier."*

The group exchanged looks, communicating without words their mixture of feelings. All were unwilling to trust Mazael, but if his story was true, then they would be walking needlessly into danger, and even if they were able to overcome the beast, Cali would be long gone. None of them had spoken about what would happen if Cali reached the Six-Ringed City before they caught her, but Alan knew the consequences would be dire. Despite his innate curiosity, a curiosity that had never dimmed even with the passing of childhood into memory, he had no desire to enter the lands of Blue Light, especially when LeBarron had spoken of them in tones of terror. Alan feared for his sanity already, and he wondered if such a warping landscape would be the final nail in the coffin of his reason.

"I assume you would like some form of payment in exchange for guiding us?" Cassilda said, wearily.

Mazael's eyes brightened to a painful radiance.

"You and the warrior of Urth are lovers, are you not?" Mazael sniffed, as though their scent confirmed his suspicion.

Cassilda's expression hardened, her grip tightening on the dreaded staff. Alan always was amazed how such delicate features could become so imposingly adamantine. A fine sculpture she might be, but one sharp enough to cut even the hand of the sculptor.

"What of it?"

Mazael laughed.

"There is one dream I seek, a rare dream that blooms beyond the atavisms of forbidden desires . . . The consummation of true love. Let me see it. Let me see . . . you and he entwined. I shall capture the essence of it, and it shall be my dearest, most valuable dream."

Cassilda recoiled, sickened. She trembled head to toe with rage. Alan was too stupefied to respond, but regardless, Cassilda would have beaten him to the punch.

"What about a new deal?" she snarled. "I unmake you here and now, then resurrect you as a slave to my will, and force you to show us the way to the Emerald Mountain?"

If Mazael was threatened, his eyes betrayed nothing.

"You are welcome to try, Princess . . . " He drew out that last word, letting them know full-well he had figured out all of their secrets. *"But how will you kill that which does not live? And how will you give life to that which has no body? Long ago I sacrificed all that was unnecessary, all that was tainted. The excrescences burned for fourteen days upon the pyre. By the end of it, all that was left were the ashes of New Becoming. And my eyes—which saw ALL!"* He stood, and Alan could not but recoil, for now standing at his full height the Harvester seemed vaster, like a purple sun dawning over a distant horizon, the baleful rays of his energy blasting and blinding them. The others followed suit, stepping back, some going for weapons. Only Cassilda stood her ground, baring her teeth, stonily defying him.

"If you know who I am, then you know it would be best not to cross me," Cassilda said. "I have raised armies and broken them. The power of life and death is in my hands."

"And as I have said, I am neither living nor dead, so you have no power over me," Mazael purred. *"I never break faith. I will uphold our bargain. Give me a dream, and I shall lead you via the most Crooked of Crooked Ways to the summit of Al Qaf Saba. From there, you may do what you wish: journey to Pe'kar, or gain audience with the Old Man, if he is still alive . . . "*

"We're not interested in your bargain!" Cassilda snapped.

"Then let us depart," Petruccio said, gently touching Cassilda's arm. "It is Cali who leaves enemies wherever she goes, not you. Let us leave this spirit to his harvest and go elsewhere. There will be other guides."

Mazael laughed.

"None will lead you as I can. You go into certain death. Either the beast shall claim you, or the madness of the dreaming."

Cassilda stepped forward, as if to strike the spectre, but once again Petruccio gently but firmly gripped her arm, pulling her back.

"Let us go," the dwarf said.

"There won't be another guide. Accept the offer . . . " Alan looked around, wondering who would dare voice such an opinion in front of Cassilda, then realised that he was the one who had spoken.

Or rather, The Claw had spoken through him.

He clapped a hand to his mouth.

Cassilda looked at him in horror.

"Alan . . . "

"It's not me . . . " he said.

Mazael turned gleeful eyes upon Alan.

"Ah, the Claw-bearer speaks! That talisman is wiser than you are, Alan Chambers of Urth. There truly is no guide such as I. The way is perilous to both flesh and soul alike . . . But I can lead you through. Come, it is not as if I ask you to commit a crime. I merely ask you to allow one to observe. God's eyes are always upon you, whatever you do. And eyes are all that is left of me. So, what difference is there between God watching and I watching?"

"You would sell our love for profit!" Cassilda said, and Alan was shocked and ashamed to see that beneath her rage and strength was a terrible vulnerability, the fragility of a little girl whose innocence had been stolen by the first whisperings of the serpent. And Alan had been the one to bring her near tears, to shred her armour, to expose her weakness. *I hate you,* he thought, directing all his ire at the terrible taloned implement upon his right arm. *You are not a part of me! I shall rule you!*

"I am the strength that you need to see this through to the end . . . " The Claw whispered in reply, unmistakeably sardonic notes dripping from the secret voice. "You may hate me all you wish, but you *need* me."

I don't need you.

"You would have died a thousand times before now, were it not for me. And here I am, saving you again!"

"Alan . . . "

He blinked rapidly, returning to himself. The others looked at him with alarmed expressions. Had he been talking out-loud to himself? He didn't know, and that is what scared him most, the elisions of time as his consciousness was sucked down a wormhole into some other place, detached from reality.

"His talisman guides him," Mazael said. Did Alan see, in those horrid, crimson orbs, a softness? a pity, even? Maybe this creature knew something of Alan's pain, for he too had been consumed, given all to the fulfilment of a singular purpose. Mazael was eyes, and Alan was a hand . . .

"It doesn't guide me," Alan choked out. "It misleads me. I am so sorry, Cassilda."

The princess hung her head. She closed her eyes, and he could tell she fought back tears. She did not weep for herself; she wept for him. Alan's heart ached as though his own taloned hand had reached inside and crushed it.

"Let's away from this cretin," Roland said. "Lest he revolt us further with his predilections."

The party moved away towards the stairwell, turning their back on the Harvester. Mazael seemed unfazed.

"*Consider my offer!*" he called after them, then sat back down and returned to his graal.

Even when the spirit was long out of sight, Alan felt as though he could feel red eyes upon him, and the hunger with which they stared.

CHAPTER 7
SLEEP ON IT

THE ROOMS WERE luxuriously furnished, and, had Alan's mind not been a tumult of emotions, he might well have paused to admire them. Blood-red curtains framed a window that looked westward over dreamland. From this distance, the wastes did not look particularly dreamlike or miraculous, simply a wide yellow desert, though at odd moments, out of the corner of Alan's eye, he thought he saw strange figures skating over the surface of the sands. Whenever he looked at these spectres dead on, the mirage dispelled.

Other than the window, there was a fourposter bed, complete with red draperies; various tables and chairs; a large chest for storage; and a cabinet for changes of clothes. The room was surplus to their requirements. Though they had packed for a long journey, their priority had been dealing with the difficulty and danger of their venture, not with comfort. Hence, they had few clothes and even fewer frivolous items.

There was also an adjoining ensuite room with a brass bathtub sat by a fireplace. Alan longed for a bath. About the only thing he missed from Earth was the ease of obtaining warm water. And right now, he felt like sand resided in every crevice of his being.

Cassilda sat naked and cross-legged upon the bed. The black staff lay horizontal across her knees. Though the sight of her glorious, nubile body roused him, he knew there would be no chance of anything tonight. His shameful words, coupled with her mounting anxiety, had caused her to emotionally retreat from him.

Not only that, but all her attention was focused on the object in her hands: the mortal, black arrow they had found imbedded in the disberry tree in the Garden of Grim Knowledge. Supposedly, the arrow had killed The King In Yellow, her father, though like the others Alan had his doubts.

Alan had been loathe for Cassilda to take the deadly implement with them. A mere accidental nick of the poisoned arrow-head would be death to whoever made the error. But Cassilda had been determined, perhaps viewing the arrow as a talisman of her failure. Before bed each night, she meditated upon it, as though by concentrating her entire being upon its infinitesimally small point she might manifest her desired revenge. Perhaps, magically sensitive as she was, she did not merely see a crude object designed to take life, but rather the reified pathway of its secret origins. Perhaps she saw her sister in its venom-dewed tip. If she did, she was silent on the matter. Alan had given up trying to understand her ritual, or draw out commentary upon it. All he knew was that Cassilda had become as fixated on her arrowhead as he upon his Claw.

"She has grown too powerful," a dark voice whispered in Alan's ear. "See how she controls the entire party?"

Of course she leads us. She is the Princess of Carcosa.

"But once you had your own free will. You have merely exchanged Cali's chains for her sister's . . . "

Silence!

Of late, Alan longed to hear the softer, more comforting voice—the very voice of Carcosa, and perhaps of his true and secret self—but it remained ominously silent.

"Kill her now, then take your pleasure of the serpent-woman, that is what a man would do . . . "

Disgusted by the temptations of The Claw, Alan announced he was going to have a bath, to which Cassilda offered no response. He shuffled out of the main room and closed the door. He leaned against the door for a moment, resting his head on polished ebony. There was something grounding about the feeling of hard pressure against his skull. He wondered if that was not part of the ritualistic prayer some religions employed, in which the prayerful touched their foreheads to the earth. *Bowing the mind intelligence to something greater,* he thought. *That is what I must do. The harder I fight The Claw, the worse it will get, the harder to resist. I must find a way to submit to something bigger than myself.* But what could that be? He had met a god, The King In Yellow, but it seemed in Carcosa gods could die.

THE DREAMS OF DEMHE

He set about placing logs and small branches—which were stacked against the fireplace—into the firebox. A metal container sat at the foot of the hearth. When he opened it, he found it contained flint and iron, as he'd suspected. He struck the flint and iron together until it created a spark. After a few attempts, one of the sparks caught a twig and began to burn. Within moments, he had a warm fire.

He sat by it for a few seconds, contemplating both all that had happened and the simple joy of watching the flames consume firewood. His mind drifted, eventually finding a metaphysical thread, the old occultist in him surfacing.

Wood grew, expanding, representing new growth and beginnings. He saw himself as a child, growing like the sapling in the forest. Then he saw that same sapling uprooted, planted anew in the soil of Carcosa. The element of wood was inevitably burned in the fire, transformed. Yes, that's what had happened in the battle for the city. The fires of war had remoulded him, made him stronger. What then came next? *Ash.* Which was a cipher for earth. Ashes sowed into the soil set the stage for new fertility, for rebirth. Though he'd already been reborn in one sense, he also believed this process of transformation had only just begun, that there was yet more dead flesh to slough away before the true, glittering nature of his being was revealed. Strangely, that brought comfort to him. There was more work to do, so surely he could not die until it was done?

The water in *The Bloody Graal* was drawn up from a deep underground river via old water-pumps; Alan and Cassilda's room, being the most expensive quarters available in the inn, had one in its en suite bathroom. It was a curiously elegant thing, with its curved handle and delicately sloped nozzle. Alan spent ten hard minutes working the pump in order to draw enough water to fill half of the tub. He expected the water to be freezing cold, but to his surprise, it was delightfully warm; the underground river must have been volcanic, a hot spring.

He stripped off his clothes and settled into the bath, releasing an involuntary sigh as the waters relaxed his overtaxed muscles, seeped into his dirty pores, and soothed the blisters that had developed—especially on the inside of his thighs—from many days of riding. He rested The Claw on the edge of the bathtub. He wished he could remove it. He felt the same when he slept.

Amputees normally took off their prosthetic limbs in these situations, but Alan had no choice but to remain welded to his monstrous weapon. It meant he could never quite let go, never quite rest. And, even stranger, could never quite be alone. All his life he had felt lonely, estranged from his fellow man. But now he realised just how precious it was to have a room of one's own, and periods of grace where no one could interrupt his thoughts. The Claw was his new permanent companion. Whilst it did fall silent for stretches, he found himself constantly tensed in anticipation of its whispering speech.

He examined the crude, pink-fleshed seam where skin met metal and hideously organic textures. He had tried to remove The Claw once, in Alar, and the act had almost torn his mind apart. *One day, I will be free of The Claw. I'll find a way to safely remove it . . .*

But a dark part of him, a part growing ever more powerful, never wanted to remove it. A dark part of him loved The Claw, more than anything—or anyone—else in the world. For with it, he had grasped the coiling serpent of his own destiny.

He rested his head on the warm bronze of the tub, trying to quiet his thoughts. He listened to his heartbeat, thumping steadily. The fire crackled, whispering in a language he longed to understand. He closed his eyes.

Sleep took him.

In the dreamworld, he opened his eyes and found himself inside another memory. He stood in a dark field under balefully bright stars. The constellation of Draco gleamed like a spinal column of fourteen vertebrae. The Eye of Taurus stared down at them with malignant energy. Even then, Aldebaran's black light called to him, from far across the galaxy.

There were three others with Alan. Though all gathered were robed in sable cloaks, he knew one of them to be Rose. Even in dreaming, the thought of her caused the hair on the back of his arms and neck to rise like grass beneath Spring sunlight. His being felt electrified and illuminated in her presence, even veiled as they were.

They stood around the edges of an ouroboros, a magical circle formed by pure white salt. In the centre burned a flame, and like all fire, including the one back in *The Bloody Graal,* it whispered constantly, profound secrets of the void.

"We of the quadriga are gathered here for the Ritual of the

THE DREAMS OF DEMHE

Agape!" a voice declared. Not Rose's, but a man's voice, reverberating out of the hood of one of the other two figures about the circle.

Rose had brought Alan along to a special ritual, one that was supposed to weaken the barriers between this world and the next. Rose's secretive companions had needed a fourth member to complete the compass points, and Alan had showed great aptitude for magic. Thus, he was tentatively admitted.

He had spent months in preparation for the ritual, rehearsing his lines, practicing his visualisations, trying to open his imaginative third eye. He had also been training physically, his body at its very leanest. He practically vibrated with excitement. This could be the moment he crossed over, the moment he found what he had been searching for his whole life. Of course, he was also excited because he knew he would be consummating the ritual with Rose, and one other woman, whose face he had not yet seen. He tried to push that part of him down. Un-channeled carnality was antithetical to magical practice, or so Rose said.

"Begin!" the voice said, with thunderous power. One of the robed members—perhaps the other woman—struck a bell, and its clear note reverberated in the dark of night with ghostly brightness.

Circles were walked. Words were uttered. The cold of the night wormed its way into his bones. Alan had not quite appreciated, rehearsing only his small portion of the ritual, just how long the magical working was. Hours went by, and his feet began to tire, his eyes to droop, his concentration to wane. Deosil. Widdershins. Round and round, an endless circle turning. A brief fragment of childhood memory flashed through his mind, strange words uttered by a man Alan had longed to know: *But all things spin upon the dragon-wheel. That which is lost returns to us in glory. I look forward to that day.*

Could this be that day? Was this the dragon-wheel about which he turned?

At last, at midnight, the moment came to disrobe. Each of them shed their sable attire and stood naked about the fire, the night hugging their wan forms like a demon lover. Rose stood at the eastern point. Her black hair was deeper than the night itself. Her sloping, Asian features gave her the look of an ancient queen. She was a lithe and supple goddess, a Lilith reborn. The other two robed figures were not as Alan had expected. One was a much older woman, blonde-haired, stretch marks and wrinkles somehow augmenting and adorning her beautiful figure, the way *kintsugi* amplifies the beauty of some rare artefact. Her eyes were disturbingly bright crystals that defied the darkness. She had the look of a woman whose beauty should have faded long ago, but some internal spirit kept it living, shining from underneath her flesh. The final figure was a man, broad-chested, vaguely Middle Eastern in appearance, his flesh covered in thick curls. His hair was dark and coiled, his beard full and luscious. He would not have been out of place in the company of ancient Persian warriors. He was tall too, thick limbed and muscular. But what intrigued Alan most were his eyes.

The same bright yellow orbs he had seen as a boy in the back of a taxi cab.

He opened his mouth, longed to say something. *Ub!* But the theatrics of the ritual kept him rooted, unable to speak. He dared not break out of character. *Besides, it can't be him; he hasn't aged a day!* Yet that did not dispel his mounting terror and excitement, that this was the man, that such a mysterious encounter might finally be explained.

The man smiled at Alan, as if he knew.

"Now, the Agape shall commence, and we shall return to the primal atavisms of the Serpent. *Praise the One who is born of Serpent and Man!*"

Alan had no time to react. What came over him then was nothing short of terrifying. He had been steeling himself for the ritualistic sex-act, cleansing his mind of impurities, building his energetic carnality with the intent of rending the veil between worlds. The nature of magical sex was control, yet suddenly Alan found he had none.

Writhe, writhe, writhe like the serpent you are!

Rose was before him, then she was on the ground, spreading her legs for him, her cunt dripping wet, her dark eyes riveted to his. He trembled head to toe, overcome by a passion he could not understand. It was as though a snake had possessed him, a reptile, that knew only death and the sowing of its seed across the stars.

She seemed to read his fear, a deep tenderness in her, which he ached for.

"It's okay. You can give in. Give in to the serpent, Alan."

He could not speak, but he thanked her with his eyes.

THE DREAMS OF DEMHE

He thrust into her, and she cried out, though not with a human cry of pleasure, but with a hiss. It aroused him more than he could describe, a painful hardness that made her whimper. She gripped his neck with her soft and delicate hands, pulled his head towards hers. She put her lips to his ear and hissed once more, knowing how it drove him wild.

In times of sanity, Alan considered himself a practiced and sensitive lover. But the skin of that sanity had been sloughed off, revealing some animal beneath he did not know. They fucked like two serpents entwined in the dirt, a dismal writhing, hissing, spitting, biting. He clamped teeth about the flesh of her neck until it bled. She raked the skin from his back, and he almost felt as though the flakes of skin peeling away were scales, the dead armour of a former self.

"They saw, but other sight instead! a crowd of ugly serpents; horrour on them fell, and horrid sympathy!"

The words of *Paradise Lost* were shockingly true to his current situation. He had no mind left, only the dimmest flicker of consciousness that peered out from behind his eyes, pitying the loathsome thing he had become.

"Rejoice!" the yellow-eyed man called. Perhaps he watched Alan and Rose entwined, his own ritualistic part done. If he did, Alan did not care. He did not care about anything except the dissipation of the ophidian energy that possessed him. "Rejoice! For thou art the Serpent of Secret Becoming Himself! Remember, my son!"

Alan writhed. Rose screamed. His seed was spent with shocking force.

Calling out, both in the dream and in reality, consciousness began to return to him, the memory collapsing in on itself, like a tapestry showing a colourful scene folded and cast away to leave the stark, bare wall of reality in its stead. As Alan hovered in that place, before waking but not fully in dream, he thought he saw two blood red eyes staring down at him from the nothingness.

The eyes of Mazael, perhaps.

The harvester had come to reap.

CHAPTER 8
THE SHADOW LAND

C ALI REELED AS suddenly she found herself in a glittering kingdom of gushing waterfalls. Great cliffs rose around her, purple-hued, their granitic faces looking like they had either been hewn by giants or else the violence of asteroids. The chasmal gulfs that plummeted below those cliffs were filled with glittering, argent liquid, like molten silver. She looked skyward: strange stars wheeled overhead. *Where is this place? What secrets does the desert hold? Or is this mere illusion?*

There was no sign of her steed, Satan. The dreaming had become so strong—and she had been so foolish as to interact with it—that it had bifurcated reality. Cali cursed her weakness and curiosity.

Her first instinct was to run for those cliffs, to clamber up them to gain better vantage, but she knew that would only further mire herself in what was certainly an illusion, so instead she sat cross-legged, closed her eyes, and attempted to walk the path of involution.

The only reality is that which lies within, that which you have cultivated over eons. Reach the inner sepulchre where the Self lies dreaming.

She visualised her inner self as a great black chasm, full of rich and expansive beauty, a projected version of herself exploring its depths, trying to find the inner core. She focused on her breathing, slowing down her exhalations until they were as long and drawn out as the howling winds. At first, she named and numbered the sounds about her: the gurgling flow of those silver rivers and waterfalls, the susurration of the winds, the murmuring of the

53

stone. But after a while, she tried to leave them behind, recognising them as mere phantasmagoria, sensory phenomenon.

The desert plays tricks on you. Go inward, where you will discover what is real.

"How long are you going to sit there?"

Cali's eyes snapped opened and she started, almost falling backward with the shock of discovering she was not alone. How had she not heard their footsteps approaching? How, when her senses had been so attuned? Once more she cursed Demhe and its deceits.

She leapt up to her feet, bending her knees, ready to fight if need be. She had no sword, but her bare knuckles, still blistered from so many recent battles, would be more than enough to shatter the bones of any assailant.

But nothing could have prepared her for the person she found. Not her sister, whom she would have dearly loved to kill. Not any of the souls she had sent to perdition: Erik, her Father, nor her Mother, whose fate remained uncertain. Not even Alan Chambers, whom she could believe—though it pained her to admit it—might have found a way to reach her, so persistent, so infuriatingly resilient was he . . . No. None of these expected phantoms, someone altogether stranger—and yet familiar too.

She turned away from the spectre, unwilling to believe. It was both wondrous and crude, a mockery of her magical attainment and sorcerous power.

"You dare, Demhe?" Cali shrieked into the cold expanse of a sky she did not recognise. "You dare insult me with such a crude device?"

"That's not going to work," the spectre said. The spectre's voice dripped with sly mockery. "You should know better than most that the harder one tries to grasp something the more it slips away. The path of forgetting is the only way to attainment. You learned that dealing with Father."

Cali turned. Staring back at her was her own mirror image, a haunting shadow clad in the vestments of her flesh, naked and—unlike the original—unblemished by lightning scars.

"Is not Alan the perfect example?" the Shadow continued, nonchalant. She had placed a hand on her hip and kinked it out to one side, the very posture of a confident whore. Cali despised her, yet knew in doing so, she was only falling deeper into Demhe's twisted labyrinth, for that is what the desert wanted, for her to admit she hated herself. "The more you tried to control him, the more self-control he gained."

"And I suppose you would have done something differently, Illusionary Projection?" Cali said, tartly.

The Shadow laughed.

"Of course, my own Sweet Self. I would have fucked him. That way, he would have followed us like a loyal dog to the end of his days. But your pride would not permit it. Now look where your arrogance has landed us."

Cali snarled.

"There is no 'us'. I integrated you a long time ago."

Cali turned and stalked off towards the cliffs. If she was going to be forced to play the game, she might as well play it on her terms, rather than going through this dreary masquerade.

"I wouldn't turn your back on me, dear Self. That which we deny comes back tenfold. Remember?"

Cali paused. The Shadow, though a lie, did speak some truth. But wasn't that the way of the Devil? He knew the Scripture better than the faithful.

"Get behind me, Satan," Cali snarled, and continued to walk towards the monolithic cliff-faces towering over the mercurial landscape.

CHAPTER 9
THE JIGSAW PIECE

ALAN STARTED AWAKE to the sound of Cassilda's screams. They had settled down for the night without really speaking to one another: Cassilda lost in a meditation upon vengeance, Alan lost in the world of his past. Alan had slept well, not dreaming again, as though his oneiric faculties had been wiped out by the startling remembrance of the Serpent Ritual. But Cassilda screamed as though she had awoken from a nightmare. Cold sweat drenched her forehead and limbs. Her breath came heaving, her ribs flexing and contracting, as though some pale spectre clamped both hands around her heart, squeezing. Her eyes were so wide they were frightening to Alan. He felt he could pitch forward and become lost in them.

"Cassilda, what is the matter?"

She looked at him as though he might turn into a serpent. Then her expression of terror finally softened. She slumped, taking deep, gulping breaths.

"A dream . . . " she said, with some relief. "Oh, a dream I have not had in eons." Her eyes screwed up as though she were in physical pain. "A dream I never wished to have again." A soft wail escaped her lips. Alan pitied her. The sound resembled that of an animal wounded by the roadside.

He reached out and entwined the fingers of his left hand in hers.

"My love, my sweet, what is wrong? Tell me."

She opened her eyes and looked at him, returning his strong grip.

For a while she said nothing, then, with that impossible tenderness, like no woman he had ever known, she stroked his face, a sad smile blooming across her own.

"It's just a memory . . . But you are here now . . . that is far more important." She spoke as though her concerns were silly, but Alan knew the horrors and traumas she had endured, knew that it was no mere nightmare, but a relived terror, one she might never be free of.

"The past can trouble us," Alan whispered. "Sometimes more so than the present. I've been troubled by my past of late. It's this place! I can only imagine what it's like for you. You don't have to share, but if you do, I am here to listen . . . "

Cassilda's smile widened, and the dimples of her cheeks were adorned with pearls of tears.

"I have not treated you well of late. I . . . " She swallowed, as though fearing the words she meant to speak next. "I think I begin to understand the nature of your burden."

Alan nodded. Even now, as they lay intimately together, he was dreadfully and painfully aware of his right hand—The Claw—bent behind his back, the deadly talons tinkling as they rattled together like the overture to violence.

"Is it the staff?"

Cassilda nodded.

"It is so powerful, Alan. I pity the woman who made it, but also am in awe of her. What passion must have driven her to work such magic?"

"Does it . . . " Alan hesitated, unsure whether he should ask such a question for fear of what it might reveal about himself. " . . . talk to you?"

Cassilda paused, regarding him intently.

"Sometimes . . . Or rather, I think it is the dead I hear."

Alan felt a chill pass through him.

"Do they beg for revival?"

She shook her head.

"Not at all. But they do have requests and blocking them out has been difficult. No wonder Scarleth went mad." Cassilda sighed. "Then there are the slaves I made in Carcosa. I can still feel them, Alan, even all this distance apart. I can feel the army, feel them moving restlessly about the city. Their minds—or what is left of them—call out to me. They beg for only one thing: release. Every moment of every day their thoughts press upon me; it's like being buried alive. And all they want is for me to free them." A shadow passed across her face. "But if I do that, Carcosa will be exposed.

What if Pe'kar sends another legion? Or all his legions. One would have been enough to take the city, had we not been fortunate enough to arrive, had I not found the staff." She turned away from him, and Alan saw the staff leaning against four poster bed, the ruby winking at them like a dreadful eye. He once again thought of Mazael, whose entire existence was voyeurism personified. He shuddered. The many cameras and surveillance techniques of Earth had never bothered him. But here, in this magical land, he felt the eyes were far more invasive.

He touched Cassilda's cheek, trying to soothe her.

"Carcosa shall not fall. We shall stop Cali. If necessary, we will enter the land of Blue Light to do so." Alan hesitated. He wanted to ask Cassilda about her mother, who even now was likely suffering in the dungeons of Pe'kar. Roland had told them what happened at the start of the siege. The soldier had admitted that, upon reflection, it might well have been an elaborate ruse, a mummer in the guise of the Queen, but when she had been brought forth, he had been certain, from her face and aura, that it was Camilla herself. Whatever the case, it seemed a certainty that if they ventured into the lands of Blue Light to rescue Camilla, she would not return to Carcosa as the same woman who left it.

Cassilda, in that eerie way of hers, read his thoughts before he came to a decision about whether to ask.

"It may be too late for my mother . . . and she would want us to save Carcosa." Tears burned in Cassilda's eyes. "She would want us to put our loyalty to the great city above all else. That was her way, the way of self-sacrifice."

Suddenly, unexpectedly, the quiet voice within Alan returned.

The way of sacrifice makes man whole.

He gasped a little, so pure and strong was the thought—not a thought, but true communication, issuing from somewhere deep within himself. Who was this person? He had thought of the guide as Carcosa itself, and perhaps his secret self. It was both of these things, but something else as well. Something tantalising familiar, like the smell of an old lover's perfume, or the notes of a sad, old jazz song echoing out of the past.

"Alan?"

"I'm fine . . . Just thinking," he said.

"I am overwhelmed with thought!" Cassilda said, rolling onto her back, looking up at the bed's canopy with profound exasperation. "I sometimes wish I could not think!"

"That is what alcohol is for," Alan said.

He was delighted to see his humour tickled her, a smile breaking through the pall of misery.

"That is a dangerous road."

He nodded. He reached out and clasped her hand again, uncomfortably aware he lay in the same manner as a whorish assassin, a deadly blade behind his back, as though he waited for the opportune moment to plunge it into her heart.

"We'll bear these burdens together," Alan whispered.

"Yes," Cassilda answered, almost breathless. "Together."

The party of five met downstairs and broke their fast together. Liliya provided them with a humble breakfast of cured meats, spiced teas, and bread. Alan avoided meeting her gaze, Rose's serpentine hiss still following out of the dream and into waking reality, along with the memory of all it had done to him. He shuddered, remembering how it had debased his cognitive faculties, made him a beast of the field.

Alan was pleased to discover that Mazael was nowhere to be found, which eased his mounting anxiety a little. The Claw was also quiet this morning, as indeed was everyone else. The group had always talked volubly on their travails, no matter how taxing the road, but this morning all were silent and introspective. Alan realised that each person must have suffered the excessively vivid dreams brought on by proximity with Demhe, and the dreams had triggered reflection and rumination.

"I have a question," LeBarron said, suddenly piping up.

"Go ahead," Alan said.

"It is a simple one, really. What happens if Cali dies in the desert? Let us say The Harvester's story about this beast is true, and Cali runs afoul of it. What then?"

"It is as Mazael said," Cassilda replied. "The desert brings you to where you want to go. It will show us to her, even if it is to her corpse, though in truth I think you are too hopeful. If the Screaming Pit could not hold her, then Demhe's dreams are unlikely to be much of an obstacle. She has made the journey many times. We should have suspected her true motivations from the start. But we told ourselves we were learning more about Pe'kar than he was learning of us. Foolish!" Her elegant hands had clenched into fists so tight that the knuckles protruded like bony spikes.

"I agree," Roland said. "She will not be slain by the dreaming. She is alive, even as we prattle on and take our repast!" These last words were almost spat with bitterness. Alan realised that inaction did not sit well with Roland, even if he was a philosopher at heart. LeBarron was unperturbed by the jab, however. He smiled pleasantly.

"Oh, I do not think it likely she has perished," LeBarron said. "In fact, I am almost certain she has not. But, well, last night I dreamed that I was wandering the desert forever, looking for my . . . " He paused, like a man teetering upon the edge of a cliff.

"For what?" Alan prompted.

"My purpose," LeBarron said. "I knew it was buried somewhere in the sand. I must have wandered a thousand years but could not find it. I grew angrier and angrier. Why was it eluding me? How had I become so blind? When I woke up, I thought of Cali, dead, buried under a dune, and us all traipsing over the dreaming for a millennia. I suppose it is silly in the light of day."

"To give meaning to one's dreams is never silly," Petruccio said. "All my best paintings were born of dreams. Carcosa itself was a dream once."

"Well said." Cassilda smiled at the dwarf, who inclined his head in gratitude.

"There is one factor, however," Petruccio went on. "That perhaps you have overlooked, that maybe gives me some hope Cali *will* be delayed in the dreaming, if not killed."

Cassilda frowned. "What is that?"

"She is tormented." Petruccio could not conceal a dark smile of schadenfreude. "We all are, of course. We all bear the scars of trauma, inside and out. But Cali's torment is of a different kind. For all her power and magical attainment, she has long wrestled with a dual identity. In some ways, she has been even more the mummer than our friend LeBarron! But unlike LeBarron, she has not integrated these characters into her psyche. She is conflicted. Even though I did not see the full extent of her treachery, I saw how lying to the many men and women she fetched from Earth and brought to Carcosa tore at her. I saw how desperately she wanted to impress and appease her father, yet at the same time hated Him to the core. She is a split personality. And in the dreaming, that can be deadly."

Roland clapped Petruccio on the shoulder, a broad grin sparkling across his face.

"That *does* give me hope, Petruccio. And I think it is well reasoned. It is also a warning to us. If there are things we have repressed, now is the time to air them out, lest they consume us once we cross the border."

All nodded in agreement, though they did not speak further on the matter. Alan supposed it was left ambiguous as to whether these repressions should be publicly aired or simply aired to oneself.

Their hostess, Liliya, provided them with ample food and water supplies, which they loaded onto the quinels, and then they set off into Al Shujah. Just before they went, she drew Alan to one side.

It was an agony to look at her: she was so fair, so voluptuous, so strangely sensual despite her serpentine origins.

"I have seen the way you look at me," she purred.

"I love Cassilda," Alan said, a little too quickly.

Liliya smirked.

"I do not doubt it for a second. And your gaze was not entirely lascivious. There was a longing there, and a nostalgia too. You see something in me that reminds me of yourself, no? There is a familiarity to me, hmm?"

Alan felt heat in his face, sweat running down his palms and neck. Finally, he nodded in admission. Why deny it? She spoke the truth.

Liliya smiled.

"A wise man once told me that I would meet the serpent in the shape of a man," she whispered. "And I believe that you are he. He told me to tell you something."

Alan stared. His lust and libido fell away, replaced by a different kind of desire, a longing to know the secret puzzle-pieces that had ever been missing from the jigsaw of his being. His mouth was dry. His heart thundered.

"What did he want you to tell me?"

"This: *Remember all things spin upon the dragon-wheel. That which is lost returns to us in glory.*"

THE DREAMS OF DEMHE

Alan lurched backward. He tripped and fell, sprawling on the hardwood floor. His heart thundered so hard and fast it was painful. A whimper escaped his throat, of disbelief, of awe, of terror. He tried to say something, to speak, but a hand had clasped around his throat. His eyes shone with tears. *How, how, how?* He knew those words. They had been uttered by the strange, yellow-eyed taxi driver, the man who had haunted Alan's life. Indeed, perhaps the deepest mystery of Alan's existence . . . And here Alan saw the tantalising glimpse of an answer.

Liliya extended a hand to help Alan rise. He clasped it, and she hauled him to his feet. He glanced around and saw the others watching in confusion. Liliya drew his eyes back to hers with final parting words.

"Alan, at the Mount of Al Qaf Saba, seek the Old Man. He'll tell you what you need to know if you are to fulfill your destiny." She wrapped her arms about him and placed her lips to his ear—her embrace sent shivers down his spine. The human part of her was soft and voluptuous, pressed tightly against him. Her scales were warm, as though they'd trapped the sun. He understood perfectly why men would be willing to die for one night's embrace. Liliya whispered into his ear, "From one serpentkin to another, I wish you good fortune, flesh of my flesh!"

Then she released him. He stared at her in wonder, before finally tearing his eyes away. The others were waiting.

They travelled west through the town with their quinels, towards the border, searching for a guide to take them by a safe road through the desert of dreaming.

CHAPTER 10
DREAM-STORM

AL SHUJAH HELD many curiosities and wonders, but the party were increasingly blind to them, their eyes set upon the westward gate, and their minds upon their foe, who had likely not slept, driving on with infernal willpower towards her goal. Alan hoped that even a being as powerful as Cali would, at some stage, have to rest, exhaustion catching up with her. It was the only chance they had of reaching her before she reached the lands of Blue Light. That, or the dreaming embroiling her in its subterfuges.

Leading their quinels, they passed several market stalls, some selling esoteric foods—mostly based upon insects and arachnids, though there were also many colourful eggs belonging to birds Alan could not name. Many stalls sold great ropes with numerous knots tied along their length.

"For those who are only venturing a short way into the dreaming, rather than crossing over," Petruccio explained to Alan.

"Like the thread of Ariadne in the Labyrinth of the Minotaur," Alan muttered.

"Exactly." Petruccio nodded. "One may find one's way back to sanity."

"The ropes are also used to bind people to their fellows, so as not to be separated by the dreaming," LeBarron said. "But I have seen entire parties consign themselves to death because they were bound together. It is safer for each of us to face our own dreams, but to be united in bearing, our hearts and minds turned towards the Emerald Mountain. Unity of purpose and intent will bring us through."

"Is the dreaming really so overwhelming?"

THE DREAMS OF DEMHE

"It depends how far you go," LeBarron answered. The actor stared out at the horizon beyond the western gate. Clouds were gathering. The air was thick and humid, pressurised, as though an explosion were imminent. Shapes and shadows flickered across the horizon.

And danced through the streets.

More than once, Alan thought he saw strange, theriomorphic children skipping between the stalls, but when he directed his attention toward them, they vanished.

"I think the dreaming is infiltrating the town . . . " Alan said.

"The Harvester was wrong. Or maybe things have changed," LeBarron said. "The dreaming is strong today. And getting stronger."

"Is that . . . a dream storm?" Roland asked.

Thunder answered, making the heavens themselves reverberate. Black clouds coalesced, pregnant with viridian shards of lightning. Sand blew in winds that moaned the poetry of dead eons.

LeBarron turned to them with gritted teeth.

"This is going to make finding a guide infinitely more difficult."

They met with many dead ends. No one seemed willing to brave the dreaming, no matter how much coin or renown they offered, or how Cassilda threatened the wrath of Carcosa. It seemed that the auguries for such an adventure were ill and boded dark fortune. To be fair, the storm would have turned Alan away in a heartbeat; it brooded with a malevolence that went far beyond simple weather.

"We cannot let my sister get any farther ahead than she already has," Cassilda said. "She will likely not have stopped to rest as we have. We must keep going, even if it means braving the storm."

LeBarron nodded.

"I have crossed the dreaming before. I could guide you. But I fear that much has changed since I was last here."

"It is a risk we have to take," Cassilda said.

"I trust you, LeBarron." Alan clapped a hand on the actor's shoulder. "Though if there is something you should tell us about the dreaming, or your personal motivations, maybe now is the time? We wouldn't want a repeat of Alar."

LeBarron grinned, somehow both roguish and sheepish at once.

"You will never let me live that down, will you?"

"Not in a million years." Alan grinned in return.

"Very well, I solemnly swear—by the Pallid Mask of the Stranger—that I have no ulterior motive! And in his name, I shall lead you, donning the cloak of a guide!"

LeBarron turned and adopted the posture of a heroic scout, a master of beast, field, and fell, but after a few steps he suddenly collapsed, his face wrought with agony. He clutched his side, where the old wound dwelt, a scar that spoke of a journey no man should return from. Yet LeBarron had, thanks to Cassilda and the black staff she held in her lily-white hands. Alan rushed forward to help the actor, but LeBarron growled like a snarling felid, and Alan withdrew. The group waited in painful and sympathetic silence for him to rise.

The ease with which LeBarron had once bent his face and being into new shapes was no more. For some reason, his sojourn into the afterlife had robbed him of the ability to wear masks as he once did. The pain it caused him seemed greater than any physical torture a man could endure. Alan pitied him, and wondered if they had truly made the right decision in bringing him back when it caused him such grief to be less than he was.

"No matter . . . " LeBarron said, rising slowly. "I suppose I must venture on as myself—and only myself."

He trudged forward, leading his quinel by the reins. The others followed, respectfully silent. The despair in LeBarron's voice was a worse omen than the storm clouds battering the borderlands of Demhe.

Soon, they reached the western gate of Al Shujah. Peering through it, they beheld what had become a roiling tempest. The wave-like dunes were struck with titanic force by descending bolts of green lightning. Shapes and faces danced in the cyclones of sand and grit. Alan shuddered; so many of them were familiar. For a while, none of them could move or speak. All saw haunting images of past lives, past loves, and past terrors revealed in the darkly lit whirlwind of black atoms. The flashes of lightning created afterimages upon the retina that burned with the intensity of magically charged sigils.

"How could I have been so blind," the dwarf muttered.

"What is it?"

"Demhe *dreams*," Petruccio said emphatically. "The *oneiric* pigment. It must be here. The pigment is *why* the desert dreams."

THE DREAMS OF DEMHE

Cassilda's eyes widened.

"I must say, that is quite the cogent theory. But why have none considered this before?"

"They have," Petruccio said. "But the dreaming disorients them. Not only that, but it distorts their memory, for what are dreams but memories plucked from time and place? The dreaming has re-written our history, making us believe it was always this way. But it is not so! Ah, I must hold fast to my purpose!"

He took out his sketchbook and pen and began to descry a sigil upon the paper.

"A glyph of memory," the dwarf explained. "When I look upon this, I shall remember my purpose in the desert, and therefore, find the oneiric pigment at last!"

"It appears my sister's tutelage was not without some benefits," Cassilda observed, tilting her head towards the expertly wrought magical sigil.

The dwarf nodded, though he could not bring himself to speak on the matter.

"Careful," LeBarron said. "If we enter the dreaming with dispirit purpose, we will be separated."

Petruccio looked darkly at LeBarron, and the actor was not able to hold his gaze. Alan knew that nothing could stand between Petruccio and his goal. If he believed the oneiric pigment lay in Demhe, then he would look beneath every grain of sand to find it, whether it took him a thousand years or not.

"Well then," LeBarron said, breaking eye-contact with Petruccio and instead looking at the wrathful storm they saw before them. "I suppose I had better go first. The Way is not a way—not like any Way you know. Just make sure you keep me in your eyeline. If we lose each other, bear the Emerald Mountain your heart and recite the mantra *Al Qaf Saba* over and over. We will all meet there!"

"Wait!" Alan called.

But LeBarron had already strode forward into the cyclones, finding some impossibly narrow sliver between two proud columns of twisting sand, a sliver so narrow it seemed the slit of a serpent's eye, no more. Immediately, Roland set off after him, followed very closely by Petruccio. Alan and Cassilda clasped hands, shared a last look, and then hurried after them, the rage of the desert swallowing them with its fury.

CHAPTER 11
THE CROOKED PATH

A T FIRST, their path seemed ordinary. Difficult, dangerous, painful, but thoroughly material. Sand swallowed their feet. Sand blistered their exposed cheeks. Sand found its way into their throats. Even the quinels, naturally equipped to deal with the desert, seemed aggravated.

Cassilda quickly wrapped her light, turquoise kaftan about her face, but Alan's robes were not so expansive or loose, and so he had to endure the harsh grating of his flesh, squinting his eyes so as not to be blinded by the dervish of glittering grit. The wind shrieked at them, accompanied by a monotonous droning sound, as though some miserable sufferer in the wastes warned them to turn back. Lighting strobed through the maelstrom, making Alan's heart jump whenever it struck.

"This is the strongest I have ever known the storms!" LeBarron bellowed.

Alan could only just see the actor's form ahead. His blue robes were a smear of colour beside the black shadow of his quinel. His posture was hunched as he bent into the wind. Roland marched next to him, his posture stronger—for he was used to walking with heavy armour—but still leaning into the wind.

"If only the desert had been like this the last week!" Petruccio roared. Despite his diminutive stature, he stood firmest of all of them, merely tugging his grey robes a little about his face; his feet were so sure, it seemed not even a lightning bolt could shake him. "Then Cali would have made very little progress indeed!"

Roland and LeBarron laughed bitterly.

They soldiered on. Though Alan had no sense of direction—there being no sun, moon, or stars by which to guide his path, and the whole landscape dissolved behind a veil of yellow atoms—he did manage to discern a small pattern in LeBarron's movements.

He was leading them in a spiral.

At first, Alan thought that LeBarron had once again betrayed their trust, pursuing some bizarre ulterior motive. But then Alan realised that though they were essentially moving in a circle, the landscape *was* changing. A tree here. A large boulder there. New features emerged from the roiling chaos, despite the fact their footfalls wended ever leftwards. Not only that, but the circles—or corners—of the spiral were getting smaller, yet somehow they were not treading old ground. It was then Alan realised that the droning sound was LeBarron *counting*.

Crooked indeed, Alan thought. *A spiral that moves us forward . . .*

"Something's wrong," LeBarron said.

"What?" Alan struggled to hear him.

"Something's wrong!" LeBarron repeated, louder. He'd halted, and now looked left and right, as though they'd reached a crossroads. Alan could not discern the ground let alone a pathway.

"What is it?" Cassilda said, raising her voice to equal the storm.

LeBarron's acetylene eyes blazed.

"None of us are dreaming yet."

"Isn't that a good thing?" Alan said, unable to stop hope tinging his words with a childish inflection. "Maybe we're able to resist it?"

"No," LeBarron said. "Nothing resists it. Something is blocking the dreams. Something that cannot dream, perhaps . . . "

As if in answer, a great roar cut through the wind and thunder. Tectonic in its depth, it shook Alan's sternum. His ears rang with tinnitus in the aftermath. The quinels moaned and stirred. Alan had to grip the reins of his own quinel tightly to prevent the creature scarpering.

"The beast!" Roland cried.

"So the old harvester did not lie," Petruccio muttered, darkly.

LeBarron drew his scimitar. Roland raised his spear. Petruccio unsheathed his jewelled dagger. Cassilda upreared her staff and the ruby at its crown pulsed hungrily, with eagerness. Alan felt energy surge through his body, down his right arm, into The Claw, which crackled with a lightning equal to that of the storm raging above them. Though Alan knew it was dangerous to be overconfident, he could not stop himself thinking that whatever came out of the veil of the sandstorm would die a piteous and ignominious death faced with their awesome power and arsenal.

O, how wrong he was.

A shadow impressed itself upon the swirling layers of sand and grit. It's enormity threw them all off-kilter for a moment. Surely, this was no creature, but the Emerald Mountain itself? Then a flash of jade lightning struck the ground before them, throwing illumination across the monstrosity. And monstrous it was, in every conceivable way.

"Ancient damnation!" Roland cursed, and then he was diving to one side as the creature came among them.

A sprawling thing. Every animal at once. A shifting river-rapid of emergent form. Eagle beak, crow talon, jaguar flesh, lion mane, spider jaws, cockroach wings—a synaesthesia of ugly beings. Faces. Eyes. Orifices. Crimson bile that itself seemed a living fester. Alan thought that the creature looked like a cross between a fungal monstrosity and a carcass, or more accurately several carcases stitched together by a grim mycelial network. Degenerate limbs sprouted from its back, flexing like spider legs, some ending in human hands. One limb held a terrifying sword, one that was eerily familiar to Alan . . .

There was no time for thought. The quinels bolted. Alan considered running after them, but knew he would become lost in Demhe's labyrinth. He gritted his teeth and kept his focus on the monster before them.

Another spider-limb, ending in a goblin-like claw, swept up LeBarron in a death-grip. The actor's scimitar flashed, severing the limb, and he fell back to the ground. The stump of the creature's arm disgorged reeking fluid, green and red, and then before their eyes two slithering appendages forced their way out of the wound, like blind serpents drawn by the smell of freshly laid eggs. These two grotesque serpents sucked at the air with lamprey mouths.

Cassilda lowered her staff, screaming monosyllabic sounds that reverberated with such power they shook Alan's bones. He felt a similar sense of pressure to that of the elemental storm above, a concentrated power, and then the ruby flashed once, discharging a dreadful red bolt.

But the beast was more cunning than it seemed. Its mess of a face, composed of miss-mashed body parts—predominantly eyes—sloughing into one another, turned and fixed on the approaching projectile. With a reflexive motion the horrid, too-thin arm bearing the sword swung upwards and cut the red energy in half, sending two fractal zags of magical power careening off into the desert storm. The beast let out a howl, the roar of a living corpse.

Alan snarled, raising The Claw.

"For Carcosa!" A great yellow blast shot out from the palm of his hand.

His bolt stuck true, and for a moment he thought he had succeeded where Cassilda had failed. A dinner-plate sized tunnel blasted through the monster's ever-changing, porous flesh— passing clean through its roiling body, end to end.

The creature staggered for a moment, and then, before Alan's horrified eyes, the wound became a womb, red offspring birthing, scrambling down the side of the creature's flanks, some scorpion-like, some like worms, others more like crabs with gilded, crimson carapaces. LeBarron and Petruccio leapt forward, their weapons sweeping to and fro, cutting apart the creatures, which parted all too easily into gloopy, almost formless putty.

Cassilda lowered her staff, was staring in abject horror at the creature.

"This is no natural thing . . . This is magic of the blackest kind."

"How do we kill it?" Alan asked.

"We must destroy every part of it."

"Fire, then?" Alan said, but he knew it would be almost impossible by natural means. He wondered if Cassilda would be able to magically generate flame, but even if that were the case, the winds were so terrible he doubted any flame could endure for long.

Roland had regained his footing. Lowering his spear, he heroically charged towards the beast.

The creature wheeled around with disgusting speed for something so massive, its form not obeying the roadmap of physiology. Limbs answered Roland's charge even though the creature's eyes were elsewhere. Tendrils wrapped about his legs and arms, and he shrieked as unseen teeth bit deeply into his flesh, causing black blood to flow down across the sands. The tendrils lifted Roland, and his shrieking magnified to a pitch so high it caused Alan's teeth to vibrate.

"We must free him!" Alan ran forward, raising The Claw, and brought it down in an arc of yellow lightning, cutting easily through a tentacle, freeing Roland's left leg. The soldier kicked and struggled, but it was as though a python had him.

LeBarron saw Roland in danger and looked once at Petruccio. The dwarf nodded that he had the spawns under control, the tiny red creatures still coming in waves, and the actor set off at a sprint, leaping into the air and bringing his scimitar down in a two-handed slash. With another limb severed, the creature was no longer able to hold Roland. He plummeted to the ground with a heavy thump. Moments later he was on his feet, his limbs lacerated and robe torn.

He grabbed his spear, raised it like a javelin, and hurled.

The spear lodged in the creature's flanks, parting flesh. From the wound spilled tiny spider-like creatures that raced toward them over the sand.

"This is pointless!" LeBarron said. "This thing is change itself! We should withdraw."

"Agreed!" Alan replied. "You must lead us!"

But the beast had other ideas than letting them go. Suddenly pivoting, it reared up on legs they had not known were folded beneath its bulk. Now it towered over them, the size of a small house propped up on six-foot stilts. The legs buckled and broke beneath its stupendous weight, and more of its vile offspring spilled from the wounds.

Alan looked across the battlefield and saw Cassilda had rushed in to help Petruccio, her staff sending sweeps of red energy across the dunes that obliterated the swarming newborns.

The beast's eyes were on Cassilda. In fact, its eyes had been on her the whole time, despite their best efforts to antagonise and hurt the thing. It cared only for her. *No, not Cassilda. The staff!*

It suddenly clicked, and Alan had to catch a breath lest the pure horror drowned him. All this time, there had been something familiar about the mutating beast, but he hadn't been able to place it. That's because he had only seen a glimpse, emerging through cracks in shorn armour . . . Ultimately, it was the dark sword, serrated with lamprey teeth, still clutched in a vaguely human hand, that confirmed the identity of the monster.

"It's Haercus!" he cried.

For a moment, the beast's eyes swivelled away from their focus-point, landing on Alan, regarding him with a revolting mixture of recognition, pain, and pure, unadulterated rage. Alan did not delude himself for a second that there was still a man deep within this creature. Whoever Haercus had truly been, he had died long ago in the dungeons of Pe'kar. What remained was this: his flesh as the vehicle for some magical entity that knew change and only change.

Alan raised his Claw, but Haercus was already turning away from him, his multitude of eyes alighting on the black staff. Alan realised Haercus' obsession was simple in nature: the staff had previously hurt him. Haercus wanted to destroy it, before it destroyed him.

"The staff. It is vulnerable to the staff!" Alan said. "Protect Cassilda!"

He leapt forward, carving four deep rivulets in one of the creature's bulbous, fleshy legs. Though the beast might not die from his attacks, it clearly still felt pain, for it shrieked in agony. The limb crumpled, as though boneless, and Haercus toppled lopsidedly to the ground, like a young fawn with a broken leg. Alan quickly retreated as four arms emerged from the shattered rubble of its flesh and sinew, sleeved in a fluid that looked amniotic.

Roland ran up to the creature's flanks and wrenched his spear from where it lay imbedded. He clambered up the beast, using its many gyring faces and protrusions as handholds.

"Madman!" LeBarron cried.

Cassilda roared and aimed her staff. A blast of red light nearly blinded them all. The ruby blazed. Haercus shrieked, but once more his blade—the legendary sword forged by Pe'kar himself— cut the projectile in twain. Alan leapt, tackling LeBarron, forcing him to the ground as the now rogue fragment of Cassilda's magical energy zagged mere inches over their heads and exploded in a nearby dune.

"Thank you!" The actor scrambled to his feet. Alan did likewise.

Haercus was now rising, the limb Alan had destroyed not so much repaired but replaced by new probing digits. Roland rode upon its back, raising his spear and driving it down vertically into what, on a normal creature, might have been a spine.

Haercus bucked, keen to throw off his interloper. Roland clung to his spear to maintain his footing. His eyes were demon-bright, a savage grin splitting his features. Alan thought him every inch the military hero, a man who—in the heat of the moment—could do anything circumstances commanded of them.

But then Alan saw what Roland had missed.

"Roland! Behind!"

The soldier turned, but did not see in time. Haercus's great blade, wielded at the end of that horribly long spider-limb, had risen up behind like a scorpion's stinger. For a moment it remained poised, the very image of Scorpio about to strike, then it shot forward. Roland tried to dodge, but his footing was treacherous and uneven, and the blade passed clean through his chest, a spray of arterial blood spewing out from his ruptured spine. The blade passed through him all the way to the hilt. He was lifted off his feet, and then shaken off the blade's end, tumbling through the air, landing with a terrifying thud upon the ground. He did not rise.

Blinking, Alan swore that Roland's blood descried a sigil as it hovered for flickering moments the air. The Yellow Sign. The glory of Carcosa. Even in death, his very lifeblood remained symbolic of loyalty. Then Alan blinked again, shaking himself back to reality, and there was only wind and rage.

"Roland!" he cried, sprinting towards where the soldier lay.

Cassilda stared in horror at the fallen defender.

"Back to Al Shujah!" LeBarron cried, trying to rally them.

Petruccio answered, immediately seeing sense in the actor's words. Cassilda began to mutter a sibilant spell-speech, her staff glowing brighter than ever before.

Alan knelt by Roland. The soldier was dead, his eyes wide and still, mouth open in a look of surprise. The universe had granted him no parting words of philosophy or poetry. No honourable end. It made Alan want to rage, to break the heavens, and to tear the monster that had done this limb from limb—though what good would that do? It would only gain new form.

"Alan, come on!" LeBarron said, grabbing Alan's shoulder. Alan glanced behind him. He saw Cassilda had thrown up some kind of red barrier, gridlines of energy reminding him of the entoptic lights seen in drug-induced visions. Haercus feared to cross the barrier, probing with disgusting limbs and tendrils. But Alan knew it would not last. The ever-changing creature would find a way around or through it.

Alan also knew they could not leave Roland, not out here, in the desert, where no one would ever find his corpse—give it proper burial. And certainly not to the mercy of Haercus—or rather, the beast born from the womb of his flesh—that was unthinkable. He grabbed the soldier's corpse and hoisted him up. Roland's blood soaked through his robes instantly, the great open wound over his heart still pumping out gore.

"Ever the damned saint!" LeBarron cursed, but he sheathed his sword and grabbed Roland's other arm, helping Alan. "Walk where I walk! Quickly!"

Cassilda and Petruccio followed close behind as they retraced the steps of the spiral path, leaving the beast behind them in the storm, shrieking its misery across the desolate sands.

CHAPTER 12
HELLBOUND

CALI GAINED THE edge of the cliff, hauled herself up, only to discover her shadow waiting for her at the top.

She gritted her teeth, fists clenched.

"If you were really a part of me, you would know how foolish this is."

Her Shadow smirked.

"I really am a part of you, but I think you have inherited the foolish element."

Cali laughed then, hysterically. Her voice reverberated off the crystalline bluffs, descending into a darkness below illuminated only by the sound of gushing mercury.

"Uboth, see what has become of all your great works!" She bellowed the mocking words to the sky. "All the majesty of your creation has been reduced to nothing more than crude psychoanalysis."

The Shadow regarded Cali with a cool indifference that made her skin seethe. Cali's flesh still did not feel right after performing the forbidden rite of *shimen'nehah,* and she was beginning to think it never would.

"Psychoanalysis?" the Shadow purred. "You may deride it, but honestly you could do with some, my other half. And it isn't Uboth's pigment that's doing this to you. Not really. It's *you*. The oneiric pigment is named so for a reason. This is what's in your psyche." The Shadow's smile became poisonous. "And I know you know that, because *I* know it."

Cali spat.

"I'll hear no more of your intellectual flourishes. It's all very pretty and Jungian, but ultimately your illusions will not deter me from my purpose."

"Illusions?" For the first time, the Shadow seemed genuinely angry. "Illusions, Cali? Since when did you become so dull, so base? I had thought you fashioned from gold and onyx, not lead and common stone. *Does it look, to you, like the palaces of imagination have crumbled? Behold them in everlasting splendour! Behold them in undying hideousness!*" As she echoed Cali's own words back to her, a dark light bloomed around the Shadow. It was as though the Shadow were paint still wet upon a canvas, and an unseen hand had used their brush to slowly extend the bounds of her form into a living and sinuous flame. Like an eight-pointed star she blazed. Cali was forced to avert her eyes, wounded by baleful noctilucence.

"Enough!"

The Shadow abated, and just as soon as she had cloaked herself in black splendour, she was earthly again, bitterly smirking.

"You have forgotten yourself," the Shadow said. "Wars are not won with flesh or strength of arm. They are won with spirit! You think of me as your enemy, but I come to remind you of who you truly are!"

Cali's eyes widened. Perhaps she had misread the situation. The illusions of Demhe, after all, were indeed products of the mind, fantasies and fears fuelled by the pigment to the extent they became impossibly real—some said *realer* than real. She had come to the desert fleeing capture. Therefore, she had interpreted all its phenomenon as irritating obstacles at best, or harmful enemies at worst. But what if she could bend these delusions to good use? This Shadow, it seemed, offered her a degree of insight she greatly needed. She had been defeated at every turn. She had failed to dominate Alan Chambers. Failed to take Carcosa. And most likely she had failed to kill her father, galling as it was to admit. In all of these instances she had possessed every advantage. She *should* have won.

"Fine then. If you know something of the truth, then speak it," Cali said.

"The truth is . . . you are bound in chains of your own making."

"Like the old Devil of the Tarot?"

The Shadow grinned.

"Something like that."

As suddenly as serpents striking, the manacles clamped around her wrists. Where they came from was anathema—the air itself, perhaps. The nameless metal bit deep into Cali's flesh and she suppressed a yowl of pain. On chains that seemed connected to the very sky themselves, like the ladders of light climbed by shamans in the depths of their ayahuasca visions, the manacles were hoisted into the air. Cali screamed as her arms were wrenched upwards, nearly dislocated out of their sockets. Her toes brushed the ground as she was suspended from the rain-torn sky. She struggled for a moment, but it was useless. The metal felt realer than any steel that ever kissed her flesh.

The Shadow laughed.

"Let me go." Cali hated herself for saying the words. All of this was an illusion, a fabrication. Yet she, better perhaps than anyone, knew the horrid power of the mind over the flesh.

"Oh, I think not." The Shadow paced slowly towards Cali.

Cali flexed, turning her wrist to apply pressure upon the metal, but it did not give an inch, merely scoring a deep cut in her skin. She sang a direful, shattering note, but the chains held firm against her magic.

"Funny, isn't it?" the Shadow remarked, eyeing Cali up and down with a lasciviousness that made Cali's guts twist. Was she really so narcissistic?

"Don't play games."

The Shadow's smile was a gibbous moon-sickle.

"But you so *love* to play games. Like the little games you played with Alan Chambers."

Cali realised what point her Shadow was driving at. Her whole misadventure had begun with the Ritual of Five, which she had performed upon Alan in the secret dungeon of *The Black Star,* in another reality, and what felt like another eon. The ritual had begun with Cali stringing Alan up with magical chains from the ceiling. She was now similarly strung up by the wrists, suspended and at the mercy of whatever twisted designs her shadowy unconscious had in store for her. Not the Devil of the Tarot, but the Hanged Man.

"You shouldn't do this." Cali couldn't keep her voice from trembling with real fear. Though no one knew the true depths of their own unconscious, of their absolute Shadow, she had probed further into its dark recesses than most. She had an inkling of the horrors there. She had an inkling of what the twisted grin on her Shadow's face might be in anticipation of . . .

"I know," the Shadow replied. "That is the very reason I'm going to do it."

The Shadow whispered dark words. Not a spell, but a quiet, almost tender invitation, as though she were encouraging a timid pet out into the open. This proved not far from the truth, for out of the Shadow's loins slithered a black serpent. The Shadow moaned languorously as the serpent's immense girth pushed wide her sex. It reared up like a phallus before the Shadow, still attached to its host, it dark eyes glittering. The Shadow's smile was dreamy, half-conscious, the smile of an opium addict slipping into their inner world.

Bow-legged, bearing the rearing serpent, the Shadow walked towards Cali. Cali fought with her chains. She shrieked, letting loose blasts of magical power, but with the dreadful inevitability of a nightmare, none of it seemed to have any effect.

The Shadow stood before Cali for a moment, the serpent's tongue flicking against her naval, its broad head unmistakeably phallic, its eyes unmistakeably intelligent.

Slowly, the Shadow circled Cali, taking up position behind her.

"No!" Cali said, finally unable to stop herself from begging. Unshed tears burned in her eyes. This was her worst fear. The very worst. Not the act itself, but the meaning. She lived in abject terror of being sexually dominated. All her life, her father had broken her and subjugated her with the force of his magical will. No matter how many men and women, gods or demons, she killed in battle, she'd always known that her father could destroy her. Even shooting him with the arrow had felt like the hollowest of victories, as though he had ultimately allowed her deadly projectile to fly towards him.

But sex was one realm in which she always got what she wanted, in which she was always in control even if it appeared otherwise.

Not now. Now she was helpless, at the mercy of her own inner darkness.

"If you kill me, you kill yourself!" Cali screamed, as she felt the serpent's tongue now caressing her buttocks.

"The old self has to die for the new one to be born. You'll thank me!" the Shadow said, ecstatic tones in her voice, as though she were already on the edge of orgasm. "Now, you're mine."

Cali squealed as the huge serpent's head—far, far too broad—forced its way into her anus. There was no pleasure, only pain, and the sensation that the deepest and most vulnerable part of her might be ripped asunder. The Shadow gripped Cali's hair and pulled it back, as though Cali were just some common whore to be fucked. Tears ran down Cali's face as she realised that her humiliation was only just beginning: the Shadow was going to debase her in every way imaginable.

The Shadow raped her with merciless vigour. Cali could not move away or fight it off; her wrists bled as she continued to struggle to no avail. Cali felt the huge snake writhing, searching out something within her, careless of what it tore apart. Her blood sluiced its passage. She knew she was haemorrhaging from a deep internal wound. Her screams reached the sky but were not answered.

Then the serpent began to bite.

CHAPTER 13
RESURRECTION

THEY EMERGED FROM the whirling storm like vomit from the mouth of a plague-bearer. Alan and LeBarron collapsed almost as soon as they saw the arched gateway of Al Shujah. Roland fell to the floor, undignified, his corpse slopping forward with the bonelessness of a beached fish. It was an awful sight, wounding to Alan's soul. He deserved more. They had failed him.

Cassilda and Petruccio appeared with more grace. Cassilda saw Alan kneeling, his head hung in the posture of grief. She gently approached, placing her hand upon his shoulder. She spoke no words, because there were no words adequate to describe what they had been through.

"Haercus . . . " Petruccio said. His eyes did not look at Roland nor at the others, but upon some shore within himself, abutting the black waves of subconscious terrors. "What did Pe'kar do to him?"

"We saw the first signs of it in Alar," Cassilda said. "But even I did not see the full extent. That armour wasn't to protect him, it was to cage his monstrosity."

"Those children . . . " LeBarron began.

"It's best not to think of it," Cassilda said, cutting him short. "Besides, we have work to do first."

"Work?"

Cassilda ignored the actor's puzzled look. Taking her hand from Alan, she marched towards Roland's corpse.

"Alan, could you help me roll him onto his back?"

Alan nodded, gently rolling Roland over with his good hand. Cassilda stared down at the bloodied warrior, whose chest was deformed by a cavity to the size of a fist.

"You mean to . . . resurrect him?" LeBarron whispered.

Cassilda nodded.

"Unless there is a reason I shouldn't?"

LeBarron looked down at Roland. The actor seemed to be studying his features, the terrible wound in his chest, though what information he gleaned from such inspection was a mystery to Alan.

"It has long been said that the great magicians of old had power over life and death. There are many poems that speak of their wonders and miracles. I can still remember a few, even with the fog, even though I am not quite myself . . . " The actor swallowed down a bolus of emotion. "But I wonder, were they really miracles, or were they rather abominations? The power warped Scarleth. I saw it before, when I left her. And from what you've told me, she only grew worse as time went on, becoming truly monstrous."

"What are you saying, LeBarron?" Cassilda's tone was somehow firm yet also tender. Alan could not help the Freudian association of a mother figure.

"I suppose I am saying that I fear for your soul, Princess."

"*My* soul?" Cassilda sounded surprised, and Alan was too. He had expected LeBarron to speak of his own experience of being brought back, how it seemed not all of him had returned.

The actor nodded.

"As much as I lament what I lost when you brought me back, the gains still outweigh those losses. I have life. I have my friends. And I have the opportunity to see Cali finally defeated. I would not miss that for the world." LeBarron grinned, and something of the old swagger lived again in his twinkling eyes. "But that staff is like Alan's Claw. It grants power, but too much power warps the receptacle. You are the best of us, dear Princess. If you fall, we're all for the pit."

The actor bowed, conveying such humility it almost took Alan's breath away. Cassilda inclined her head in acknowledgement. Her eyes shone with passion and grief intermixed.

"If you really did lose a part of yourself in the land of the dead, LeBarron, then what a magnificent whole you must have been, if this is you reduced. I gave you too little credit. But please, take my gratitude now. You are right to fear the staff." Her eye flicked to Alan, and as is often the case with lovers, a thousand words passed between them without one ever being spoken aloud. "I fear it too.

THE DREAMS OF DEMHE

But we need Roland. And we need its power for a little longer. But I swear to you, LeBarron, by the Yellow Sign and the blood of Carcosa, that once we have finally defeated Cali . . . " Alan knew she spoke in euphemism: Cali could not be imprisoned or contained, nor could she be forgiven, she had to be killed—it was the only way. " . . . once we have defeated my sister, I shall break this staff. The Fires of Manifestation can unmake even talismans such as The Claw. I'll cast it into the fire. You have my word."

LeBarron bowed once again.

"Then proceed, daughter of Carcosa."

Cassilda smiled sadly.

"Stand back."

Alan, LeBarron, and Petruccio all took a step backward, allowing Cassilda to stand over Roland's corpse. LeBarron had died from a poisoned wound, and thus, his resurrection had seemed more a resuscitation, somehow believable. Roland, however, had been torn apart. The gaping hole in his chest leaked arterial blood. How would the staff's magic fare against such damaged flesh? Alan took a deep, steadying breath. They were about to find out.

Cassilda closed her eyes, and the ruby at the crown of the staff began to pulse, like the planet Mars seen on a clear night's sky, a bloody eye winking across the black gulf.

"I bid thee rise, servant of The Yellow King!" Cassilda intoned. "Take up thy spear once more. The war is not ended, nor thy part in it! Rise, rise, rise, warrior and philosopher, soldier and friend. The realm of nothingness is not thine; I call thee forth from the foaming blackness into this vessel. The battle is not ended! The battle is everlasting! I bid thee rise, if thou art a true servant of The Yellow King! Rise, Roland, for thy part in the war is not yet done!"

The ruby light became a bright sphere, painful to look upon, and then it shot forward, blasting Roland, enveloping his body in crimson flames. Before Alan's eyes, the wound shut, not merely cauterised but re-knitted as though by an invisible seamstress's hand. The red flames rose higher and higher. And then, as with LeBarron, something rose from the ground and plunged into the corpse.

LeBarron let out a horrified gasp at this. Alan realised he was seeing, for the first time, what all of them had seen beside Lake Hali, a profane thing, a desecration of natural order.

The thing that had emerged from the ground was not truly

visible. It defeated the eye, which, after all, was the most treacherous of sensory organs. The nearest descriptor Alan could give was of a two-dimensional silhouette—a true shadow. Whether it was a soul, the animating spirit, or something far darker was a secret none could say.

As suddenly as they arose, the flames died. Roland's eyes snapped open and he gasped. His first breath was horrid, ragged, as though his throat were clagged with blood. He rolled onto his side and vomited a mixture of bile, blood, and sand. He wiped his mouth with the back of his hand. Then he stared at his hands, as though its wrinkles and flesh were strange to him.

"I . . . I . . . "

"You live, Roland," Cassilda said. She knelt slowly beside him. Her eyes were lambent with pity, concern, hope, all these at once. Alan's heart ached to see her tenderness. LeBarron was right: she was the best of them. He would do all in his power to protect her.

"You must protect her from them . . . " the Claw whispered.

Not now!

"If not now, then when?" The Claw was becoming more verbally dextrous, turning Alan's dismissive remark on its head. "LeBarron clearly desires her, and Roland too. And what will you do when LeBarron comes to her chambers. He is more man than you."

Silence!

The Claw strangely obeyed his mental command, but the damage was done, the dark seed planted. Alan remembered all too well LeBarron's massive manhood. A violent spike of jealousy drove into his heart. *You're being ridiculous. Cassilda would never betray you like Cali did.* But try as he might, he could not dislodge the pernicious thorn from his mind.

Roland was getting his bearings, still disorientated and confused. Petruccio knelt by his side, helping him sit upright. The dwarf offered him water from a canteen which the soldier accepted gratefully. LeBarron watched Roland with a strange intensity. The two men shared a dark secret, had both glimpsed what lay beyond the border of life.

"Did you see *him*?" LeBarron asked. Alan did not understand the cryptic question, but he could have sworn that for a second— less even than that—LeBarron's eyes had flicked towards him.

Roland frowned quizzically.

"Who?"

LeBarron's face shadowed.

"Nevermind."

"I suggest we take some time to regroup," Cassilda said. She looked weary, leaning on her staff. Alan noted that not only were her eyes flecked with ruby, as they had been the day they met, but also the whites were tinged a faint crimson, as though she were about to weep tears of blood. He strode toward her and, with instincts bordering on a sixth sense, suddenly lunged—just in time to catch her as she fell. Blearily, she looked up at him. He lowered her gently to the ground, cradling her. "I will be fine in a moment," she said. "The energy . . . it is quite something."

"She's still controlling the slaves back at Carcosa," Petruccio said. "Our lady is stretching her powers thin."

"If she lets them go, Carcosa will be vulnerable," Roland said, trying to clamber to his feet, as though that very moment he intended to march back across the desert and defend his city. LeBarron forced him back down.

"Rest, soldier. There's little we can do. Cassilda, perhaps you can let some of the slaves go? I'm sure Carcosa is even now building up its defences again. Gril'dakken and his people will also defend the city with their lives. You're no good to us dead." LeBarron suddenly smiled. "After all, who necromances the necromancer?"

Cassilda smiled wanly. Alan thought she looked feverous. Despite how weak she seemed, her hand remained clenched tightly about her staff, as though letting it go were the last thing before death itself.

"We must regroup," LeBarron said, getting to his feet. "Consider our options. I yearn for vengeance on Cali as much as any of you, but with that beast guarding the Crooked Path . . . We'll have to find another way through."

"Agreed," Roland said. He sat with his head in his hands, as though nursing a pounding headache. Periodically, one hand flicked to his chest, exploring the place where there should have been a mortal wound. "The heart is willing, but the body . . . not so much. Apologies, my friends."

"I'm sorry," Alan said. "But we can't wait. We have no time."

"Cali already had a head-start on us," Petruccio said. The dwarf watched Cassilda and Alan intently, concern etched into his stony features. "I think a day or two of reprieve is no bad idea."

"No," Alan said. "I'm not talking about Cali. Haercus, he—it—wants The Claw. That's how he found us out there in the storm. And now he knows we're here. It's only a matter of time before he comes to Al Shujah. While we linger here, everyone is in danger."

The company all regarded Alan. They knew he was right, but none wanted to admit it.

"Perhaps a day," LeBarron said, after a while. "One day to regroup."

"You know it's too risky. He was hot on our heels. Do you think the guards here will deter him? He'll cut through them like a shark through sardines."

"But he fears the staff," LeBarron interjected. "He was wary of it."

"Not wary enough to hold back." Alan was surprised to hear Petruccio come to his aid. "Alan *is* right. Once again." The dwarf cracked the faintest, thinnest of smiles. "It is irritating, you do know that?"

Alan smiled in return.

"You remind me of my mother."

"Ha!" A bark of laughter. "Then you had an ugly mother indeed!"

"Then what do you propose?" LeBarron said, bringing them back to the seriousness of the situation. "We have lost the quinels, and therefore our supplies. We might be able to procure more, but at cost. The only road we know is blocked. I know of no other path through Demhe. I *might* be able to find one, given time, but that is what you say we do not have."

"The Claw's talons are deeper in Haercus' mind than even mine," Alan said. "Trust me, he will raze this village to the ground in search of it."

"Alan, it's okay, you can let me go."

Alan looked down at Cassilda, who was smiling sweetly—albeit with a slight twist of pain. She did look haler, or as hale as the milk-white woman could look. Her eyes had regained some of their purity, the crimson glow ebbing. Gently, Alan helped her to her feet. "Thank you," she whispered, squeezing his hand. He noted how quickly she returned her grip to the staff. Alan felt ashamed at the fact he was beginning to become jealous of an inanimate object.

"But it is not inanimate . . . " The Claw whispered. "You know that well. Everything has a soul. The great works of the Old Kings more than most."

Quiet! Alan did not like to be reminded that his weapon—now surgically attached to him—had been made by Pe'kar.

"My proposal is this," Alan began. He faltered, looking once at Cassilda, knowing his next words would pain her beyond measure. "We accept Mazael's offer."

The others shared dark glances, though they said nothing, knowing it was not their matter to comment on. Cassilda showed teeth, but before she could shout at him, Alan continued, "But with a condition. He will only receive payment on completion of the mission."

"You intend to deceive him? To renege on the agreement?" Petruccio said.

Alan made a *comme ci comme ça* gesture.

"We will have to cross that bridge when we come to it. He is clearly powerful, I am not sure we want to fight with him. I doubt we will be able to lose him either; this is his territory. But I will do everything in my power to avoid having to give him what he wants."

Cassilda looked like a sculpture of ice. The coldness of her gaze frightened him. But finally, she nodded.

"It is the only way, I think. Though I am loathe to admit it."

"Then it is woefully agreed," LeBarron said. "We will take Mazael as our guide."

CHAPTER 14
SHEDDING THE SNAKESKIN

CALI HAD BEEN tortured many times. She had never been truly broken by her captors or abusers. She had always retained a secret kingdom within herself, however small, that remained uncorrupted and inaccessible to her tormentors. When she was in a philosophical mood she regarded this final piece of Selfhood as her soul—the indestructible consciousness that was the true puppeteer of her being. At other times, she simply regarded it as evidence of her mind's indomitability, of how far she had come along the magical path.

Her Shadow, however, came the closest of anyone to breaking her mind, to destroying the final wall within her psyche, and accessing that most secret place within herself. Cali supposed that the ultimate evidence of a soul's existence was the fact that it could be lost. Though she had done terrible things, betrayed those she loved, contended with greater demons, made bargains and pacts in exchange for powers and knowledge that would terrify even the most potent of Earth's sorcerers, she had never compromised that tiny sliver, that miraculous and secret kingdom. She had never, in other words, given up her soul. She had scorched that soul, burned it, lashed it to a blazing ship coming apart in the midst of a dark ocean, but never given it into the hands of the enemy.

But now, she was almost ready to surrender. She knew that was what it would take to make the pain end.

The torture was of course made worst by the fact that she had no demarcation of time. No sun rose, no sun set. No moon shone. The eerie, mercurial landscape remained a fixed image, a frozen unreality that she was yet incapable of escaping. She had tried every spell she could think of—save for one. She was loathe to perform it again, but it was perhaps the only way. Better than losing her soul.

"You think you have a soul?" her Shadow whispered, knowing even her most intimate of thoughts.

Cali's battered eyes open. They had been crusted shut with blood. Her whole body was smeared with blood. The lower half of her body felt ruptured yet numb at the same time. She was torn in too many places. She felt dizzy, lightheaded, yet at times the agony would return with dreadful clarity, as though her nerves, having rested, once more awoke to their true condition. Not an inch of her onyx flesh remained un-bruised. But that was only a minor complaint compared to what had taken place within, to how her Shadow had mastered her.

Through the veil of blood-crusted vision, Cali saw the dark silhouette of her Shadow Self, swollen with hideous pride, grinning ear to ear, and showing no signs of tiring.

"All things have souls," Cali replied. She spat blood. There might have been teeth in the mixture too. "The colour of one's skin does not determine the worthiness of their spirit."

"I make no reference to your origins, Cali," the Shadow purred. "It is your *actions* that have compromised your soul. Betrayal. Murder. Villainy upon villainy. You may think that none of them were absolute bargains, that you never traded your full soul, but piece by piece you auctioned your innermost sacred being to the highest bidder. Now, there's very little left, if anything at all."

"The infinite cannot be divided," Cali said. "If I have even a sliver, it is still the whole."

"Now who is the one using intellectual flourishes?" The Shadow laughed. "You know full well that a soul can be reduced. Think of the men and women whom you dominated before, who you brought to Carcosa and then abandoned when their minds collapsed . . . They wander the black planet as shells of their former glory."

The Shadow's words were true enough, yet they did not wound as intended. Cali found herself thinking not of the others, but of Alan, the only one who had not died or gone mad, the only one who had not only survived but *thrived* in Carcosa. She had thought him her greatest failure, but now she realised he was her greatest success. And in that epiphany, she found a dismal flicker of hope.

"You have had your way with me, Shadow," Cali snarled. "But now it's my turn."

Before the Shadow could act, Cali cried out the magical words, "SHIMEN'NEHAH!"

With a disgusting noise, skin peeled from meat. Cali's flesh unseamed down the middle, crown to groin, and opened like the folds of a vaginal flower. Unfurling, the black curtain of flesh revealed its sopping, muscular secret, a red being of savage lunacy, grinning without lips and staring without eyelids. Freed from flesh, the horror of nerves and tendons and veins and revolting musculature slipped from its bondage and descended towards the ground, leaving behind the black ribbons of discarded skin.

And so the snake sheds its skin! Cali thought, with a triumph surge.

But there was no impact. Her feet met nothing like solid ground. Rather, they passed through the seemingly hard stone. Suddenly, she was plunging down a wormhole, the entire reality of the mercury-tinged realm sucked down with her, as though she were the central peg that had held up the carnival tent's imaginative canvas—as she fell, so too did the entire structure. Down she went into the sinkhole, and with her came the cosmic dreamworld, a swirling blend of entoptic colours spiralling down to a black depth below her.

Buffeted to and fro, she spun, barely able to draw breath into her lungs to shriek. She saw a black shadow flying through the whirlpool with her, and at first thought it was her enemy, her projected shadow self, but soon she realised it was her discarded flesh, swimming like some disgusting pink and black jellyfish through the interstitial sea between dreams.

She reached out and grabbed her flesh. As one would a cloak, she donned it, feeling the skin gratefully and eagerly solder itself back to her muscles. Still falling, she grinned in triumph. She had escaped. She had overcome her Shadow. And though she had suffered greatly, she had not given up that which lay deepest within her.

A new horror awaited. Of that, she had no doubt. Even as she fell, light began to bubble up from the darkness below: yellow, orange, red, all colours of warning and danger. Grit stung her face. The sound of a dreadful wind rose and rose. She wondered if she would meet hard ground, whether, in her dream-state, she had unknowingly cast herself from a high precipice. *No! That will not be my end! No end so ignoble for Cali!*

THE DREAMS OF DEMHE

As suddenly as she had entered the wormhole, she breached out of the other side. Bright light wounded her eyes. Twin suns shone overhead. A desert stretched endlessly in all the cardinal directions. She stood enfleshed and exhausted in the midst of this barrenness.

But not alone.

Before her stood a figure. Not her Shadow, but something far greater. Only now did Cali realise her Shadow had been merely a disguise worn by a greater power. Only now did she realise that her true suspicion—that there was more to her torturous episode than purely the dreaming machinations of Demhe—had been founded on truth.

It took all her strength not to bow, not to fall down in a posture of total obeisance. Unlike her father, whose psychic aura overpowered all who stood in its presence, the figure before her ensorcelled with his physical beauty. The King In Yellow's power was *felt* at the level of bone and gut.

But Pe'kar's power was seen and heard.

An indescribable beauty—that of an archangel—combined with the sensuality of a demonic lover. Turquoise light radiated from his body as though his skin were eternally afire, still burning with the heat of the universe's creation. In his form was remembered the perfection and terror of that first cosmic act of formation. For if she stared too long, she began to see the kiss of suns colliding, the radiance of moons fractured and broken apart, and the chasms of black holes widening—all glyphed upon his living flesh.

His shape was humanoid in all ways save two: firstly, the perfection of his features made them seem somehow alien—no human being could have a face so chiseled, limbs so perfectly in proportion, eyes so bright, or a smile so beatific; secondly, he possessed a scaly tail, crowned with the head of a dark serpent. Before Cali flashed the icon of the Star of David: six points upon the star, representing man-perfected. And here stood that perfect man—or almost perfect. Yes, that was the truth of Pe'kar's being as well as the tragedy of his existence: he was perfection, yet in the womb of the Great Mother his seed had conceived demons. And The King In Yellow, who concealed his hideous and twisted form behind a grey cowl: He, of all people, had been the one to conceive beautiful mankind. Yin and yang, action and reaction, dark and light, Horus and Set, all polarities reversed and intertwined. If there was a God who reigned beyond the stars, as her father so believed, then He had no small sense of irony.

"Pe'kar," she whispered.

The bright being smiled. O, how she longed to kiss those lips once more! But she knew she must resist. He had possessed her once, and in exchange he had taught her the very powers she had just used to make her escape. Had he been testing her, then? Testing what she remembered? Or had he simply been probing her for information.

"*Dear Cali,*" the Demon King said. "*My warrior princess . . .*" The descriptor seemed to amuse him, for he laughed, a sound sweeter than all the music of Carcosa. "*How long I have waited for our reunion. I had begun to worry you had forgotten me, and forgotten our agreement.*"

"Never, Great King," Cali said, inclining her head. She dared not bow lower, for fear she would never rise. Her eyes were already beginning to hurt. She felt they might be plucked from their sockets in their eagerness to drink his beauty. "But I have been delayed and obstructed at every turn." An idea blazed across her mind. "I need . . . I need help, O King! Your help!" She fell to her knees. "Please!"

Pe'kar—or perhaps it was merely his projection—laughed even louder at this, yet somehow nothing in his tone seemed derisory. She felt her heart tremble, uncertain of its beating. She remembered their nights in his palace, his ravishment, his seed like honey on her tongue. *No, Cali. Do not succumb to his seductions.*

"*You have never once asked anyone for help, Cali.*"

"I have never been this desperate!" Her words were not entirely untruthful. "Alan Chambers . . . he has become unstoppable. He has The Claw. And so many allies, my sister among them. I am alone. But even so . . . " She smiled darkly now. "I killed the King In Yellow! Yes, I did as you asked! I overthrew my father. Carcosa may still stand, but it grows weaker and weaker by the day. If you were but to lend me aid . . . "

Pe'kar considered her, and though his veneer was ever sweet and beatific, she saw through the outward beauty an awareness as cold as the reptilian tail with which he had been cursed or gifted, depending on whom you asked.

"*It is true that I no longer sense my brother . . . And I see no reason to doubt it was your hand that struck the killing blow. But, my dear warrior princess, my generals tell me you fought against my army, that you slew a great many Pe'karians. That was ill done."*

"Look like the innocent flower, but be the serpent under it," Cali said. With a surge of both pride and shame, she realised that quoting *Macbeth* was exactly what Alan Chambers might have done. *Well, if we cannot learn from our enemies—those who best us—who can we learn from?* If Alan Chambers was her greatest success, then she could stand to take advice from his actions. Maybe then she could find out what made him tick, and thereby undo him.

Pe'kar smiled.

"So you did this only to maintain your deception, is that the truth you peddle?"

"Yes, Great King. And please, forgive me!" She touched her forehead to the ground, the gesture of absolute obeisance, though she quickly reared herself up from it, scared that if she lingered his powers would begin to dominate her mind once again. And there was nothing she hated and feared more.

To her surprise, when she lifted her head, she found Pe'kar now stood right before her, mere inches away. His serpent-headed tail regarded her with cold indifference, and his angelic face stared down, an ancient sky-god drawn to the prayers of a penitent soul. He extended a hand, phosphorescent, shimmering with light.

"Come, Cali. We have much to discuss about your future."

CHAPTER 15
THE SECRET PATH

THEY STOOD ONCE more at the threshold of Demhe. This time, Mazael stood with them, like the spectre of Death himself. It had taken some persuading for him to agree to their offer of delayed payment, but in the end he had acquiesced.

"But should you try to deceive me, I shall scoop out every dream from your skull," he'd said.

Alan had grimaced. "It shall not come to that."

Now, the dark spectre knelt and ran his fingers over the soft sand. His phylacteries rattled whenever he moved, a reminder of the grim promise Alan had made to him.

"You say that the beast hunts you, Claw-bearer?"

Alan nodded.

"Then we must move swifter than thought."

"There is something wrong with the dreaming—or rather, with Haercus." Alan had been forced to reveal the beast's true identity to Mazael to explain why the beast sought him so ardently, but Mazael seemed uninterested in the reappearance of a figure from ancient lore. "LeBarron says that the creature is immune to the dreams."

Mazael looked sharply at Alan, then to LeBarron.

"All things dream. Even the lowly ant. Even mindless creatures. Even the most hateful soul."

"Not this thing," LeBarron replied, calmly.

"Then its nature has been corrupted beyond the threshold of understanding. The Demon King has violated all spiritual accords . . . He has debased life in ways that should never be known."

Alan could not help but think that perhaps Cali did not need to be stopped after all. She was presumably travelling headlong into the sanctuary of the Demon King. If Pe'kar was as maniacal and treacherous as all the stories suggested, then surely he would inflict horrors upon her beyond their darkest dreams. Alan almost began to feel pity for her. She had suffered much. True, it was largely by her own hand, but still, he almost always felt empathy for those in pain. *But there would always be a risk she survived, perhaps even that she overthrew Pe'kar. The only way to be sure is to catch her, to stop her, to see it with your own eyes.*

"Kill her," the Claw whispered.

For once, he and the weapon were in agreement.

"We waste time," Cassilda prompted.

Mazael rose. Demhe's storm still raged, and the flashes of viridian lightning played off his cowl, reaching into the shadowy interior of his hood, but finding no face—only eyes.

"Yes. Time flows on. Come with me. Follow exactly. When the dreaming takes you, speak forth the name of Al Qaf Saba, and that is where we shall meet!"

Before they could muster themselves, Mazael set off. His limbs—visible only because of how they were bandaged—were long and spidery, covering great distance despite the fact he hardly seemed to move. In seconds the sandstorm had swallowed him. Alan, Cassilda, LeBarron, Roland, and Petruccio scrambled after.

Once again, dust and grit assailed them. Once again, they walked through a maelstrom illuminated by flashes of ungodly lightning. But whereas LeBarron's path through the storm had been a curiously measured spiral, moving ever inward on a path of involution, Mazael's path was—as far as Alan's aching feet could discern—a crazed zigzag. It was like following the path of a killer's slashing knife. Left, then right. Right, then left. Back and forth. A blind, furious, blood-drunk assault. Sometimes the zags were so small that Mazael barely took half a step before pirouetting, like a ballet dancer, upon the ball of his foot, then shooting off in another direction. Other times it seemed they walked miles before turning again. As they reached one crook in the path, Mazael turned and looked back at them, his crimson eyes a disturbing clarity in the otherwise inchoate storm.

"Crawl!" was all he said.

And so, on their hands and knees, they did. After what felt like several miles, Mazael leapt to his feet, and they resumed their quicktime march.

Alan checked constantly to make sure the others were following. He couldn't imagine anything worse than being left behind in this madness.

Petruccio marched at the rear as the most unshakeable and surefooted of the group. Roland walked in front of him. Without his proud spear, the soldier seemed diminished, though he still walked resolutely through the battering winds. Alan wondered what was going through his head, what he'd seen on the other side. LeBarron said he could not speak of what he'd seen in the land of the dead, as though he were under some cosmic dictate. But after Roland had come back, he had dropped a sliver of a clue. *Did you see him?* LeBarron had asked. Who did LeBarron mean? And why did Alan feel sure that LeBarron had glanced his way as he asked the question? Was that pure narcissism, or was there a mystery he wasn't seeing?

Then there was Cassilda. She had hardly spoken a word to him since he had suggested the plan of using Mazael. It seemed his every action and decision jeopardised their relationship further. He knew Cassilda was the reason he had come to Carcosa, that he was meant to meet her, but even destiny could be overthrown if the soul in question was not strong enough to live up to what was demanded of them. Was Alan failing?

"The only thing you have failed to do is exorcise true power," the Claw growled. "Cast off your shackles. See beyond one woman, and make all women bow to you. First, Liliya. Then all the whores of Carcosa. And finally, Cali herself!"

Alan could not deny a thrill of terror and pleasure ran through him.

You would have me make love to a woman who called me "kin"? How incestuous.

"Did not the mighty pharaohs marry their siblings?" The Claw sounded eager, perhaps because Alan was no longer dismissing its suggestions out of hand. It sensed his willingness to engage, that his iron resolve was bending slightly to accommodate the Claw's mandates. The door was no longer entirely shut. "But you miss my point. Would not Cali make a fine slave?"

You indulge in too much fantasy.

"No, Alan. You have not indulged enough. I am power. You are will. What is the use of power if it is not wielded? And what is the use of will if it cannot focus upon what we truly want? *We* are The Claw. All you need ever do is reach out and grasp that which your heart most desires . . . "

The Claw fell silent again of its own accord, which unnerved Alan, for he assumed that meant The Claw was satisfied it had made its point felt. And that wasn't far from the truth. The thought of Cali, submissive and pliant before him, her throat gripped in the dark talons of The Claw, helpless, at his mercy . . .

Enough! These thoughts are twisted and dark. You love Cassilda . . .

But perhaps Cassilda no longer loved him?

He had been so deep in thought that he had not realised Mazael was no longer in sight. Panicked, Alan staggered forward, the footing ever more treacherous, his feet sinking deep into the sand, more like walking through a bog than across a dune. His face ached from the lashes of the wind-borne grit. No matter how fast he ran, he could not find Mazael's shadow.

Curse him! Had they been betrayed?

He turned back to the others, but found they were also gone. He stood alone in the midst of the raging storm, the very nightmare he had feared for another come true for himself.

"Cassilda! LeBarron! Petruccio!"

The desert did not answer him, save that its borders seemed to be shrinking. He watched in horror as the horizon, already limited by the swirling sand, began to approach, a cavalry charge led by the King of Nothingness. Only darkness lay beyond its edge. What happened when he fell over the rim of eternity? He turned to run, but found another horizon approaching him, faster than the first. He was surrounded by a shrinking universe. *The end,* he thought. *The end of everything.* The walls of reality closed in.

Suddenly, a new fear speared through Alan's heart, this one eclipsing all others, making death seem but a blessed sleep. What if, when the borders of this collapsing world enveloped him, he woke up back on Earth? What if this had all been a fantastical dream, a flight of insane fantasy, elongated by his damaged brain? To awake again in his old, mundane life—that was a fate worse than death, worse than anything. He raised The Claw to his throat. He'd rip it out if it came to that. *I choose my fate! I choose Carcosa!*

The horizon was almost upon him now, gathering momentum,

the black horses of the void rearing their heads, their manes whipping like onyx flames, and suddenly he saw, in the great yawning darkness, two blood red eyes piercing him with the sharpness of arrows. He sucked in a breath.

"Mazael!" he cried.

Then the dreaming took him.

CHAPTER 16
I DID NOT BID HIM COME

FOR A MOMENT, barely a flicker, Alan thought he had tumbled into another memory. He crouched in the dip of a dune, like some oversized toad—though what amphibian would inhabit these parched lands was a mystery his intellect was currently incapable of solving. In fact, no sooner than he had the thought of being a toad, than he became one, a grossly-fleshed, squat thing blinking stupidly against the glare of twin suns.

He observed a secret rendezvous.

Before him was his enemy. Cali. She looked as though she had crawled through the nine levels of Dante's hell. Her skin looked as though it had been pulverised with a meat tenderiser. Her scars shone as bright as the lightning that'd inhabited Demhe's dreaming storms. But even bloodied and broken, she was beautiful, a black goddess of death and lust, voluptuous, muscular, and terrible.

He felt hatred for her with an emotional venom equal to the porous, oily liquid coating his toad-flesh. But he was partly distracted by another presence.

The figure opposite Cali was a man, the most beautiful man Alan had ever seen. His naked flesh shone with a radiance that made starlight seem ugly. How Alan envied him! He was dimly reminded of watching LeBarron and Cali in their tryst, that fateful first night he'd departed from Carcosa in search of The Claw—naive of Cali's true motives.

But unlike a normal man, this beautiful angel-being was gifted with a long serpent tail, crowned with a lazy-eyed head.

"There is a place for you in my city," the man said.

Cali smiled.

"As your whore?"

"*As my queen.*" The man took a step towards Cali, and Alan noted that she withdrew, afraid. Even standing against her own father, The King In Yellow himself, Cali had shown defiance, but she *feared* this being, and that caused Alan's flesh to prickle. "*Why do you withdraw? We were together once. We whispered secrets together once . . .* "

"No one is ever with you," Cali said, shuddering. "You are always the master." She bowed her head. "I'm grateful, truly. Your spell-ways allowed me to escape my enemies. But I can't . . . "

Cali was *crying.* Had Alan been possessed of his true body, his mouth might have widened in surprise. Instead, his horrible maw opened and emitted a thunderous croak.

No sooner than she heard the croak, Cali's eyes swivelled to the toad. At first, she appeared confused, but then, her expression morphed into one of blind rage. The man looked on mildly.

She's seen me, Alan thought, *her eyes see through my disguise.* And her next words proved his fears right.

"What is *he* doing here?" she hissed.

"*I did not bid him come,*" the beautiful man replied. "*Perhaps he is here of his own volition?*"

"Impossible. The dreams are a solitary experience." She turned back to the man, though Alan knew she watched him from her periphery. "You've conjured his phantom to torment me."

"*If dreams are always solitary, then you might ask how I came to find you here. And if this is your dream, then you are the one who has conjured him. Bid him depart.*"

Cali closed her eyes, Alan felt a sudden pain, as though he were experiencing the aches and strains of bones expanding in childhood, but all at once. He tried to let out a fearful croak but instead a spluttering, human groan escaped his lips. *Lips!* He now had them, and legs, arms, feet, all encased in bronze flesh. He was himself, again.

His right hand—The Claw—crackled with dangerous potential.

Cali opened her eyes. She showed gleaming teeth upon discovering that Alan had not departed, merely changed his form.

"Why?"

"I don't know," Alan said, perhaps too honestly. "I suppose the dreaming has brought us together." That sounded wrong in Alan's ears. He didn't want to be together with Cali, he wanted to kill her. Reading his thoughts, The Claw kindled with eye-searing wreaths of lightning.

THE DREAMS OF DEMHE

Cali beat him to the punch. She emitted a sonic scream. The sound became thick and tangible, a flame hovering in the air, light bending and refracting in strange patterns around it, sword-shaped. In the blink of an eye, it sailed towards him. His dream-self was sluggish, and he did not move out of the way. The blade passed clean through his chest.

To no effect.

He was only dreamstuff.

Cali shrieked and cursed.

"A plague upon your house! I hope you and all your progeny die in misery!"

Alan only smiled.

"Misery comes only to those who court it. When we meet again, Cali, I shall be the one who strikes, and my bolt shall strike truer than yours!"

"The time has not yet come for that battle, Alan Chambers," the mysterious snake-tailed man said. With that, he snapped his fingers. Alan felt as though a rope was tied around his waist, connected to a great trebuchet, which had suddenly swung its throwing arm aloft, catapulting him out of the scene. He barely suppressed a scream as he sailed through the air.

Cali and the mysterious man grew smaller and smaller until they were mere specks, like hardened gemstones sitting upon forgotten sand-slopes. All at once, he realised he was not looking at something far away, but something very close. Yes, without landing, without falling, he was on solid ground again: good soil, dashed with stones. He felt no fear, only a giddy excitement for what he'd next see. He began to understand the desert was showing him answers to the deep questions of his mind. And while he travelled in this way, he could not be harmed.

Raising his eyes, he found himself in a field. A single tree stood at its centre. Walking through the long grass surrounding the tree was a familiar figure: Petruccio.

What is that sound, music? Alan wondered.

Gentle notes drifted upon the air, light as falling leaves, sweet as birdsong. It dimly reminded him of Cali and her magical instrument, the way she had played for him, thereby ushering him to this strange world. For all his hatred of Cali, he was grateful to her for this one act. Even evil could perform good in ignorance.

Petruccio walked towards the tree, a smile upon his face. It was easy to see why. Beneath the shadow of the tree's canopy of bright leaves, a maiden sat, wearing a beauteous white dress that shimmered translucently, revealing whiter skin beneath. Soft brunette curls fell down about her shoulders. It was she who played, a sitar-like instrument similar to Cali's balanced on her lap. When she opened her mouth, the notes she sang caused the hairs on Alan's forearms to rise, his blood to run swift. The beauty almost overwhelmed him.

Alan followed Petruccio towards the singing maiden. If the dwarf had perceived Alan's presence, he gave no sign.

Petruccio paused a few feet away from the singing maiden. Though she was lost in her song, her eyes occasionally flitted to Petruccio, a smile causing the corners of her lips to rise as she formed bright-sounding syllables that seemed to originate from a language not of the Earth. The dwarf shifted tentatively from foot to foot. Alan could tell he wanted to speak, to address the woman, but he could not bring himself to break the spell.

At last, the woman allowed her voice to fall away, like the sun passing behind a cloud, or falling into the deep shadow beyond the horizon. She plucked a final note upon the supernatural strings of her instrument and bowed her head.

"My lady," Petruccio whispered, breathlessly. "You are the very Abyssinian maiden. I am ensorcelled! Please, permit me the honour of serving you." He dropped to one knee, bowing his own head. "I am faithful and will do your bidding—whatever you ask. Only, permit me to hear you sing once more!"

The lady began to laugh, light and soft. But soon, the music of her voice began to sour. Like a tune changing from major to minor key, her laughter grew harsh, biting the hearts of those who heard. As the laugh became more bitter, its volume increased, until the woman's once-sweet voice now rang stridently over the empty fields. Petruccio looked in dismay at first, then in pure anger. He rose shaking, with clenched fists.

"I may be a dwarf," he spat. "But no less worthy of honest work, of life, or *love!*"

At this, the woman howled, and the notes of her hilarity were now unmistakably mocking. Petruccio turned blood red, redder than Cassilda's ruby-crowned staff.

"A curse upon you!" Petruccio snarled.

The woman raised her head; even Alan recoiled. Her face had

split open, perhaps from the sheer exertion of her remorseless laughter, and revealed another face beneath.

Cali.

Shedding the pale skin as though it were no more than rags, Cali rose before Petruccio, sneering as he retreated from her. The great warrior and magician now cowered like a small child. This seemed at odds with the stone-hard Petruccio Alan knew, but of course, if this was Petruccio's dream, Alan was seeing a secret version of the dwarf, perhaps seeing his deepest fears. Alan also could not help but wonder if there was not some hint of memory about this dream. Was this how Cali had seduced Petruccio into her service—as a sweet maiden with a siren song? Only to one day turn into the black goddess who had betrayed and humiliated him? Alan was struck by overwhelming pangs of sympathy.

"You little maggot," Cali snarled. "How you fawn and abase thyself before me! Not worthy to lick faecal matter from my foot. Not worthy to live as a coprophage in the lowest dungeon of Carcosa's inner hells. Even the cannibals would reject your stunted form." She grinned. "Better to live as a celibate. Better never to sow your execrable seed. Disgusting thing!"

Alan bared his teeth, leaping forward. He would not have his friend treated so. But he found Cali did not even look at him, did not even seem aware. Alan frowned. Was this, then, merely a dream-projection, not the true Cali? Merely a projection of Petruccio's fears and memories, not the real enemy herself? Alan's thoughts were interrupted by Petruccio's exclamation.

"Alan!"

Petruccio, at least, was real then.

"Yes, I'm here, friend. Do not listen to her! She speaks poison. And she thinks because her heart knows only loneliness and self-hatred, that all beings must feel the same!" Alan smiled, raising The Claw. "Begone!"

With a blast of light, the phantom was incinerated.

An unceremonious end, Alan thought, knowing in his heart the real confrontation between them would be far more arduous.

Alan turned and found Petruccio grinning ear to ear. The dwarf chuckled, and though it sounded like pebblestones avalanching, Alan couldn't help but find a kind of music in it.

"What's so funny?" Alan asked.

"This is a dream, isn't it?"

Alan's smile remained, though now his eyes conveyed his sorrow.

"I'm afraid so."

"Well, it was a good one. I shan't forget that you looked out for me even while I slept." Petruccio frowned and chewed his lip, an uncharacteristically childish gesture. "You're a strange one, aren't you Mr Chambers? You always turn up in the most unexpected places."

"I do my be—"

Alan did not get a chance to finish his sentence, for suddenly, he was flying again. Petruccio waved to him from the fields below, smiling happily, as Alan soared into the darkness of a night sky. Since when had it become night? The stars surrounded him. Their brightness was almost too much to bear, enveloping him, until suddenly the light had obliterated all of existence, leaving only a canvas white as snow and anticipation of what was to come.

CHAPTER 17
DARK ROOMS
AND DARK THOUGHTS

ALAN BLINKED. He sat in a high-backed wooden chair, situated in the corner of a boudoir. The room was so exquisitely furnished, it was surely the secret bedroom of some king or emperor. Although, if Alan wracked his brain, he was sure the room bore some similarity with the one he had occupied in *The Bloody Graal*. A fourposter bed dominated one side of the room, situated between two windows. Four animals were carved into its pillars: a bird of some kind, a lion, an ox, and a scorpion. On the beam spanning its two forward-facing poles, a fifth creature was emblemed, though Alan could not make head nor tail of it.

Crimson curtains hung over the two large windows, though they needn't have been drawn, for it was not only night outside, but dark within too, as though the air itself had congealed to a molasses-thick syrup. Melting candles were situated on virtually every surface: bedside table, cabinet, table, empty chairs. Yet, despite the array of flickering lights, the gloom remained imperturbable. This brought Alan a paradoxical double sense of foreboding and safety. He was hidden in the shadows, yet also the darkness promised hidden deeds.

The room was, at present, empty save for Alan himself. But from beyond the thick door of ebony wood, Alan heard footsteps approaching. A key turned, the door was unlocked and swung open, and in strode LeBarron. He was dressed rather differently. Gone were his blue travelling robes. Instead, he wore a white tunic, open at the chest to reveal his muscular, hairless chest, along with faded britches. On another man, the clothes might have seemed slovenly, but on LeBarron they seemed enchantingly free, an invitation to live and carouse a little.

Alan was almost tempted to call out to LeBarron then and there. The idea of talking to LeBarron in this dark, secret room appealed to him. Though they had enjoyed several heart-to-heart conversations, there was always some pressing danger that cut short their conversation. That, or Alan feared the attentive ears of their other comrades. Not that Alan resented or disliked the others, but he felt a special curiosity about LeBarron. Perhaps, he reasoned, it was because he had shared his very blood with the actor as he lay near death in the swamps of Yhtill.

Before Alan plucked up the courage to reveal himself to LeBarron, or else his dream incarnation, LeBarron stood beside the door and motioned for someone else to step through.

Alan's mouth hung open.

Five women traipsed into the hidden boudoir, each more gorgeous than the last. They wore scant clothing: loincloths, stylised golden brassieres, glittering chains, strips of cloth, but even these they discarded at once. The five women clambered onto the bed, giggling, smiling at LeBarron, who shut the door furtively and ensured it was bolted, so they would not be disturbed.

Once again you play the part of the voyeur, Alan chastised himself. In that moment, he almost thought he could see Mazael's eyes, shining out from the dark. There was a concerning thought: where was the Harvester, their so-called guide? Alan supposed in time he would be privy to all his companions' dreams. He wasn't sure how he knew this, or why it made so much sense. He supposed this was dream-knowing.

The first woman was willowy like a tree. The second played with flaming red tresses. The third had Nubian skin the colour of the earth, with bright green eyes. The fourth had steely silver running through her hair, though she was young and lithe. The last of them was pale as winter's snow, with black curls and lips blue as the colour of grave oceans. Each of them was lovely, impossibly lovely, to the point where it seemed they could have no equal. But as the next one moved into the foreground, and the former one faded, Alan's lustful attention would shift, magnifying the present woman as the most fair and beautiful of them all.

"Ladies," LeBarron said, opening his arms wide like a master of ceremonies.

THE DREAMS OF DEMHE

Even in dreams, LeBarron's confidence radiated forth. Unlike Petruccio, who had revealed a slightly more frightened version of himself in the encounter with the fake maiden, it seemed LeBarron even dreamed himself a prince among men.

"Me first," the willowy woman said.

She knelt before LeBarron. The other women set about to kissing and caressing each other while the first showered her attentions upon the actor. She unzipped his britches and pulled out his member, which was perhaps even more preposterously large in this dream-realm. *No deep-seated fears of inadequacy then, LeBarron?* Alan thought, wryly.

"No," LeBarron said, holding up one finger to indicate the woman stop in her ministrations. "Ladies always come first."

The women giggled but were suggestible. Alan watched dumbfounded, jealous, and painfully aroused as the first woman returned to the bed, and each of the women turned over onto their front, lifting their perfectly formed behinds into the air. LeBarron's eyes glittered with dark delight.

"What a feast!"

LeBarron set about to pleasuring the first with his mouth. Her moans ran through Alan like an electrical current. Instinctively, Alan found his right hand wandering to his groin, then pulled it back sharply, pricked by pain. He'd almost castrated himself with the taloned fingers of The Claw.

Shame was defeated as laughter broke from Alan's lips. The situation was so ridiculous, *he* was so ridiculous, he could not help it. There was something strangely freeing in laughing at one's perversions rather than recriminating them.

LeBarron looked up, staring into the dark in Alan's direction. "Who's there?" He squinted, peering into the gloom.

Alan remained silent, rigid in his chair, more a statue than a man.

"Don't stop now," the first woman said.

LeBarron forced a grin and returned to his ministrations. Alan wondered why the dream was showing him this. Was it because, when he had seen Cali and that strange man, he had recalled her rendezvous with LeBarron on the shores of Lake Hali? But that made little sense, because the dreaming had next shown him Petruccio, a markedly different scene.

LeBarron's attentions were diligent, with tongue, finger, and eventually his tremendous cock. The first woman moaned, then cried out. Having satisfied the first he moved to the second. Alan was in awe of LeBarron's stamina, though he reminded himself that this was a dream, pure fantasy.

After agonising minutes—well, agonising for Alan but very pleasurable for LeBarron and his "friends"—the red-haired woman cried out in orgasm. She and the first woman played together as LeBarron moved to the third. Whereas LeBarron had passionately, almost frantically made love to the second, the third was slower, heavier, almost as if he were tiring, though Alan knew he was not, simply that he was responding intuitively to the preferences and perhaps essential nature of each of these magical women.

The minutes dragged on. Alan remained painfully aroused, flushed head to toe, yet he did not feel brave enough to interrupt—and perhaps a secret part of him did not want to. More than anything, he would have liked to have joined in, but he knew he would never be allowed. His presence would scare the women, if indeed they could see him at all. Certainly, he had already scared LeBarron. And was it any wonder? Alan sometimes forgot that now his silhouette was not entirely that of a man, that always he carried with him the cruel, gleaming knives of The Claw's hideously potent fingers. *I am that which children have nightmares about,* he thought, a terrible sadness finally weighing down the arousal, causing him to quite literally deflate.

LeBarron had finished with the fourth woman and moved onto the fifth and final one. Perhaps this ordeal would be over soon? The actor knelt down to pleasure her orally, his tongue flicking across her glistening labia. The paleness of her skin made the secret inner folds of her cunt so brightly pink they were intoxicating to the eye. Yet suddenly, LeBarron pulled back, aghast.

"What is it, my love?" the fifth woman asked.

He went to speak, but found his voice muffled. He spat, and skating across the hardwood floor towards Alan went a bright blue stone.

Alan frowned. Had that been *inside* the woman?

"What was that?" LeBarron said, echoing Alan's confusion.

"A gift, my love," the woman said, but now her smile was dark, her blue lips eerily evocative of the kiss of Death herself.

LeBarron opened his mouth to demand more information, but all that emerged was a strange noise, almost like the hooting of an owl, but deeper.

"Oogh!"

The woman smiled. All the women, in fact, were smiling. They stood and circled LeBarron.

"What was that, my dear?"

"Ooogh! Oogh! Oooogh!" LeBarron said.

Alan felt his hairs stand on end. Now, there was no mistaking the sound: the low, throaty grunting of an orangutang.

And indeed, bright orange hair was now growing on LeBarron's face and chest. His arms were lengthening. His posture stooped. His impossible handsomeness was contorted as those full and luscious lips ballooned to monkey-proportions. His sockets retreated deep into his skull. His toes extended and gripped the floor.

But what remained was the fear in his eyes. Terror, in fact.

"Ooogh! Ooogh! Ooogh!"

He beat his chest, bared his teeth. But speech was impossible to him.

The women began to laugh. The cruelty of the sound cut through Alan like a blade.

Alan leapt from the chair, intending to comfort the poor animal that had once been his friend, but no sooner than he got to his feet than all the candles snuffed out, and he was left alone in absolute darkness.

Not absolute. There were bodies pressed around him, men in armour, men bloodied and muddied head to toe, screaming, their tongues like red serpents, their eyes bright as stars. Darkness overhead, comets streaking through the heavens, and high walls under siege. Carcosa? Or some other fortress lost in the midst of the black planet's impossibly ancient history.

"Captain Roland!" a voice cried.

Alan fought his way out of the press of bodies, and there, upon the upper battlements of the wall, he saw Roland, alone, wielding a sword in one hand and a spear in the other. A horde of Pe'karians surged toward him—their lips uttering protestations of devotion to the Demon King, hungry for blood and vengeance. A stone stairway led up to the wall. If Alan could reach him in time . . .

Before he could remember that this was mere dream, or process what he had just seen in the darkest corner of LeBarron's mind, his feet were in motion, hurtling up the steps. "With me!" he called to the other soldiers, but strangely they would not come, lingering below, locked in some senseless struggle that deceived his eye if he looked at it too long.

Alan heard Roland issuing war-cries. Heard blades singing through the air, metal carving flesh. The ring of steel on steel. The crack of broken bones.

Alan gained the upper battlements and saw Roland carving a vicious path through the horde. The wall's width only permitted the enemy to come three or four at a time; Roland's spear kept them at bay. Corpses already littered the battlements, making footing treacherous. Blood covered every stone.

"I'll help you!" Alan said.

If Roland was aware of him, he gave no sign, never breaking focus, killing with merciless swiftness, the very living incarnation of war.

Alan set about the Pe'karians, The Claw ripping and tearing. He could not deny it felt good. Shadows lunged at him and with tiger-like strokes he rent them asunder. Another came and Alan picked up a sword in his left hand, blocking their downward swing. He reached into their stomach with his dreadful talisman, hooked his talons about their guts, and pulled. Though they had made themselves in the image of demons, they died as men.

As suddenly as it had begun, the battle was over. Roland and Alan stood amidst a field of carnage, the bodies piled three corpses high in places. Alan grinned savagely. Still, Roland did not look at or perceive him. His eurypterid plate was crusted with gore and bile.

But they were not alone on the bridge. A new figure had appeared, walking over the strewn dead. The way they moved did not suggest aggression, and therefore Alan waited in breathless anticipation. Roland, it seemed, had some prescient of who this person was.

The darkness lifted, as though some unseen hand had turned a spotlight upon this new visitation, and Alan beheld a woman who bared some resemblance to Cali, though it was evidently not her. Her serpent-eyes were cast down to the ground as she walked. Her onyx skin was tinted with deep viridian, unlike Cali's, which had the blackness of night, dark space itself. This new woman was slender, too, her footfalls as dainty and timid as those of a fawn. A white dress floated around her with the ethereality of spirit. At last, standing a few paces from Roland, she stopped. Slowly, she lifted her head. Roland gasped. The soldier knew this woman.

"M-mother?"

She smiled, sadly.

"Yes, Roland. I am here."

"But . . . but you died. Pe'kar . . . Ordered your death. And I was sent to Carcosa . . . "

Had Alan not been so invested in this revelation, he might have wondered how Roland knew what his mother looked like, how he recognised her when in truth he had never known her, but of course that was the way of dreams, faces were given to those without, and those with faces had them taken away. Perhaps that was why, at this present moment, Roland could not see him?

"No, Roland. I live. Though I now wish I did not."

"Why do you speak so, mother?" Roland sounded heartbroken, yet her next words would cleave him even further asunder.

"You have slain your brothers. Look . . . "

Roland cast his eyes, and Alan saw—to his horror too—that each Pe'karian they had slain was gifted with Roland's own face.

Roland looked back to his mother.

"No! *No!*"

His mother nodded sadly, tears falling from her ophidian eyes.

"Yes. And now me too."

She leapt, and Roland seemed powerless to stop it. He screamed, a sound so chillingly full of despair Alan could barely stand. Alan wanted to throw up, but the dream denied him that release.

Roland's mother impaled herself fully upon the soldier's spear. Blood flowed from a gaping wound in her stomach, as well as from her mouth, which opened one last time to utter a low yet earth-shattering curse, *"I hate you."*

Roland took his mother in his arms, falling to his knees, sobbing and sobbing. His wails were loud enough to batter down the walls of Jerusalem. His anguish was such that Alan felt his own heart breaking into thousands of tiny pieces. He could not say or do anything.

"I'm sorry," Alan said.

The wall exploded, struck by some catapulted meteor. Stone, blood, and the dead rose into the air, and Alan was cast down. He did not fall long, a gateway yawned wide beneath him, and he suddenly found himself once more sat in a dark bedroom, only this was one he recognised.

Cassilda's room.

Now, a knot of dread formed in his chest too tight to unwind. His breathing became so shallow he was sure he would pass out, whether in a dream or not. His heart thundered with painful force.

The room was as he remembered it. Translucent silver curtains cobwebbed between the furniture and windows. A fourposter bed, that seemed likely to spring to life, hibernated in the centre of the room. The great living cabinet, Do'ledon, stood sentinel in one corner. Alan wondered what other secrets Do'ledon hid for Cassilda. She had taken the staff with her on their journey, but surely Do'ledon guarded other treasures.

Lastly, Alan remembered the chaise longue with black velvet cushioning and golden trim, which he and Cassilda had performed such erotic acts upon. If only Cali had not escaped! They might have stayed in that room forever, taking pleasure of one another, healing old wounds.

The door to the chamber creaked open.

Alan held his breath in expectation of what was to come.

CHAPTER 18
A STRANGER TO YOURSELF

THERE SHE WAS, his love, his dear Cassilda. Though things were strained between them, no sooner did he see her, than he knew he had to make everything right; for all Alan's failings there was a heart within that was true and loyal, capable of love.

She wore a simple gown, the kind of elegant and relaxed dress he had never seen her wear, tormented as she was by reminders of the past. She carried another dress with her, this one a lavish garment in white and cream, studded with pearls and opals, the price of the kingdom in one sequinned masterpiece: a wedding dress. Alan's heart tore. He knew now what scene approached, what terror he was about to witness.

Cassilda, like the other dreamers, did not immediately see Alan. It seemed he was in control of whether they perceived him or not. She carried the dress almost ritualistically over to the chaise longue and laid it down. The impish delight upon her face would have warmed Alan's heart, but knowing what was to come, and knowing, too, how infrequently she allowed such innocent pleasure to show on her face these days, his heart instead felt as though it had calcified into a stone in his chest.

Spare her, he found himself thinking. *Spare her please.* Then he realised that, as with the others, he could take action. True, he'd failed to help LeBarron and Roland, but he'd helped Petruccio. Maybe he could help Cassilda too. His feelings for her were strong, almost overwhelmingly strong. *Yes, when he appears, I shall act.* The Claw was a dreadful weight, a part of him still quite alien. He was always aware of its presence, like an aching scab on the flesh.

The door swung shut, guided by a gust of wind that should not exist. Cassilda did not jump but straightened. Her eyes held a languid excitement that—to Alan's discomfort—reminded him of Cali's raw sensuality. Had the two sisters once been more alike?

Without turning around or looking into the darkened corners of the room, she spoke. "'Tis bad luck to see the bride on the night before the wedding."

"A crude custom of Earth."

Alan's heart pounded. The voice, it was so rich, so dark, so full, like ancient honey, plumbed from some sacred grove of old gods. He could not see who the voice belonged to, but the shadows in the room seemed to be coagulating, thickening. "We need not be bound by such trivialities. Our love is of the spirit, not of the flesh."

Cassilda smiled.

"Yet thou hast come for the flesh, hast thou not?"

The shadow behind Cassilda became painfully thick, solid beyond reasoning. And all of a sudden it was no longer shadow in the limited sense, but matter, of a dark and different kind, an energy that glided across the surface of reality but was not bound to it, the disappearing antithesis of a black hole moulded into solid shape, an aberration of physics. This dark form enveloped Cassilda, more like a cloud than a man, though a man's shape was just discernible in the vortex of his shaded being. The moan that left Cassilda's lips was one of ecstasy as she leaned back into the embrace of the darkness, many black hands running across her form. Alan—in his paroxysm of horror and arousal combined—could not help but think of Zeus, transformed into such diverse shapes in order to enter the bedchambers of beautiful women. That was the nature of this being: a god, an elemental, not flesh.

"Men call me The Stranger," the dark cloud whispered. "And yet, I no longer wish to be a stranger to thee, Cassilda." And from the blackness emerged a pale mask, at once expressionless and yet so alive with meaning that its light seemed to cut words into Alan's thundering heart. Alan could scarcely tolerate looking into the mask's chasmal depths, for it began to distort his sense of light, all other things darkening. Every moment it transformed, from lust to hate to bitter emptiness to joy, and other expressions for which Alan had no name. In the myriad forms, he thought he once glimpsed LeBarron, but perhaps that was just his mind playing tricks.

Cassilda pulled herself free of her dark lover's embrace.

"You know I love thee. But thou must wait . . . The wedding is tomorrow. And afterwards, we shall be one." She smiled, biting her lip in a way that roused Alan's desire for her all the more. "Let the red dawn surmise, what we shall do. When this blue starlight dies, and all is through."

The shadow approached Cassilda again, though in truth he was all around her, a swirling miasma upon which floated the white-golden mask, shining with such awful light.

"A kiss, then?" The Stranger said. "A kiss and all shall be well."

Alan saw conflict within Cassilda, though he knew not the full reason nor depths of it. Then, to his surprise, Cassilda turned away.

The shadow darkened, becoming a pall so black it was difficult even to see the walls of the room.

"Thou wouldst deny me?"

"Only until tomorrow."

"But what is a kiss between lovers?"

"I bid thee wait!"

The mask became terrible; Alan was rooted to the spot.

"I shall not wait to take what is mine!"

The shadow enveloped Cassilda, and the Pallid Mask swooped toward her. Though Cassilda struggled, The Stranger was not one but many, a hundred shadowy hands gripping her, as though the dead lived within the penumbra of his being. The mask planted a kiss upon her lips. Hollow, and lustless.

"There," Cassilda said, some of the familiar anger surfacing. "Art thou satisfied?"

A breathless moment passed, and Alan knew what The Stranger would say, knew how awful it would be, that he observed a moment in time that could never be reversed, where fate and love and life were irrevocably changed.

"No," the shadow whispered.

Cassilda let out a scream. The shadow fully enveloped her. But Alan finally found his courage. God or not, dream or no, he would stand against The Stranger. No sooner than he rose from his chair, than the Pallid Mask swivelled fully to apprehend Alan. He was bathed in its terrible light, feeling his flesh convulse between its unnatural power. The mask was the reverse of stasis, a chaotic dance of never-ceasing progression, a performance in itself, where the players were atoms, darkness and light, matter itself. The nearest comparison Alan could make was of a Tarot deck being shuffled with its card faces upward. The constant appearance and disappearance of archetypal forms. Yet, unlike the Tarot, these forms were also merging, convalescing, combining, creating new forms, ghostly illuminances that played before his eyes as startling circus acts. Near hypnotised, Alan raised The Claw, more to shield his eyes from its glare than to threaten.

There was something behind the Pallid Mask, however. Something terrible. A secret. The eyes that shone out through the eyeholes were familiar.

Cassilda, using The Stranger's moment of distraction, tore herself away. She leaned against the fourposter bed, holding her head.

"Alan . . . " she said, confusedly. "Alan . . . what are you doing here? A dream? Am I dreaming?"

The Stranger regarded Alan, then seemed to straighten, his form a towering monolith of solid nothingness, crowned by the pale mask that was also a masque, an eternal dance of hideous splendour.

"Thou willst not stand between me and what is mine," The Stranger thundered.

"I will," Alan said. "By the power of The Claw, I apprehend thee."

"Then let us dance!" The Stranger roared.

The two met, shadow and light, yet in each of them was a spot of the opposite. Though Alan's Claw wreathed him with violent brightness, in his eyes there shone a darkness of his secret nature. The Stranger's voluminous shadow enveloped Alan, but at its heart glowed the white coal of the Pallid Mask. With tectonic force they met. The Stranger's hands ripped at Alan, tearing flesh. But he ignored all. He knew what he had to do. He had to reach through the shadowy mire, the fog and doubt and confusion, the swampland of The Stranger's inchoate being, where nothing was ever fixed or certain save uncertainty itself. *Reach, reach, reach.* The Claw extended from him, guiding him, cutting through the blackness.

And then, he brought The Claw down upon the Pallid Mask. Its lightning-charged talons closed about the face that was no face.

The Stranger screamed.

"Take off your mask!" Alan roared.

He pulled with all his might, and the mask came loose. But it was no simple disguise: grafted to the dark face beneath, wires of tissue connecting the porcelain talisman to its moorings, thick rivulets of blood dripping down from where the seemingly ethereal flesh had yet been torn. Such was the power of The Claw, to make even the unreal real, to rend even dreams.

"No!" screamed The Stranger. "No! I wear no mask! I wear no mask!"

"Your mask belongs to me!" Alan shrieked.

He pulled with all his might, and finally the Pallid Mask was ripped from The Stranger's face. From a visage devoid of flesh, grinning with a lipless mouth, lidless eyes stared—the eyes of someone Alan knew.

Red eyes.

"Mazael!" Alan gasped, stumbling back, the Pallid Mask still in his hand.

The shadow withdrew, sucked into the centre, finally forming the silhouette of a man. There was no true face, only a horror of exposed meat, and those two terrifyingly red eyes, like twin crimson suns setting at the end of the world.

"No, Alan," Cassilda whispered, a quiver of terror in her voice. "There is no Mazael. It's him. It's truly him! How could I have been so blind? The night he came to me . . . raped me . . . I tore off his Mask. I did not see his true face, for he fled as a shadow of his former self. I destroyed the Mask in the Fires of Manifestation, so that no one again would be subject to its evil power. But still, there are those who worship The Stranger. They gathered the ashes and pieces of his Mask. Some sewed its fragments beneath their skin. Others consumed the ash. They requested powers from their dark lord . . . " Cassilda spat, some of her defiance returning. "But none of them could ever be the original. Not even The Stranger himself." Cassilda strode up to the kneeling form of the shadow. "I broke you."

Mazael might have been trying to form a snarl, but he could not without lips, so instead his horrid teeth ground over one another.

"You *did* break me," he said at last. "You left me with nothing but this merest sliver of form. For eons I wandered. I sought wisdom in the desert. Perhaps, in the dreaming, I could become whole again. And indeed, I almost was. For here, time melts away. I had the Mask again! I felt its power! O the delight of it! The splendour!" His eyes grew brighter and brighter, a sick rapture illuminating his ragged horror of a face with something akin to joy. "A cold wench such as you could not understand!"

Cassilda looked sadly upon her ancient lover and enemy.

"I couldn't then. But I do now."

Mazael, or rather The Stranger, looked hopefully upon her.

"You do? You'll let me go, then? Back to being a harvester of dreams? Back to my lifeless existence? Please. I shall not ever trouble you again. I have paid penance for my great sin."

Alan snarled.

"If you have, then it has not been enough. To lure us into the dream to reclaim the Mask is one thing, but to reenact your sin? That is unforgiveable."

Mazael hung his head.

"Claw-bearer . . . how can I answer you? I am contemptible."

Alan raised The Claw, its light charging.

"Wait!"

Alan turned sharply. Cassilda had placed her hand upon his arm. Her eyes implored him to hold back. How could it be? Her abuser, the one who had violated her, she sought to spare him, to show mercy. Alan was more than ready to destroy him on her behalf, eager even to taste justice and vengeance.

"*Alan.*" It seemed, for a moment, Cassilda spoke not just with her own voice, but also the deep, quiet voice that had guided him through his worst ordeals in Carcosa. The spirit of Carcosa, Cassilda, and his conscience were all one, it seemed, in this perfect dreaming moment. "*Alan, you would kill him only to avenge your own honour. Kill him now, and I will never be free. The path of forgiveness is the true path. We must let him go.*"

"He wronged you in unimaginable ways, and then he tried again! He tricked us into following him. He has tormented each of us."

"No!" The Stranger cried. "No! The dreaming is what the dreaming is. All the dreams you have experienced, they were not within my power to control. If anything, it is *you* that brought us together, that made this moment possible! I had no intention of using the dreaming at first. I wished to act when the time came for you to fulfil your end of our agreement."

"Which will never happen," Alan snarled.

Cassilda was frowning.

THE DREAMS OF DEMHE

"What do you mean that Alan brought us together in the dreams?"

Mazael looked from one to the other. He could not smile, but his teeth became even more ghastly.

"You still do not know what he is?" The crimson orbs swung to Alan. "I knew from the moment I saw you."

"Tell me," Alan said. Though how could he trust anything The Stranger said?

Mazael lowered his eyes.

"It is not for me to do so. You would not understand, nor accept it from my mouth. But I shall lead you to the mountain of Al Qaf Saba, as promised."

"You shall get nothing in return," Cassilda said, eyes narrowing.

"Except my life." The room began to fade, darkness settling in, like deep night after a long summer's day. "For eons, all I wanted was to see your face again, Cassilda. But now I see, I am not worthy to gaze upon it. Nor shall I ever wear the Pallid Mask again. I go forth from here finally divested of my disguise. I go forth from here as a stranger to myself—as Mazael in truth becoming."

A flash of light, and the dream ended.

CHAPTER 19
THE EMERALD MOUNTAIN

OR A FEW MOMENTS, Alan could hardly remember who he was, where he was, or why. The disorientation was less like waking from a dream, and more like being bound and gagged, tossed into a stormy sea, turned hither and thither in the relentless fury of the waves, and finally spat out upon some unknown shore.

Blinking, he looked about him, as if searching for some lifebuoy, still feeling cast adrift. Though he could see, what he saw made no impression, held no significance, like staring at script in a language he did not know. Yes, there was sand. Yes, there were suns in the sky. Yes, there was a shimmer of high heat rising off the baked desert. And yes, there were figures he recognised. But they were merely colours and shapes impressed upon his retina—his brain had lost its interpretive faculties. A strange green glow tarnished everything. It took him a moment to realise its source.

"Jesus," he said. A rare instance that name came to his lips. He had become increasingly acculturated to Carcosa, thinking in terms of its gods and myths and stars. But sometimes he experienced something that shocked him out of the present and into his past. "Jesus Christ."

Before he and the others reared a mountain of godlike proportions. Its stone was a deep and dark emerald. The glancing rays of the sun reflecting off the mountain's formidable sides cast the surrounding area in paradoxically underwater hues, so that the sand looked more like that of an ocean bed than a desert. What augmented the peak's already imposing height was how unnaturally it dwelt in the surrounding landscape. It stood alone, rising from desert sand without valley, ridge, or crevasse to explain its formation. Alan was reminded of the manmade mountain, Kailash, which stood with haunting grandeur in the Ngari Prefecture of Tibet. *Men should not be able to build such things,* he thought.

But the mountain was not only forbiddingly mighty, but beautiful. The deep lustre of the emerald stone made it seem as though some green planet had been cored out and its heart set like a jewel in the midst of Demhe. Girdling the mountain's colossal heights were flowers: yellow, blue, white, black, purple. The smell that came from them enlivened Alan's senses, and at last dispelled his confusion.

"This is Al Qaf Saba?" he said.

Cassilda, who now stood by his side, smiled and nodded. He noted that—unlike her dream self—she was once more armed with the black staff, clutching it in her right hand as though letting go would mean her death. She touched him with her left hand, though, with such striking tenderness he felt his strange jealousy quelled—at least for the moment.

"Thank you, Alan. For defending me."

He inclined his head.

"I am at the service of my lady."

Cassilda's smile became a grin.

"You are learning the ways of formal speech."

"And you are learning to speak like a commoner," Alan teased. "How far you have lowered yourself in my perverse company."

Cassilda saddened at that.

"You are not perverse, and I was wrong to say that. Yours is a noble heart. I begin to see that what is strange to the spirit is ordinary to the flesh, and what is ordinary to the flesh is strange to the spirit. I must let you be that which you are." She swallowed and leaned in close, as though she had a secret to impart. "When this is done, we must speak about what you saw in my dream."

Alan nodded.

"You did what I could not," he said. "I wonder if that is why I feel so stuck?"

"Stuck?"

"Yes," Alan said bitterly. "I am pulled this way and that by The Claw, by my conscience, by vengeance and love, by power and weakness . . . Who am I beneath that? I cannot always be torn in two." He knew those final words were not his own, but for the moment their source escaped him. *You still have not quite shed the chrysalis,* he thought. *Your transformation is not finished.*

"Alan . . . "

But Cassilda was interrupted by LeBarron and Roland, who marched over to check all were well. Petruccio stood off on his own. He seemed to have recovered quickest, and was staring up at the mountain, as though committing it to memory. And perhaps he was; Alan had no doubt such an inspiring sight would make for a good painting, when all this was through.

Alan noted with some guilt that both Roland and LeBarron looked haunted, with dark rings beneath their eyes, and an unsettled energy draped about their shoulders, as obvious to any who looked upon them as the bloodied furs of a dead animal.

"I'm glad to see you here," LeBarron said. "I have never known the dreams to be so treacherously potent. Some dark magic is at work here, I swear it."

"You mean that was not usual?" Alan asked.

LeBarron shook his head. "You think that Pe'kar's armies could have marched upon Carcosa so swiftly if each individual soldier had to go through *that*? It would be chaos. No, something is at work here." LeBarron cast his eyes about the party. "What of Mazael?"

Alan and Cassilda exchanged a look.

"He isn't coming," Alan finally said.

"The pigment!" Petruccio cried.

All turned to see the dwarf beaming delightedly at the glyph of memory he had inscribed upon the roll of parchment. He turned and grinned at all of them, rolling the parchment back up and stuffing it into one of his deceptively deep pockets.

"You remembered?" Roland said, jovially.

"Yes. The glyph helped. And I think perhaps it answers your question, LeBarron. The oneiric pigment resides here. This is what has caused the dreaming. I'm sure of it. Perhaps someone is tampering with it, causing the dreams to rise and fall in potency?" Petruccio's expression darkened. "Perhaps it's Cali?"

"That would be bad news, indeed," Cassilda said.

"I think it unlikely," Alan said. "I saw Cali in the dreaming."

Now all eyes swivelled to Alan, alarm etched into every face, save for LeBarron's.

"I would not read too much into what you saw, Alan. It would not have been the real Cali, just a dream projection."

"No," Petruccio said. "Alan was there in my dream. Not just a projection. It was the real him. I'm sure of it."

"Me too," Cassilda said.

LeBarron frowned.

"I did not see him."

"Nor I," Roland added.

"As I said," LeBarron said, seeming to relax. "Dream projections and no more."

Alan shook his head.

"I saw you. Both of you." Alan hesitated. Did he dare reveal such personal insights before the whole group?

LeBarron had turned pale.

"Speak of what you saw, then."

Alan swallowed.

"A blue stone," he said.

LeBarron lowered his eyes.

"Then you really did see . . . "

"And what of me?" Roland asked, his words as sharp as his sword.

"Death," Alan replied simply. "And guilt."

Roland's nostrils flared, and he let out a deep sigh.

"So you have seen us all at our most vulnerable, then?"

"I did not wish to," Alan said, perhaps a little too hastily. "I did not have any control. I was simply there. And then as soon as one vision seemed to approach a crisis, I was forced into the next. But yes, I did see all of you. And Cali . . . "

"And what was Cali doing?" Cassilda asked, her voice like steel.

"She was speaking with someone; I don't know who. He did not seem to be a projection, for he was aware of me." Alan brightened. "Maybe this explains why our dreams linked?"

LeBarron shook his head.

"Let us be careful now, and not get terms confused. Our dreams were not linked. *Only you* were able to move between our dreams. But I take your point, if there was an interloper, perhaps they distorted the dreaming, and your connection to Cali caused the disruption."

"This is too much speculation," Petruccio said, after a few moments of silence. "Even for one who watches the stars. I think we will find answers upon the mountain . . . "

"And your precious pigment," Roland remarked.

"A man may dream."

"And speaking of dreams: you say Mazael is lost to us?" LeBarron said. Alan tried to read his eyes. The actor was highly intelligent, and as a servant of The Stranger—who had walked with them unbeknownst to his most devoted follower—could read deceptions better than most. LeBarron sensed something was missing from Cassilda's cryptic answer. But they were spared having to address the issue further.

"We are glad to be rid of him," Roland said, giving the impression he would have liked to have been the one to remove Mazael himself.

"Agreed," Cassilda added quickly.

"Let us hope he does not catch up with us," Petruccio said.

If he does, Alan thought, *I shall kill him, demigod or no.*

The thought gave him no little pleasure.

CHAPTER 20

THE PATH OF FLOWERS

THEY BEGAN THEIR ASCENT, feeling like sea-legged sailors stepping off from a ship that had been adrift for years. It was not that the stone of the mountain didn't feel solid. In fact, quite the reverse. The mountain's very concreteness was such a sharp juxtaposition to the ephemerality of the dreaming realm they had just traversed that it seemed alien. The flowers swayed about them in the black planet's mysterious winds, resembling crowds of waving and cheering people. Their colours mesmerised Alan to the point he had to close his eyes, feeling as though staring too long might trigger an epileptic fit.

"Are you alright, Alan?" Cassilda said.

He opened his eyes and forced himself to continue the climb. LeBarron and Roland walked a little way in front. Petruccio marched at the very head of the party, most eager of all to climb the mountain's summit, convinced of what he would find there. His eyes blazed like the twin suns themselves. Alan prayed the dwarf was not disappointed a third time.

"I'm okay," he managed. "But I can't shake this feeling . . . "

He dared not speak what the feeling was, for its implications were truly terrible, beyond the reach of his mind.

"You have always known, Alan," The Claw whispered. "You were never of Earth."

"Deja vu is just an illusion of the brain," Alan replied, through gritted teeth.

The Claw laughed at him, a sound like chains rattling in a dungeon.

"After all you've experienced you reach for the rationalist's feeble excuse? I expected better, Alan."

The Claw's use of the word "I" chilled Alan.

He turned his attention to the flowers growing up the sides of the mountain, their wild banks forming a pathway that serpentined its way up towards what Alan suspected would be an entrance into the mountain itself. The flowers were of different varieties, roses and Aaron's beards and daisies, and but there was one dominant species, showing soft yellow petals with faint purple lines at the throat. *Alyssa.* The name came unbidden to him. It brought with it warmth but also further pangs of doubt and confusion, for his sense of *deja vu* was only increasing as he looked at the flowers.

Cassilda watched Alan with dark-eyed concern.

At last, the path terminated, just as Alan had suspected, in a warm-looking cave mouth. The exterior of the mountain was glittering green, but the tunnel showed orange light that made Alan think of campfires and childhood stories and warm spaces where one might curl up and sleep.

"I have come too far to let courage fail now," Petruccio said. There was a mania in his face at odds with the sculpt of his features, and his usually stoic expressions, as though a younger man were trying to shed the skin of the older one.

Without further words, the artist marched into the cave mouth.

LeBarron and Roland exchanged glances. The two had always had a strange chemistry, despite the fact that Roland had professed to not trusting LeBarron. Their mutual experience of what lay beyond death had bonded them further.

"Petruccio is right," LeBarron said. "It would be pointless to venture on without discovering the mountain's secret."

Roland nodded.

"As one," the soldier said, simply. LeBarron smiled. The two strode together into the cave.

Alan and Cassilda remained. Alan was reminded of another moment, what seemed so long ago, where the two of them had been the last to descend down the xanthimum, into the secret city of Alar. A mad urge came upon Alan to beg Cassilda to turn away. For the two of them to run, to leave the others behind. Let Petruccio have his oneiric pigment. Let Roland has his vengeance on Cali. And let LeBarron find his true self. But he and Cassilda, they would run, back to Earth if need be, forging a new life. He did not want to enter the cave, did not want to look. He sensed the whole universe was pushing him toward this point, and that could only mean something life-changing, something he had denied and avoided his whole life, waited to finally ensnare him. Deep within his heart he had a dark suspicion of what it might be, but he could not confess it to anyone, not even himself.

Cassilda put a delicate hand upon his arm.

"You are scared?" she asked.

He closed his eyes, held her to him.

"I am."

"Me too."

He opened his eyes and looked down at her sweet face in surprise.

"Why?"

"I don't want to lose you. And I fear whatever we are about to discover, whatever is about to come to light, may take you from me forever." Her voice was near hoarse, a whispered promise. Alan found his lips dry, his heart racing.

"I don't want to lose you either. You are all that makes sense to me. You are my black star, my guiding light . . . "

"Then let us swear that whatever happens, we will not be lost to each other."

"Yes. I swear it."

"And I too."

They kissed, and in her flower-sweet mouth, the world itself was momentarily forgotten.

They held hands and faced the cave-mouth.

"Together."

"Yes."

They walked within.

At first, there was nothing unusual about the cave. Soft light played off the walls. The stone was rugged but unmistakeably beautiful in the half-light of the fire. They were not walking through tunnels long before they entered a broad, open space, a circular "room", though it had evidently been formed naturally. A campfire burned at its centre, around which were what looked like pink-white porcelain fragments. A hole in the ceiling allowed the smoke to flow out, and a small trickle of light in. LeBarron, Roland, and Petruccio all stood around the fire, their faces perplexed.

Crack.

Alan looked down and found one of the porcelain fragments had broken beneath his feet. He stooped and picked up the fragment. It was vaguely oily and sticky. Not porcelain at all, but an egg-shell, though the original egg must have been tremendously large, larger than an ostrich's egg.

A flash of memory. A cave. Yellow eyes. Crawling through massive pieces of shell . . .

"It's all . . . familiar . . . " Alan swallowed.

"Familiar?" LeBarron said, a note of almost terror in his voice.

"It must be some T.V. show . . . Something . . . " Alan said. But that could not explain the clarity with which he felt that he had trodden these steep slopes before, had smelled these flowers, had stood—no, crawled—in this very same cave.

"What's T . . . V . . . ?" Cassilda whispered.

Before Alan could answer her, a voice caused them all to swivel sharply.

"Greetings, friends."

In their very midst, arriving via no discernible entrance, an apparition: a wizened old man, his features flat and broad—suggesting a person who smiled a great deal yet also weathered the elements—and adorned by the most extravagant whiskered moustache, the kind worn by ancient Chinese emperors. He wore what looked like an emerald fez and glittering silken robes, embroidered with images of serpents and dragons intertwined, coiling and uncoiling, soaring through clouds of pearlescent white. His eyes seemed tiny in his face, like black jewels, only reflecting the smallest sliver of firelight.

The old man sat upon a log—which Alan was fairly sure had not been there before—facing the fire.

"Please, have a seat," the old man said.

"Who are you?" Cassilda asked, her words ringing around the cave walls.

To Alan's surprise, the old man's gaze fixed upon Petruccio.

"I am the guardian of the pigment, appointed by the Great Master Uboth himself. For eons, I have kept vigil, awaiting the right seeker." The flame in the centre of the room suddenly exploded with impossible brightness, illuminating the walls of the cave, showing them not to be dull, but rather painted and daubed with hypnotic, phantasmagorical images. Creatures whose names were unknown to Alan seemed to materialise from out of the rock itself, their horns gleaming, their eyes brighter and more alive than those of the living souls who stared back at them. Sleek, furred flanks darted and danced through fantastical trees. Glistening scales encircled the cavern. Shadowy figures danced in darkness and flame. Alan's heart was like a cup filled up with awe as the art came alive about him, a host of wild and ever-living forms, each more beautiful and graceful than the last, and each holding some indecipherable secret of being itself.

Petruccio fell to his knees, prostrated himself in the posture of obeisance.

"I have come so far, noble guardian. I have met with disappointment time and time again." He raised tear-filled eyes. "But do you tell me, truly, that you guard the pigment?"

The old man smiled.

"I tell you truly, that if you pass the trial set by the Grand Master Uboth, then the pigment shall be yours, and with it, the power of all dreaming."

Petruccio wept. The others looked on in astonishment.

"Come," the old man said. "Have a seat about the fire. I have waited a long time as well. You will no doubt have many questions. Some answers I can give you now. Some only when the trial is done."

One by one, each of them took a seat about the fire. Round about them, the shadows of ideal form danced and leapt and raced and slithered and sang, a memory of dreams that had been, and a promise of dreams yet to come.

CHAPTER 21
MASTER HAO

L IKE CHILDREN BEFORE their parent, the party sat cross-legged, awaiting the strange old man's next words.

"Only one may be permitted to undergo the trial," the old man said. "Which of you would step forth?"

Despite asking the question, his eyes lingered on Petruccio. But before the artist could answer, Cassilda interrupted.

"Our aim is to stop Cali, not to seek the pigment," Cassilda warned.

Petruccio wheeled savagely.

"How short-sighted can you be!" the dwarf snapped. "With the pigment, stopping Cali will be a mere thought! Universes beckon! The light of stars yet unborn is seeded in the pigment!"

Alan felt his hackles rise in alarm. Never had Petruccio spoken so rudely to the princess.

"The Claw and the staff are enough," Cassilda replied, keeping her cool.

Petruccio turned away, as though disgusted.

"Perhaps they are enough," the old man mused. "But is stopping Cali enough? Does the overthrow of one tyrant or enemy ensure peace? No, a new one steps into their place. Only with a dream of the future can things change for the better."

Cassilda paused, reflecting on what he had said. Alan saw much truth in the words, and clearly Cassilda did too. Were they being too shortsighted, as Petruccio had said? Yes, they could kill Cali, but what then? There was still Pe'kar. There were still many other problems, some Alan probably wasn't even aware of with his limited knowledge.

THE DREAMS OF DEMHE

"I would like to know who *you* are," Roland rumbled.

The old man smiled.

"I am the guardian, as I said, appointed by Grand Master Uboth himself. But if you are looking for a name, you may call me Master Hao."

Alan could not suppress a smile at the homonym for the word "how". *Okay, universe, you have made your point. Cali is the why. This strange old man is the "how". And perhaps, perhaps the thing he guards is the "what".*

"Well then, Master Hao," Roland said. "How came you to know Uboth?"

Alan could tell from the soldier's tone he was more than merely curious. Roland, too, guarded a piece of Uboth's legacy in the form of the banner. And, having been used by Cali, he had every right to suspect *everyone*.

"The story is long—tediously so. Enlightenment is not obtained in one dramatic moment or instant. True, it may seem to manifest in the instant—the lightning bolt of descending inspiration—but it is only through the hard and slow path of the upward ascending flame that one may catalyst such a moment to occur in the first place. In truth, enlightenment is acquired over a lifetime of dedicated study and hard work. Suffice to say, that as a young man utterly lost to the world, I sought the mountain peak wherein we all sit now, and there I met Uboth, undergoing his own spiritual pilgrimage, though much farther along the path than I. We studied together. He illuminated me, awakened my innermost being. Then, he left. He had great purpose in the world. Anyone with second sight could see it." Master Hao's eyes remained impenetrably hard, and yet Alan thought he saw the faintest clues as to a secret grief haunting the old man: the crow's feet deepening, the lip fractionally trembling. "One day he returned, and with him a woman, a beautiful nagini, pregnant. She laid her divine egg—fertile with the seed of Uboth—within this very cave. And lo, from the egg came the oneiric pigment!" Master Hao smiled, his expression timelessly avuncular. "It was entrusted to me, to keep hidden, to keep safe. Until the stars were right." He drew in a deep breath, and when he released it, the mighty fire burning at the heart of the cave quivered as though a terrific wind had nearly battered it into extinction. "Those stars now reign in the sky. The time is now. The pigment must be reclaimed and used once again

130

by those who would build a better future for the Uboth's beloved Carcosa."

"It will be so," Petruccio said, in a voice of rapt zeal.

Master Hao's smile became mischievous, that of a wicked boy who had just played a toilet prank. "We shall see whether your mettle is equal to the call of virtue."

"But if only one person can undergo the trial, what shall we do?" Cassilda said, now biting her lip, revealing the girlishness beneath her iron-hard exterior.

Master Hao's stare became diamond-hard.

"Wait or go, it makes no difference to me. Your friend will brave the trial. He may return. But then again, he may not. In a sense, none return from such a trial, for in order to pass it, one must transubstantiate one's being . . . " The old man seemed to fall off a precipice into a deep world of inner imagination, bowing his head, closing his eyes, mumbling to himself, words and phrases so arcane they perplexed even Cassilda. After a moment, he roused. "Yes, he must go forth. If he is ready . . . ?"

All eyes turned to Petruccio.

The dwarf stood, then bowed. His face had resumed its stony solemnity: the Petruccio Alan had first met in *The Black Star*, what seemed decades ago.

"I am," the dwarf intoned.

"Then behold the way!" Master Hao cried, raising his hand.

A black part of the cave, a corner that the brightened fire hadn't touched, suddenly ruptured. A sound like tectonic plates moving, the wheels of a dismal engine turning, roared around them, causing Alan's teeth to buzz and his sternum vibrate. The whole mountain seemed to be shuddering, as if with anticipation. Then, as quickly as it began, it ceased, and a secret tunnel lay opened before them, its walls lined with bright lamps, though what it was that burned so brightly in the lamps was impossible to discern. The tunnel curved away, beyond sight, sloping softly downwards.

"Another labyrinth," LeBarron muttered.

Petruccio stood, staring at the concealed entrance. Alan walked up and gently put his left hand upon the dwarf's shoulder. Without looking back at Alan, the dwarf reached up and clasped it, the closest thing to an embrace they had shared.

"Are you sure about this?" Alan whispered, knowing the answer before it came.

THE DREAMS OF DEMHE

"I know you, of all people, will understand," Petruccio said. "I *must* do this."

"I do. We will wait for you."

"If I'm not back within three days, go on," the dwarf said, and Alan's heart tore to hear the slight tremble in Petruccio's voice, the tiniest wavering of courage. But no sooner than it came, it was gone, and Petruccio drew in a deep breath. Squeezing Alan's hand once, he stepped forward, pulling away from the safety of his embrace. Like Orpheus, he strode towards the darkly gleaming passageway, though unlike the ancient singer, Petruccio did not look back at his friends.

Alan had never been much of an artist, for though he was imaginative he lacked the capacity to enshrine meaning in an image. Yet, the sight of Petruccio, so small yet dauntless, striding into the chasmal unknown, his face set—sterner than the very mountain in which they stood—seemed to flash and burn itself upon his mind's eye, to sear itself into his very being. Never once did the dwarf's step falter, or his resolution waver, not even when the mountain once more began to grind and roar, as the black stone began to rise from the floor behind the lone dwarf, like a wave rearing up to drown a tiny skiff clinging to life upon a storm-tossed sea, cutting him off from their sight.

And any possibility of turning back.

CHAPTER 22
THE TEMPLE OF
THE SERPENTKIN

PETRUCCIO BLINKED, his eyes adjusting to the gloom. Once, he had worn glasses, until Cali had taught him a spell to heal his vision. The effects of the spell were sadly not permanent, and he had to use it every month or so to restore his eyes to perfect function. Therefore, though the tunnel was lined with bright lamps, he could feel his tired eyes struggling to scour the darker depths. He would soon need to recast the spell. But not before he saw this trial to its end—all things waited upon his final attainment.

He felt naked, especially without Alan by his side. Petruccio had never enjoyed many friends. His fellow palaeontologists and archaeologists had been mere acquaintances, brought together out of professional necessity, and many of them made no secret of the fact they disliked Petruccio for his artistic flair and were jealous of his eidetic memory. Cali had been a mentor, a guru, in other words: not his friend but his master—that was, until she betrayed him. There were a few souls in Carcosa whom he regarded highly. But their relationship always consisted of some kind of transactional element, information for information, trinket for trinket. Pleasant, to be sure. But not true friendship, not what he felt might bind him and Alan Chambers.

His footsteps seemed preposterously loud in this confined space, though in truth he had no idea how long the tunnel ran for. It appeared to curve slightly to the right, at a constant downward slope. A spiral, then. A spiral winding its way down into the heart of the mountain. He could already feel the oppressive weight of millions of tons of rock above his head. How deep did this internal structure go? He dreaded to think. *Surely it cannot be deeper than my own mind. You braved Demhe, you can survive this.* Somehow he doubted that to be true. Demhe had posed many psychological dangers, but this posed magical ones. Compared to Cassilda and Cali, in whom the royal blood flowed, augmenting their magical prowess, he was but a journeyman of sorcery, perhaps even less than that. He'd always known Cali held back much in her teachings, only giving him enough that he might be of adequate service to her. What she had perhaps failed to realise was that he, too, held back parts of himself. He had dedicated much to her and her path, but not all.

He walked the tunnels for so long it began to become tedious. Surely, no sane mind would design a structure so monotonous or repetitive. Perhaps there were further hidden entrances the initiated could open with magical words? Perhaps he was merely fantasising, his mind exhausted from the ordeal in Demhe, from emotional upheaval, and the repetition before him.

No, all was *not* exactly the same. Paying attention to the small details, he noticed the space between the lamps was getting wider. Yes, the patches of shadow were larger and deeper. The lamps were incrementally being spaced further and further apart. Petruccio smiled to himself.

Very well then, if you wish to play games.

He reached up and plucked a lamp off its iron hook.

Immediately, all the other lamps snapped out of existence. Petruccio sucked in a sharp breath of fear and excitement. He now stood in total darkness save for the pale, white light of the lamp in his hand. It was a heavy talisman to bear, made of crude iron, swinging pendulously from its handle.

"Change is good," he said, wondering whether the darkness would answer him.

He walked on, bearing the light before him, its feeble illumination only enough to reveal the next five or six feet of the path. *I must be the very image of The Hermit Tarot,* he thought. Well, it was an apt card to be thinking about: isolation, meditation, the path of involution. That was his road, not only deeper into the mountain, but deeper into his own heart.

The tunnel was disturbingly quiet, only the sound of the lamp-handle creaking, his heart pulsating, and his shuffling footfalls penetrated the veil of silence. He found himself struggling to hold on to his thoughts. No sooner did they come than they vanished, as though the darkness had opened doorways hitherto closed, out of which the shadows of his mind slipped gleefully, to revel and dance beyond his grasp. *Alan. Cassilda. LeBarron. Roland. Cali. Cali. Cali.* The names were a mantra to keep him focused, to keep him clear. Brotherhood and vengeance. Love and hate. The twin pillars of his being, holding him upright as surely as his muscular—though stout—legs. *No, there is something else. Something more that drives you.* It seemed a ghost whispered to him. Yes, in the darkness, his thoughts became externalised, seemed not to *originate* within the brain but rather to be *received* by it. Wasn't that one of the fundamentals of all magic? The brain as receiver, not generator. The levels of reality all radio-stations broadcasting at the same time—and the adept might tune in to the particular frequency they wanted to hear. He smiled wondering what FM frequency Carcosa would be tuned to. *666 seems apt.* But hush, his thoughts were getting away from him again. What had the ghost being tried to tell him? Something else driving? Yes. *Desire.* Not of a sexual kind, not like the others, who were all subject to their ids, even Cassilda. No, Petruccio was purer. LeBarron had tried to persuade him after the battle at Carcosa, and he had been sorely tempted. So many willing women, libidos kindled by the endorphin rush of survival. The oldest story in the book: we live another night, so let us propagate. But Petruccio, above such things, above the promises of the serpent.

Or so he thought.

"I desire the pigment," he whispered. "I desire to build something new."

The force with which he whispered the words seemed to manifest his will, for all of a sudden, he saw light winking at him from around the bend. *Light!* How easily one became accustomed to its absence and longed for its return. How often he had taken it for granted as he stayed up late in his office, researching, researching, researching, the dull electric bulb on his desk buzzing like a fly, yet for all its crudeness managing to hold back the night.

The light growing as he began to round the bend, a doorway, between two pillars. Around each pillar was the stone sculpture of the serpent. He was reminded of the bannister in Liliya's tavern, *The Bloody Graal.*

And beyond the door, flames burning in bronze braziers, a

135

sense of vastness that would have dwarfed even a giant. Cavernous space. Stairwells rising into blackness. Temples. Colonnaded paths. All of it draped in dancing shadow, as though a cloak made out of still-living beetles had been thrown over the massive architecture.

He stepped through the door, setting down his lantern, and allowed his neck to crane as he tracked some of the colossal pillars up into the vast dark hovering above. The flame-light washed the structure's stone in a warming glow that belied the deadly cold, which Petruccio now seemed to sense more keenly, drawing his cloak about him.

A paved road extended before him. To the right of this path rose the steps of a temple so vast it might have rivalled the palace of Carcosa in size. To the right were a series of smaller buildings, many of them circular and supported by ionic columns, interconnected by colonnaded paths, descending a subtle slope, down into a yet deeper basin of the mountain.

Coming down the main paved road were two figures, both nagas, gifted with serpentine lower halves. One was a woman, grey-haired yet still beautiful, wearing a golden robe that fell diagonally across her torso and shimmered in the firelight. Her serpentine half had scales of a dark, lustrous purple. The other was a young man, brown-haired, with the human aspect of a young Greek warrior. He slithered on a tail bright green, with a whiter underbelly. His human torso was bare-chested, though a bright necklace fell between his muscular pectorals. Petruccio did not read hostile intent in their approach, and so he exorcised restraint, holding back his defensive urge and bowing low when they drew near.

"Welcome," the old woman said, inclining her head in acknowledgement of Petruccio's bow. "Seeker of the Pigment."

"Welcome," the young man echoed. His smile was a terrible radiance. "You have come far."

"Braved many trials."

"To reach the Temple of the Serpentkin."

Petruccio's eyes widened.

The old woman cocked her head.

"You have heard this term before? You have seen one of us before?"

Petruccio nodded.

"In a tavern, in the town of Al Shujah, I met one of your kind."

"Liliya," the young man said. "Ah, ever she knows just what to say to direct Seekers to our door, though of course, few have made it here alive."

"There *were* others?"

"Oh yes. Do you imagine you are the only one to ever have discovered the source of Demhe's dreaming?"

Petruccio lowered his eyes, abashed.

"I imagined, perhaps, that I was the only one who had discovered a way of circumnavigating the dreaming's disorientation."

The old woman laughed.

"Do not be embarrassed, for it was well done, and like we have said, very few ever make it this far. To have been greeted on the threshold of the Temple is, itself, one of the greatest attainments a soul can aspire to."

"Now we must apprise you of the risks," the young man said. "There is still time to turn back."

"And no shame in doing so."

"For there are three possibilities before you."

"Firstly, that you pass the trial, and we reveal to you the secret of the pigment."

"Secondly, that you die in the trial, your journey ends here, and you are buried with the honoured dead."

"Or thirdly, that you fail, and thus are banished from here, *never again to set foot in the Temple.*"

Petruccio swallowed, his spit tasting thicker than tar.

"It seems you know my mind, for the third option is by far the worst. To die in the attempt is nothing. But to live on, knowing where the secret lies, but never again able to attempt it . . . That is unbearable."

The two serpentkin nodded, the old woman smiling sadly.

"I see that wisdom is yours as well as strength and courage. Well, what say you?"

"I have not come this far to waver now," Petruccio said, and he felt the fire kindle in his belly, a supernova in the night sky of his being. "I shall attempt it. And if I fail, then I will humbly ask you for death, for it is better than the alternative."

The two guardians exchanged a look. The old woman sighed.

"How much I prefer you already to the last soul to venture here. As I am in no way involved in the officiation of the trial, I can say without consequence that I do sorely hope you succeed. Come, with us."

"Wait . . . " Petruccio said, holding up his hand as the two serpentkin turned to lead him down the long road, towards whatever doom he had spent his entire life preparing for. "The last soul . . . " Then all became clear to him, with the same power and certainty of dream-knowing. The fire that had begun in his belly rocketed up his spine and entered his brain, where it seethed, its burning an intermixed ecstasy and agony. *"Cali?"* Her name was a curse on his lips.

The old woman and the younger man exchanged another glance. Then, silently, the young serpent nodded.

"She hid it from me!" the dwarf raged. "She knew and she *hid* the knowledge! That viper! That whore! That monster!"

"Your anger burns brightly, Seeker. But perhaps there is one comfort to your distress?"

Petruccio looked at the young serpent wild-eyed. He could not imagine anything could quell or soothe the burning fire. He was practically beyond speech, the incandescence of his hatred cindering his very soul.

The young snake, however, did not let Petruccio's anger dissuade his mirth.

"Remember, Seeker: Cali *failed.*"

CHAPTER 23
THE STORM BEFORE THE QUIET

"SOON," PE'KAR—or rather his astral phantom— said, *"The dream-storm will quieten."*
"Is this your doing?" Cali said.
"No, but you can trust that it is the truth."

Their interview had continued after Alan's strange interruption. Cali did not know the significance of seeing him here, but it perturbed her, for her understanding of the dreaming was that it belonged to the individual, a private visionary universe, a personal hell. *It makes sense that Alan would be in your personal hell,* she thought, not without a small spark of her old humour. But she had felt, palpably, that it was not merely a dream-projection of Alan, but the real thing she was seeing. And Pe'kar's reaction confirmed as much. *"I did not bid him come,"* Pe'kar had said. *"Perhaps he is here of his own volition?"* Those words were enough to strike terror into her soul.

"And what do you want me to do?" There was always a catch with the Demon King, always something to be given in exchange. His plans seemed crude and primitive, but he had survived eons, contested the King In Yellow himself, and whilst his armies had twice been defeated by Carcosa in recent times, there were many more legions and generals, and darker secrets held in the Six Ringed City.

"Do as you already planned and come to my city. But do not come in desperation, as a fugitive, skulking in the shadows, hiding from your enemies. Come as my bride-to-be, come to my arms willingly, and I will complete what we began together."

Cali battered her eyelashes and pulled a coquettish pose.

"My Great King, you flatter me. But surely you cannot mean

139

the final secrets of your magic? What could you possibly gain by sharing such prizes with me?"

The beautiful being, man perfected and harmonious with the serpent, seemed to occlude for a moment, as though his form were more cloud than matter, enveloping itself in dark thunderheads, a roiling nest of energy within ready to explode into forked lightning. But then, the skies cleared, and once more he was perfect, turquoise radiance sloughing off his flesh like the oily iridescence of a serpent's scales.

"In exchange for the one secret I would never divulge to you, I ask for the one secret you would never divulge to me . . . We shall whisper such secrets to each other in the marital bed. And then we shall claim such power as is befitting twin gods . . . For that is what I, and I alone, can make you, Cali. You say you have slain a god . . . Someone must take his place. It should be you."

Cali shuddered. The one secret, she knew what he meant by that: the location of the oneiric pigment. The one power Pe'kar did not possess was the power to create. His genius was in the re-sculpting of forms—indeed, he had taught an entire civilisation the art of self-mutilation in the name of perfection—yet, he could not create that which was new. To her knowledge, he also could no longer conceive. He had been permitted one act of fertile sexual union, with the great Mother, and then all had been spent. The true-born demons were a dying race in that regard, immortal but unable to procreate alone. Thus, they resorted to mating with other orders of beings; hence her father's deception, and hence her own birth: half-demon, half-Carcosan.

She understood full well why Pe'kar would crave such power. And as it was the only thing he did not possess, it was the one power Cali had over him, the one reason he had not killed her after taking his fill, and the reason he had been so generous with his profane, magical teachings.

She wondered, at times, whether he could not have found the pigment's location himself. There were plenty of clues. And the desert held little terror for a being a powerful as Pe'kar. Then again, maybe she was wrong. Maybe the strength of the desert's trials equalled the strength of the seeker's mind. What horrors would be unleashed, therefore, upon a god?

Whatever the reasons, he had not found the pigment, nor its serpentkin guardians. Cali's blood boiled in remembrance of them.

Arrogant. Pretentious. Small-minded. Hypocritical. She loathed that her own ophidian eyes were a constant reminder of their patronising dismissal.

But a new thought was born out of the scum of that memory, a dark and terrible question she had never considered before—perhaps because she had never had so many pieces together in one place, and perhaps because Demhe was forcing her brain into new shapes, contorting her perception the longer she remained in its thrall.

"Why serpents?" she asked.

Pe'kar cocked his beautiful head.

"Is that the answer you would give such a proposal?"

"Forgive me, Great King. But my mind reels. I require more information. And I know, with your near-infinite knowledge, that you will have the answer. Why serpents? You bear the serpent, and so do many of your sons and daughters, those who have inherited the demon's blood. Yet the serpentkin, those who hide the pigment from you, they too bear the forms of snakes. Why? Is there something that links us?"

"The very answer to that question is what I propose to share with you, should you accept my offer. Come, give me an answer. I shall not be so generous again, nor should a king be left waiting."

Cali prostrated herself.

"I accept, O Great King! Your generosity overwhelms me! I submit to you, that I will tell you the secret, whisper it to you, as you desire, in the warmth of our marriage bed."

Pe'kar's smile was a wound. The twin suns dimmed for a moment. Demhe's winds howled with pain.

"My warrior princess, soon you shall be more than a queen, more than an empress: you shall be a goddess! Come swiftly to my palace. The way shall be open to you."

And with that, the apparition of the Demon King vanished, and the desert—devoid of feature or substance—revealed itself for the hollowness it was. Its edges folded inward like an unwanted sheet of paper, and Cali descended once again into a blackness like the womb.

CHAPTER 24
THE WAIT

ALAN PACED RESTLESSLY. Mazael, Liliya, and others had told him that the answers to his burning questions would be found at Al Qaf Saba, the Emerald Mountain, yet now Master Hao remained frustratingly mute and impenetrable, only answering his queries with monosyllabic words, sometimes not at all. Alan sensed that the guardian awaited Petruccio's return before anything further could be divulged. Alan wondered if he should do the same, but inaction felt intolerable to him.

Finally, he flung himself down on the floor next to Cassilda. She stroked his cheek, and he felt the animal inside partly cooled by her touch.

"Sometimes, when we suffer, there is nothing we can do to alleviate the suffering. We can only endure by enduring."

Alan was reminded of Cassilda's trauma, of the dark scene in Demhe's visions he had witnessed but then changed the course of. He gripped her hand with his good one. The Claw lay by his side, like a spider lurking, waiting for the optimal time to crawl into the shadows and escape his sight.

"I alternate between being worried about Petruccio and worried that we are the ones in a trap . . . "

Cassilda smiled.

"You have waited your entire life for answers. When I first met you, I could see how they burned within you. What is a few more days?"

Alan smiled back.

"It is easily said by one who has lived thousands of years!"

"Perhaps it is easier. But still, eternity awaits you as well if you stay in Carcosa . . . " She paused for a moment, biting her lip. " . . . with me."

He kissed her. Warmth passed between them. Alan felt with the meeting and parting of their lips they had been stitched together, their souls knitted.

Suddenly, LeBarron's face appeared between them.

"My lovebirds, if you could confine your intimacies to the bedroom, that would be well for all of us."

Both Cassilda and Alan burst out laughing. LeBarron grinned roguishly.

"Now," he went on. "I have something to show you."

Alan and Cassilda got to their feet. LeBarron pointed towards a part of the cave-wall. Looking around him, Alan realised Roland was nowhere to be found.

"He went scouting and foraging," LeBarron said.

"He need not go far," Master Hao chimed. "The mountainside is abundant not just with flowers, but berries and fruits too. Many trees grow here."

"Are berries all that constitute your diet?" Alan queried.

Master Hao smiled inscrutably.

"Why, no. One does not need berries when one has life itself as nourishment."

Alan's eyes widened. He knew there was so much Master Hao could teach him, beyond his paltry occult explorations back on Earth, but Hao would not share his secrets now, that was for sure. *Petruccio will return,* Alan thought. *I have faith in him.*

"But what if he does not return?" The Claw chided. "What then will you do?"

Alan felt as though a shadow had fallen over his soul. The Claw's voice seemed stronger, more powerful, as though it were gusting through him.

As LeBarron pointed to one of the shimmering, living illustrations upon the cave-wall, explaining it resembled a curious or rare creature he had once encountered, Alan's mind zoned out, his senses shut down, and he became consumed by his internal world, a world where no one could reach him save the dreaded talisman he carried—the burden of his soul.

"Cease your fear-mongering," Alan replied, anger mixed with his anxiety.

"I do not fear. Nor should you. We are *action.* That which

would threaten, we destroy. That which we desire, we take. I am the hand that grasps . . . "

"I choose life," Alan said, though he felt as though he were speaking into a gale, his voice swallowed up by the fury of howling winds.

"Life is the choice of one who does not know the power of Death. Life is the choice of the naive boy you were, not the man you have become. If you had done as you desired, and slain Cali where she stood, then none of this would have been necessary."

"She had surrendered. She was unarmed."

"Not true. For did I not stop her deadly bolt from destroying the King In Yellow? She should not have been allowed to attempt the assassination again. You stood by and allowed the others to make their cowardly moral decisions, decisions which have caused further loss of life, hardship, pain."

"You have heard the others. We are resolved to end her life when we next find her."

"By then it will be far too late. I know whom Cali spoke with in the desert, the 'man' with the serpent's tail . . . Would you like to know who it was?"

Alan felt his teeth grinding, his fists clenched.

"Speak your truth or be silent."

The Claw laughed, though it was like no human laughter, a mechanical sound, gears creaking as they turned upon a torture rack.

"It was Pe'kar . . . "

Alan felt pain ripple through his chest, as though his own Claw had reached into his ribcage and squeezed his heart.

"No . . . "

"Yes . . . you know I am right. I was made by Pe'kar. I know him, better perhaps than anyone . . . The Lord of the Six-Ringed City, King of Demons, Emperor of the Land of Blue Light . . . She goes to him now. Either he will reveal his secrets to her, or she will take them from him, it makes little difference. The Cali you meet in the Six Ringed City will not be the same animal who left you in Carcosa."

"We will prevail."

"No, my dear Abracadabra, you will not. You will fall. Unless you do now as I instruct . . . "

Alan closed his eyes. Pain lanced through his skull. His body tingled with dire precognition.

"Speak . . . "

"Kill Cassilda and take her staff. Then kill LeBarron in the same instant. Armed with myself and the black staff, you shall have little trouble overpowering Master Hao, powerful though he is. Drink his blood, and you shall inherit some of that life force he was moments before crowing about." The Claw laughed softly. "Use the staff to bring all of them back as your slaves. March the undead army—which will now reside under your control—out of Carcosa and besiege Pe'kar's palace."

Alan could scarcely hold back his rage, but he did so, for he wished to know the full mind of the monster grafted to his flesh.

"And what of Petruccio?"

"Petruccio is about to learn a truth that will drive him mad."

"A truth about me?"

"Why, yes."

"You have known all along?"

"It has taken time for our minds to fully meld. There is an interstitial period where a transplanted organ must be integrated and accepted by the host. We draw close now to full integration . . . When we are One, *nothing* shall stand in our path."

Alan shuddered. He'd known for a while now that he was on a ticking clock, but he had not quite realised just how rapidly the timer was running down, nor how close to doomsday he drifted. He knew full integration with The Claw meant madness of the same kind that had infected Haercus, though Haercus was able to escape The Claw's hold for a time by removing it—something Alan did not feel he had the strength to do.

"I would never betray Cassilda," Alan said. "Nor the others. I love her."

The Claw laughed again—prisoners shrieking in a deep cell, somewhere miles beneath the earth.

"You do not love her. You do not even know what love is. First, you were infatuated with Cali. Then Cassilda. But in Al Shujah, the first sight of exotic beauty enflamed your arousal to an almost embarrassing degree."

"One can be sexually attracted to other women but love truly in one's soul . . . "

"No, my dear Abracadabra. You have betrayed her in your mind because you don't truly love her. She is pretty enough to have taken your fancy. And she is wild in the secrecy of a boudoir . . . "

Alan felt himself flush with shame and anger. To think that The Claw had been a voyeur to his most intimate experiences was almost too much to bear. "Oh yes," The Claw whispered, now gleeful. "And soon I will not merely be a voyeur. The time will come when you will wish to use me upon your women. Yes. To wrap my pretty talons about their pretty throats. They will ask for it. You will see! They will ask to be mastered! For that is what we are, Abracadabra, we are the hand that grips reality itself, that commands wordlessly, that subjugates without remorse."

"NO!"

It took Alan a few moments to realise he had opened his eyes and screamed this final word aloud. Cassilda and LeBarron stared at him with shocked faces. Master Hao looked up mildly from the fire as though he had heard the cry of an interesting bird.

Sweat covered Alan's face. He felt clammy, cold even, unsteady on his limbs. He swayed and as he fell LeBarron and Cassilda both caught him.

"What has happened?" Cassilda said, breathlessly.

A gleam of recognition in LeBarron's eyes betrayed that he knew more than he would say

They lay Alan down upon the floor. He felt weak as though with a fever.

"A spiritual battle rages within him," Master Hao said. "The Claw has given him power, but its price is high."

Alan trembled so violently that his legs kicked against the hard stone, almost like a seizure. Foam bubbled from his lips. His veins stood out under his skin, as though rebelling against the architecture of human form. Cassilda cooed and tried to soothe him by stroking his brow. LeBarron knelt nearby, his eyes wet with empathy.

"I should never have let you take that thing," LeBarron whispered. "I would rather cut off my own hand than watch you suffer like this."

"Then your roles would merely have been reversed," Cassilda said, sharply. "It were better The Claw had never been made."

Cassilda began to sing, her voice sounding fuller and richer than ever before, the cave walls seeming to sing *with* her, forming a chorus of ghostly voices. Yet, for all its beauty, the magic had no effect, and Alan began to shake more violently. *God, so cold, the cold so deep* . . . Was The Claw torturing him for his stubbornness?

"Can you do something?" she said, breaking off her singing and imploring Master Hao.

"I will not and cannot help him until your friend returns."

"Why?" LeBarron snapped. "Is this some kind of execrable law you must follow?"

Master Hao smiled, but with terrible sadness, like a jester who saw the dark comedy of their own miseries.

"No. The reason is both more cosmic and more practical than that: I cannot help him because the dwarf's success or failure is inextricably tied up with his . . . "

CHAPTER 25
AWAN

PETRUCCIO WAS USHERED into a room—he had no way of knowing its dimensions. They had placed a hood over his head of sable cloth before leading him through what seemed like measureless passageways, longer by far than the path of his initial descent, and labyrinthine, travelling both upward and downward—left, right, back, and forth—until all sense of orientation was lost. His nose had partially guided him, for the air was thicker here, as though they were perhaps inside a building; incense burned, a sweet smell that reminded him of jasmine, though no doubt it was a far stranger flower growing upon the mountain.

He felt soft hands on his shoulders. The old nagini, perhaps.

"To pass this trial, you must be prepared to give up everything," she whispered. Her tenderness astonished him. But at the same time, his suspicions were roused. Was this, perhaps, another part of the test? Was she lulling him into a false sense of security, pretending to be his ally, when in fact she meant his ruin, like so many other souls who had come through here. *You cannot act on what you do not know,* he reasoned. He breathed in deeply and allowed the breath to escape in a sigh. Ever logic was his ward against evil, the chaos of his emotions, indeed, the chaos of reality itself. But he felt its fragility, at times, how it threatened to snap and break the moment the winds of his universe rose to a tempest. Alan said Petruccio was made of stone. But in truth, Petruccio felt he was made of brittle glass, and every wound was a new crack—what would be the final blow to cause him to shatter?

Still, you must go on, dauntless!

"I am ready," he said.

"Very well."

Swift as a magician's trick, the hood was plucked from his head. He heard a sharp slithering, scale on stone, and suddenly he was alone. A door slammed—though it was not the sound of metal locks chiming, but rather of great stone sealing.

Mist hovered at knee-level, perhaps leaking in through some secret and concealed vent. He wondered if the mists were endowed with hallucinogenic properties. He knew of the mysteries of Eleusis. But he suspected the mysteries here would be grander, and not solely reliant on alchemical concoctions, valid and potent as they were for inducing religious experience.

The chamber was dark and unadorned. It stretched away an absurd distance, dreamlike. His only comfort was the sweet smell, which still beckoned to him. *Perhaps I should follow it?*

Petruccio made his way forward, feeling as though he had to wade through the mist, as though it had physical texture. He remembered the dismal descent into the Temple of Namtar, the battle with the eurypterid. Then another descent, into the underwater city of Alar. He was more than accustomed to terror and danger. Yet, somehow, he felt a far greater dread now. Perhaps because he was alone. Perhaps because there was a sense of finality in this place, the deathly coolness of a mausoleum, the blank walls, the grey mists; the place had the unmistakeable feeling of a crypt. The ceiling was lost in darkness. The only light came from torches which burned ghastly white along the lefthand wall—the only wall he could see—much like the lamps in the tunnel leading down to the heart of the mountain. They washed everything with a pallid bleach. Petruccio hoped not to see his reflection, for he imagined he would look revoltingly pale and sepulchral.

The serpentkin had told him very little about his trial. He had been tempted a few times on his blind journey here to ask, but always he'd held off. The nature of a trial was the unknown. What could they tell him other than cliches and riddles? No. Better to focus on clearing his head rather than anticipating what was to come.

To pass this trial, you must be prepared to give up everything . . .

What had she meant by that? His life? His morality? That which he held most sacred? *Better for her not to have said anything at all!* he thought.

THE DREAMS OF DEMHE

From the mists, a shape loomed. Solid. A rectangular block of stone, the size of a large tomb. *A crypt indeed.* But what was that light on top? No, not light, but the reflection of light, the torches at each corner of the tomb, burning in sconces casting flame-light over naked flesh.

Petruccio sucked in a breath.

A beautiful nagini lay stretched out over the tomb, her back arched, her languorous coils billowing over the side of the stone sepulchre and pooling upon the ground. Slowly, as Petruccio approached, she raised herself on one forearm. His eyes were mesmerised by her cascade of raven-black hair, by the lusciously serpentine form undulating from her midriff downward. Her eyes were heavy-lidded, as though she had woken recently from a slumber. Her blood-red lips invited a kiss.

With one finger, she beckoned him. He stood his ground. He had kept his vow, all this time. Was this what the old nagini had meant by being prepared to give up everything?

"Come to me," the young nagini on the tomb said. "I am Awan. You must please me if you wish to be granted the secret of the pigment."

With a motion so delicate it seemed magical, she caressed the scales just beneath the human, fleshy part of her torso, where the lines of her hips became indistinct, merging with scale. There, an opening appeared, glisteningly pink, widening like a flower to the sun, a warm invitation to secret delights beyond anything Petruccio had imagined or experienced.

Still, he hesitated. He had come so far. It seemed reckless and absurd to give up his vow now. Like an alcoholic who had managed to maintain decades of sobriety, there was too much weight behind capitulating to desire, and not only that, but the desire had begun to recede. Eighty years was a long time. The urges did not come as strongly as they once did. Less and less he required breathing to calm his excited senses.

But the pigment. The thought brought him crashing back to the immediate now with the force of a hammer upon an anvil. If he did not do this deed, he risked losing his one and only chance at obtaining the pigment. He *had* to go through with it, even if it shamed him, even if it brought agony upon him.

He took a step forward, and the young nagini playfully held up a finger, bidding him wait one moment more.

"But if you spill a single drop of seed, you will also have failed."

Petruccio felt his heart blacken, his breathing become shallow. So this, then, was the *true* trial. Self-restraint whilst in the throes of pleasure. Order in the very womb of chaos. *Curse my vow! Curse my celibacy!* He had thought he spent a lifetime preparing for the challenge of obtaining the pigment, but now he saw the cruel, almost malignant, irony of his plight. *If I'd fucked a thousand whores, I would be better prepared!* He was unpracticed, uninitiated. And now, staring at the beautiful, labial opening in the nagini's serpentine lower body, he felt painful arousal, super sensitivity. Her heavy breasts glistened with a sheen of dew bestowed by the mist. Her dark eyes called to him, invited him to sup of delicacies he had never tasted. The primordial, reptilian impulse of his brain gathered energy in his groin until he felt he would burst. With an effort of will, he regulated his breathing, calmed his nerves. God, how was he going to succeed in this? He could barely look at her without cumming. A lifetime of repressed sexuality was welling up inside him. He had lied to himself that he was redirecting the energy, sublimating it into art and poetry and music and magic, but the truth was now laid bare: nothing was ever lost, and every fleeting sexual fantasy now rose, like an imaginal serpent within him, and bid him spit his venom into the void.

"Come, my sweet," she whispered. "I will be gentle."

"That is what I am afraid of," he said.

But he could not turn back now, not with the pigment in reach. He had to make the attempt. And if he failed, either the serpentkin would kill him as he asked, or he would cast himself from the peak of Al Qaf Saba. Better to die than to live with shame forever.

He reached her, feeling like a supplicant before their goddess. Her wide hips, and the strange gooey orifice between them, were like an idol which he was about to kiss. Her hands reached his face, cupping his chin.

"So many scars," she said. "You have seen more war than love."

Petruccio nodded.

Slowly, she undressed him. First, she removed the skullcap, so that the Yellow Sign blazed forth in the deep darkness of that place. She admired it for a time, running her delicate fingers over the scar-tissue of its formation. Then, she helped him remove his robe, with its many pockets; his belt with its many satchels and a scabbard for the bejewelled dagger of Carcosa's court; finally, his trousers and shoes, until he was stood, bare as the day he was born, his cock proudly erect, his breath misting before him.

"I . . . I cannot reach . . . " He stumbled over his words, felt fresh influx of shame.

But she knew his meaning immediately: the tomb was too high for him to climb atop. Instead, she lowered herself, her back against the side wall of the stone obelisk, her strange sexual organ open to him; he need only bend his knees a little to push into her sumptuous folds.

A cry left his lips as he entered her. God, she was so soft, wet. Unimaginable to one who had never known it. In times gone by, men were hyper-fixated on the female hymen, the first breaking of the virginal veil, but Petruccio realised that he was the one in whom a veil had been broken—a psychological veil, wool pulled over his eyes. Oh, how much more difficult he would find it to return to celibacy now he had actually tasted the forbidden fruit! It had been easy—so easy—to deny pleasures he didn't understand. But now, in a blinking flash, he knew them—and knew why empires had fallen to them.

He sucked in breath, let it out in hissing exhales. He must control the muscles in his groin. He must hold back the dam that wanted so desperately to burst. He pushed into her slowly. Rhythm was impossible, for the sensation was simply overwhelming. He was forced to stop to master his impulse. *There must be magic at work here,* he thought. *Surely.* He could have laughed at the idea— a magical cunt proving his undoing—but no, deep down he knew the answer lay in his own mind, his own repressions. He had never loosed the beast, and now it yearned to be free.

"Oh God!" he cried. It was as though every vein his body was near to rupturing. But he maintained, almost inexplicably maintained, control over his organ. He would not release himself to pleasure.

Looking at Awan's face, so soft, so open, so languidly sensuous, was liable to make him spill, so he clamped his eyes shut.

And then he seemed to crest a wave. Having fought down the initial surge, he was in possession again—of sanity and control.

He began to thrust more rhythmically. But now, a new challenge emerged: Awan moaned. He was giving her pleasure. He, Petruccio, was pleasuring this goddess. The pride that accompanied that thought almost caused him to lose control, and once more he had to stop. Slowly he withdrew his cock, pressed the secret meridian at the top of his engorged member. He had never been so painfully hard. The tip of his penis was an almost alarming purple.

Pressing the meridian cooled him. Once more, Cali's profane teachings had come in use. He grinned savagely at the thought of how Cali had underestimated him. She had failed this trial—though what that meant in terms of female pleasure he had no idea. He would not fail. He re-entered Awan. She placed her arms on his shoulders, stroking his muscles. He felt her wordless appreciation of him, a feeling he'd never known before. Always he had seen the way women's eyes passed over him, deeming him small, unworthy, stunted. But she saw him, felt him, cried out for him. *Yes!*

"Keep going," Awan whispered.

He could do it—he felt she was almost there. But as a result, her cunt began to contract around his cock, squeezing, wringing even more delicious sensations out of their strange union. Pleasure that was suspiciously like pain surged up his spine, travelling up from the very root of him to the crown, like lightning in reverse. His entire body trembled. He teetered on the precipice. He was going to fail, to give in. *Hold, hold.* The pleasure deepened, intensified, like a serpent coiling about his guts. *Hold, you fucking ingrate. Hold!* He could feel his temples throbbing, muscles tearing. Had he the experience and control of a seasoned lover, he might have easily been able to turn off and on the secret muscle that controlled male ejaculation, but he was not seasoned, and therefore his entire body was used up in the effort of restraint.

"I'm close, so close," Awan whispered in his ear, pressing his breasts against his chest. "You can do it. You can."

He did the only thing he could: savagely bite down upon his own forearm until blood began to run. The pain trumped the pleasure, set him free. He thrust as hard as he could, and Awan let out a breathy exhalation, her whole being seeming to tighten around him like the death-grip of an anaconda. She trembled and he trembled with her, still barely in control. *Not one drop, not one drop.* A scream of frustration but also victory left his bloody lips.

He withdrew from her glistening cunt, flecked with juices both unnatural and natural.

THE DREAMS OF DEMHE

He trembled, swaying for a moment on unsteady legs, then finally collapsing; breathless, near blackout.

Panting, he lay there, practically delirious. He had done it. He had vanquished the serpent within.

After a few more moments, in which his consciousness swam in and out of absolute focus, hovering dangerously close to the realm of dream, he propped himself up on his elbows.

He found himself alone.

A strange disappointment settled on him. Had Awan been real? Surely that could not have been a vision, no matter how potent the hallucinogens the mist contained, no matter how powerful Demhe's dreaming . . . His cock still felt wet with her. Yes, there, by the tomb, was the stain of their sweat and other things . . .

But she had left him.

It was only a ritual, Petruccio. Not love. You truly are a virgin!

Then he smiled. *Not anymore.*

But a part of him constantly alert to danger realised that his trial was likely not finished. No one had come to take him away. If Awan was gone, then something else was coming.

And he could hear that something else. A sound like scales on stone. Not the delicate and subtle sounds made by the serpentkin as they moved, something much larger.

In the dark before him shone two yellow eyes. Petruccio felt his heart—already sorely used this day—pounding dangerously hard, a dull ache spreading through his chest. His dagger lay only a few feet away. If he could just reach it . . .

The darkness behind those eyes shifted, and in a flash the monster was upon him. He leapt for his weapon, knowing that the true trial was about to begin.

CHAPTER 26
THE TRIAL

HE HIT THE floor with ugly force, skin scraping off his thighs and belly, knocking the wind from his already famished lungs. His fingers tightened around the hilt of his dagger just as the massive creature reached him.

A serpent, of course, of a species that no longer existed on Earth, but that Petruccio recognised from his paleontological research: the Titanoboa. Its head was nearly as large as Petruccio's torso, with an engorged gullet and small horns adorning its nostrils. Its green-scaled body extended for meters, finally swallowed by the darkness beyond—no end in sight.

As it descended, he turned onto his back and held aloft the dagger. Intelligence glimmered in its eyes, and its mighty head twisted, not limited by such concepts as "right way up". Petruccio suddenly found his arm was ensnared by the serpent's huge coils. He screamed as titanic pressure was exerted on his elbow joint. An ordinary man's arm would have broken in mere seconds beneath that vice, but Petruccio was not ordinary, and what he lacked in stature he made up for in strength. Gritting his teeth, he fought to keep his arm from bending back at an unnatural anger, maintaining a deathgrip upon his dagger.

But the greater danger came from the Titanboa's jaws, which were now perilously close to his neck. With his free hand he reached out and gripped the snake's horns, forcing it backward and away, though the effort of doing so—at an awkward angle across his body—drained him.

He tried to get his feet under him, attempting to stand, but his body was drenched with sweat and he could not gain purchase.

The Titanboa hissed at him. Yellow eyes bored into his.

THE DREAMS OF DEMHE

From the shadows, its tail slithered, beginning to wrap itself around Petruccio's legs. He kicked frantically, but soon it had fully enwrapped him. He screamed as he felt the same awful pressure now exerted upon his knees and femur bones. Its strength was hideous. An elephant would have fallen beneath its oppressive constriction. But Petruccio knew magic—though only a little. His bones were hardened. His muscles steely. And as death drew closer and closer, he closed his eyes, and began to hum. His voice did not have the striking musicality of Cassilda's magical song, nor the shrieking power of Cali's potent projections, but it contained its own resonance, like the deep murmur of a whale's heartbeat, a low and guttural evocation.

He concentrated upon a glyph of fire.

"Make my flesh as fire, my face as blinding light," he sang. *"White hot I burn, O black star of the Night!"*

Over and over he repeated the incantation, trying to shut out the hideous, hissing breaths of the serpent, the agony flooding his body. He tried to ignore the fact that his breaths were coming shallower and shallower as the snake's grip squeezed tighter, exertion draining more oxygen from his blood.

"Make my flesh as fire, my face as blinding light. White hot I burn, O black star of the Night!"

He tried to visualise his flesh igniting, bright white fire burning. But somehow the image kept slipping, his focus disturbed not only by his physical danger and struggle, but by something else: his memories of the deed he had just consummated with Awan.

The erotic fantasy he had just lived played before his mind like a movie on the silver screen. Even as the snake crushed his body, he felt not death, but her delicate hands upon him. Even as the serpent hissed with foetid breath in his ear, straining to plunge its fangs into his throat, he heard instead her sibilant, sensual encouragements.

Death and sex, forever interlinked, he thought and even had time—so blasted was his focus—to consider how it was very like something Alan might have said.

He saw the deathtrap he was caught in with new clarity—and couldn't help but admire it. Either one of the challenges could be overcome easily by a magician or warrior with the right training. But in combination, they were an exquisite ordeal. The effort of will it had taken to master his most basic impulse had drained him of psychic energy to a point he felt weak-limbed, lacklustre, dazed. His mind was not the sharp blade he was used to. He felt blunted, stupid even. But his mind was all he had against this far stronger and more powerful foe.

Merciless, the Titanboa wrapped more of its tremendous bulk around him, this time concentrating on the midriff. The pressure came so suddenly he vomited, spilling the contents of his stomach, though there was not much there to begin with. Breath left him, and he had to fight to catch it. He sounded like a corpse groaning, releasing the trapped air in its lungs.

"*Make . . . my . . . flesh as fire . . .* " he spluttered. The veins in his face and throat felt as though they were about to pop. "*My face as . . . as . . . as . . . blinding light . . .* "

He couldn't finish. The dagger dropped from his fingers. He felt his elbow-joint creaking as his arm was slowly bent backward on itself.

How, how can I beat this? Petruccio had always prided himself on his strength. Yet his strength was nothing against the serpent's. And indeed, the more he struggled, the more tired he grew, and the more thoroughly its coils ensnared him.

Foams and spit dribbled from his lips. He breathed now through clenched teeth.

The pain riddling his body was like nothing he had ever endured. They said that the tortures Pe'kar inflicted in his dungeons were beyond any other agony. If that were the case, then Petruccio did not want even to imagine them, for this pain now was like a man crushed by the rubble of a collapsing mine-shaft, yet somehow still alive to experience every broken rib and shattered joint. To feel his flesh beginning to tear away from the musculature as the twisting boa's body squeezed him out of his own skin. This pain, whilst physical, seemed merely symptomatic of a sudden and terrible shame. *You abandoned your vow. You will die pointlessly and having forsaken your oath. You could have been true to the end, but you gave it all up . . .*

He had submitted to the ophidian urge. He had defiled the temple of his being, and all for nothing.

Tighter and tighter the serpent wound. He tasted blood in his mouth. Felt his ribs collapsing. Something shattered in his ankle, his foot wrenched out of shape, and he screamed. His arm was moments away from being bent backward upon itself. Only supernatural tenacity kept him holding on.

THE DREAMS OF DEMHE

His mind, beginning to detach from the agonies in his body, began to wander far and wide. He wondered what Alan would do were their places exchanged. Sure, Alan had The Claw of Craving, but it was Alan's mind that had led them out of countless fixes: in Yhtill, in the Temple of Namtar, in Alar. Time and again Alan solved problems creatively. *What would he do? He would do the last thing one expects . . .*

And then it clicked, with the suddenness of a lightning bolt. He could have laughed, if there was any space left in his windpipe. The whole trial wasn't about overcoming, it was about *submission*. He had needed to give in to his desire with Awan. And now, here, he also needed to give in. Only by submitting could he ever escape. To obtain the pigment, he had to show he was willing to let go of control, that he was not a monomaniacal evildoer who would bend the pigment to his uncompromising will. He had to show his ability to just *let go.*

No sooner than the thought ran through his head than he heard the sickening sound of his arm breaking, cracked at the elbow joint and forced back on itself. A suppressed scream left his lips, but suddenly, floppy as the arm was and sluiced with his own blood—for a shard of bone had broken through his flesh—he was more able to move.

Hissing, the serpent came in to deliver its killing blow. Rather than pushing back against it, he allowed the serpent to move closer and enfolded it in an embrace, clutching it so closely to its chest it could not articulate its head enough to sink its fangs into him. He grinned like a madman.

He felt the boa's coils adjusting, trying to gain purchase. For once, his diminutive size was an advantage, for there was too little of him for its meters of length to come to any use. As it partially released pressure on his right leg, he seized his chance, slipping from its grasp with a disgusting, squelching sound, and more flares of agony as his broken bones rattled in their sockets. The serpent lunged, but its aim was woefully off, its own prodigious weight— no longer propped up by Petruccio—causing it to miss by a score of inches. Slick with blood, panting like a wild animal, Petruccio clambered to his feet and picked up the knife in his good hand. His right arm dangled limply, broken at the elbow. He could feel the regular, metronomic pulse of his lifeblood spitting out of a nicked vein in his arm.

The serpent gathered itself, rearing. Its coils likewise glistened with a sheen of his blood. Its yellow eyes were so unblinkingly fixed on him, he feared for a moment they might hypnotise, rob him of his sense. But he shook himself, summoning all of his power.

"Make my flesh as fire, my face as blinding light," he cried. His throat burned, but he forced the words out, vibrating with the frequencies of magic he had tried so hard to master. *"White hot I burn, O black star of the Night!"*

The serpent lunged.

But at last, the magic worked. His flesh kindled with fire, white light shining from his inner being. He felt energy traveling up from the ground, through the soles of his feet, up his mangled legs, into his belly—the seat of power. Then, guided by an exhale, it flowed down his left arm, into the palm of his hand, through the dagger hilt. He screamed as he thrust the blade forward. The metal turned white, winking in the darkness. As it made contact with the serpent's scales there was an eruption. Magmatic power exploded from the microscopic tip of the blade. Red, orange, and white light blasted through the serpent, fire licked its body with supreme eagerness, and Petruccio roared in triumph as the mighty creature was engulfed in hungry brilliance.

The flame devoured the great serpent to ashes. But fire, as any magician knew, was transformative. And as the snake's terrifying masses were burned away, every last scale consumed, beneath was revealed milk-white flesh, unearthly beauty . . . a dead woman.

Tears filled the dwarf's eyes as he gazed upon Awan. She lay naked like the choicest jewel at the heart of a dark forge, a pearl in the flaming abyss. So, there was a price be paid, even in victory. She had guarded the pigment all her life, most likely. And at last, one had come worthy of obtaining it. But having obtained it, he would be forever reminded of the profane act, of the sacrifice, required. Thus, he would never lightly use its power. Never flippantly raise dreams from their abyssal slumbers.

He watched her burn for what seemed like hours. Blood loss, pain, and exhaustion took hold, and he collapsed next to the ancient tomb, only a half-step away from the land of the dead himself.

CHAPTER 27
THE RETURNING HERO

PETRUCCIO'S DREAMS WERE DARK, with the everlasting quality of a Babushka doll, each layer of dream concealing a new one within. As such, when he awoke, he hardly knew where he was. Indeed, for a flickering moment, he expected the bare plaster walls and cruddy light-fixtures of his old apartment in London where he had lived for ten years in ignorance of Carcosa, of magic, and of the pigment. *The pigment!*

He bolted upright, but found himself not in the grand temple of the serpentkin, but rather back in the cave where he had left the others.

Astonished—and relieved—faces surrounded his. There was Cassilda, pale as moonlight, kneeling over his busted leg, her lips moving subtly as she murmured a soft healing song. He could feel the bones in his arm had already been reset. Sometimes, he feared the princess's power. Were she to turn on them, as Cali had, he doubted any of them could stop her. He nodded and Cassilda smiled ever-so-slightly. Only Alan could bring out her brightest expressions.

Roland stood by the mouth of the cave, his muscled figure cutting an imposing silhouette. Master Hao, the strange old guardian of the pigment, still sat upon his log by the fire, as though he had not moved in the time Petruccio was gone. *And how long had that been?* He had little sense of it. Time had felt very slippery indeed down in the halls of the serpentkin.

LeBarron knelt on Petruccio's other side, his face beaming with a wide rogue's grin. No doubt, some quip was forthcoming.

"I suppose I shall have to pause composition of my epic eulogy in your honour."

Petruccio smiled. Yet, as was always the way with him, his brightest skies only seemed to invite the presence of invading thunderheads. He felt the shadow fall across his soul as surely as if the mouth of the cave had closed, sealing them in darkness.

"You shall write Cali's first."

LeBarron and Petruccio clasped hands. Their eyes communicated a bond knit by hatred and revenge more clearly than any words could.

"Where's Alan?" Petruccio said, sitting up. He saw Cassilda swiftly wipe away a tear. She motioned behind her, where Petruccio saw Alan lying propped up against the cave's wall. Had he been hurt? He could see no wounds, yet Alan looked gravely ill, as though a deathly fever had come upon him.

"The Claw . . . " Cassilda said.

Petruccio sighed.

"A heavy burden." Petruccio felt his heart almost cleaved uttering those words, for he knew Alan bore the burden for their sakes.

"Petruccio!"

All eyes turned to Master Hao, who had raised his finger into the air, like a strict schoolmaster about to elucidate some obscure pearl of moral law. "The time has come," Master Hao went on. "Step forth and I shall reveal the secret to you."

With trembling legs, Petruccio rose to meet the destiny he had so long awaited.

Alan, blinking away the paralysis that had taken hold after his battle with the will of The Claw, sat upright. He watched with baited breath as Petruccio, his stone veneer partly cracked and revealing the trepidation within, stepped forward and knelt before Master Hao.

"You have mastered the serpent, within and without," Master Hao said. "You are the first soul since Grand Master Uboth hid the secret of the pigment to pass such a trial—the first and only." The old man's eyes glinted like superheated coals. The corners of his mouth twitched—was it with amusement, deceit, or some deeper awareness beyond his fathoming? "The secret of the pigment—not only its location, but also its nature—for the pigment is called such only in symbolic terms. Let us never forget the words of another great master, 'Do not mistake the mask for the face, nor the symbol for the symbolised'."

Alan recognised the quote as belonging to the Draconian sorcerer Andrew D. Chumbley. Had he visited Carcosa's shores? He had no time to ponder on such riddles. He listened with rapt attention, his own ailment forgotten in the light of Petruccio's achievement.

"Yes, the pigment *is* liquid, in many ways, but it is also of the spirit. And of course, it is utterly living."

Petruccio trembled so violently Alan thought he might have a seizure. But to his credit, the dwarf held himself in restraint, not letting impatience get the better of him. Alan wondered if this was perhaps a final part of the ordeal—a test of character. Though it seemed Petruccio had been through one already judging by the wisdom etched into his face in the form of new scars.

"Are you ready for me to bequeath the pigment to you?" Master Hao whispered. It was as though he not only sensed Petruccio's inner turmoil, but *tasted* it, perhaps was even nourished by it, disturbing as that thought was.

"Yes," the dwarf whispered.

"Alas, I cannot. For you are already the guardian of the pigment," Master Hao said.

A deafening silence followed these words.

"What? *What!*" Petruccio seethed with rage. "This had better be some tasteless joke! I will not be told that the pigment is merely some fantasy of inner power or self-belief!" Spittle flew from the dwarf's lips. "I have given more than you could imagine to reach this point, lost friends, abjured the love of women, spurned all pleasures!" Then, to Alan's surprise, he wept in a fit of passion that seemed more apt for LeBarron. "And yet I broke my vow. Smashed it to smithereens!"

Master Hao held up a single palm, not dismissing, merely bidding him be at peace. Petruccio fell silent, breathing raggedly. It was the most emotion Alan had ever seen the artist exhibit. Not even Cali's betrayal had so shaken him. Alan thought he had good reason to be angry; there was nothing so torturous as frustrated hopes.

"You misapprehend my meaning, Petruccio," Master Hao said in his infuriatingly slow and calm manner. "I am telling you that the pigment has been right under your nose the entire time. You have already fulfilled the role of a guardian and fulfilled it admirably. Thus, the trial was merely the paperwork for a worthiness you have already proved to us."

"What? Where is it?" Petruccio looked like he might lose his mind any second. He shifted his balance from foot to foot the way a cat might before pouncing.

Master Hao turned his pure and implacable gaze upon Alan.

"*There* is the oneiric pigment."

Alan looked around, expecting to find something behind or near him, but there was no mistaking where Master Hao pointed.

"No," Alan whispered. "It can't be."

"Alan?" Cassilda sounded afraid, terrified even.

"I knew one day you would return, to the very cave where you were conceived—" Hao said.

"No."

"—what better place to hide the most powerful secret in all of Carcosa than in another world?"

"No!" Alan growled. He rose to his feet. Strength and vitality flooded his body, or perhaps its nearest equivalent: rage. His mind raced. "It's not possible. I have parents. I grew up on Earth. I have memories."

"O, I'm sure you do," Master Hao said, absently, as though Alan had made an unremarkable statement about his love of dogs. "But tell me, what were the names of your parents?"

"Alyssa and Aaron."

"Mhmm. And what was the name of your first love?"

Alan glanced at Cassilda, but she simply stared at him as though he were an alien species. He shifted from foot to foot.

"Daisy . . . "

Master Hao nodded.

"A childhood sweetheart?"

"Sort of."

"And when you grew to be a man, you loved another woman?"

Alan nodded, his palms clammy, his heart thundering. Petruccio stared at Alan like he couldn't decide whether to kill him or not.

"Her name?"

"Rose." That was hardest to utter, even now sending a knife of guilt into Alan's heart.

THE DREAMS OF DEMHE

Master Hao, on the other hand, nodded matter-of-factly, as though they were merely discussing meteorological matters.

"Tell me, do you notice anything peculiar about those names?"

"No."

"You should," Hao said, smiling warmly.

"Alan . . ."

He turned to see Cassilda biting her lip, uncertain whether she should reveal the oddity, an oddity Alan could not see no matter how hard he now applied his mind to the problem. *There's nothing wrong. He's fucking with your head. You grew up on Earth. Alyssa and Aaron. Mum and dad. Alyssa, with her baking business. Aaron, the lawyer. I used to play in the garden, digging to another world, and they chided me. I used to rub pollen over my body, and they told me I was a little freak . . .*

"Alan," Cassilda whispered, putting a gentle hand on his shoulder. "All those names, they're . . . they're all *flowers.*"

Alan collapsed. He fell to his knees and then onto his face, lying flat upon the ground, almost hugging it like a child would. The emotion passed through him like a hundred thousand volts; robbed of power, almost robbed of life, he sobbed uncontrollably.

Hao smiled down kindly at him.

"None of it was real . . ." Alan wept. "My life . . ."

"It was all real, Alan," Hao said, in a soft voice like a single autumnal leaf falling. "You made it so. As you grew older, you became more and more divorced from your gift, until in your desperation to find meaning you came here. But it was all real. Your power *made* it real."

"Mother . . . Father . . . My brother . . . Just dreams?"

Hao's smile was at once the comfort of a benevolent king, the giddy yet pure happiness of a child, and something beyond Alan's understanding.

"That is all mortals are, Alan. Dreams of the living god whose true name none know, not even Uboth, not even the Yellow King."

Then Alan remembered what the King In Yellow had told him, that his secret name was Abracadabra, and it finally made sense. Abracadabra was a magic word, used by magicians to manifest their will. Whether they were trickster magicians who performed illusions at parties, or real sorcerers bending magic, the result was the same: the word indicated the return of something that had been made to disappear.

"Abracadabra," Alan whispered.

Hao smiled ear to ear.

"At last, you understand."

Alan nodded. But tears still ran down his face, for one grief had given birth to another.

"Rose, could I have saved her?"

"You did not know who or what you were."

"But if I had? Could I have stopped her from dying?"

Master Hao did not respond, his face implacable as granite. Alan hung his head.

"Death is the mystery of life, and life is the mystery of Death," Hao pronounced. The words rang with awful finality.

"But what does this mean?" Petruccio said. His voice, normally firm as stone, was riven and cracked with desperation. "How can one wield the pigment if it is a man?" Petruccio met Alan's eyes. "If it is a friend?"

"Well, you could cut him open, use his blood to paint great works . . . " Master Hao said, his benevolence was tinged with something darker, devilish and gleeful, but it was only in passing.

Petruccio bowed his head, shuffled backwards, humbled and ashamed.

"But this does not make sense." To Alan's surprise, it was Cassilda who voiced this defiance. "Petruccio is a good deal older than Alan, having dwelt in Carcosa's eternity. Indeed, you said yourself, Petruccio, that you had been looking for the pigment longer than Alan has been alive."

Petruccio looked like an electronic toy that had had its batteries replaced. He sparked to life, nodding fervently.

"Yes, yes she is right!"

Master Hao seemed unfazed by this line of argument. He turned to Alan.

"Please tell us, Abracadabra—"

"His name is Alan!" Cassilda said.

Master Hao smirked.

"*Alan* then. Please tell us, how old are you?"

"Well I'm . . . I was born in . . . "

Cassilda stared at Alan.

He reached for the numbers, but there was nothing there. He remembered a childhood, digging in the garden, but when had that truly been? What year? In what place? He'd always felt Alyssa and

THE DREAMS OF DEMHE

Aaron wanted him to be normal, wanted to help him integrate with society, but wasn't that notion really conceived within himself? Hadn't he really *known,* all along, that he was an alien upon Earth, that his true home was elsewhere, and so he had made pleasant, unremarkable phantoms to assist his transition, to assist his acclimatisation to a new reality.

But no matter how hard he tried to deny it, the true reality had crept through. He remembered the taxi driver. The man with the yellow eyes. The same man who had been Rose's "friend", who had watched as he and her lay as serpents intertwined. Not "Ub", of course, but *Uboth.*

His father.

Roland seemed to have made the same connections Alan had, for he stepped forward.

"Alan . . . I think this is yours?"

Alan rose slowly to his feet. Roland had unclasped the cylinder from his belt containing Uboth's magical banner. *No, my banner.* Alan remembered it now. A thousand memories were surfacing, shoots in Spring greedily driving up through the earth to receive the sun's light. A pain bloomed in his head, right at the crown, as though an invisible metal rod had been through down through the top of his skull.

He took the cylinder. Opened it. The dark brilliance of the banner shone forth, and he reached in and touched the sacred cloth.

Images swarmed his consciousness. Flowers upon the side of the mountain. Egg-shells. Pieces of the egg from which *he* had been born, laid by the beautiful nagini who was his mother . . . Her name, on the tip of Alan's tongue . . . Forbidden . . . Eons ago, all of this took place. As a child he was kept like a dark secret. He moved, treacle-slow, from place to place, always hidden, then inserted into a pocket of time, growing and dying, growing and dying, the new self born out of the old, always forgetting the life he led before, assuming a new face, much like The Stranger whom he'd come to detest, never truly knowing himself, in truth outside of time. He stared down at his hands—one a callous, metallic instrument of death that increasingly possessed features, a dark face—and loathed the skin-suit that cloaked him.

"Why was I rendered in flesh?" he hissed. "Why would Uboth do such a thing?"

Master Hao smiled, pityingly.

"Only that which is flesh can change the world."

"You are the reason the dreaming has been changing!" LeBarron said, not bothering to conceal his triumph at having worked it out. "Demhe was becoming dormant, but now you have returned and the dream-storms are intensifying again. It's you, Alan."

"And that is why you did not feel compelled to bow to my father," Cassilda added. "And why Carcosa welcomes you as its own. *You* made Carcosa." The tears Cassilda had fought to restrain now fell freely, but to Alan they seemed strangely happy, like pearls of joy.

"No . . . " Alan whispered. But he already knew it was true. His blood ran through the city's veins. His blood was the pigment that had painted its mad spires. He was the city's blackly beating heart. And while he lived, it could never die.

Petruccio sat rubbing his head. If his headache was anything like Alan's, he pitied the dwarf.

"What does this mean?" Alan said, directing his question at Master Hao. "Are you saying that I may paint things into being? Create *ex nihilo*?"

Master Hao considered. Alan knew it was not that he was uncertain, merely that he was weighing what would be right to tell him at this specific moment in time.

"Truths are truths, whether we know them or not. But once we bring truth into our consciousness, that is, out of the unconscious, then we may more wisely use the truth, no?" The old man smiled, satisfied he had provided a suitably cryptic reply that yet conveyed some keys.

"Your blood, your . . . spirit . . . may have been what painted Carcosa," Petruccio said, and there was a tone of dreadful defeat in his voice. "But it was guided by Uboth—an artist unparalleled in the history of any world—and without him, I doubt anything so spectacular can occur. I thought the pigment to be something inanimate, something I could imbibe and then control: in changing myself perhaps I would become capable of the same greatness as Uboth. But no, it is not to be."

"But you are forgetting one thing, Petruccio," LeBarron said, putting a hand of fellowship upon the dwarf's shoulder.

"What is that?"

THE DREAMS OF DEMHE

"Alan *has* changed you. He has changed us all. True, it is not so simple as drinking magical fluid or painting it upon your skin . . . But Alan has touched each of us, and we have shaped him in turn. Perhaps, all together, we might still build these worlds you dream of, might still build the future of Carcosa."

Petruccio grinned, ear to ear.

"You know, LeBarron, sometimes I think you might genuinely be wise."

The actor gave a mock bow.

"Any wisdom that leaves my lips is the wisdom of The Stranger, not I."

Alan and Cassilda's eyes met at this remark, both agreeing wordlessly to maintain their secret. There was warmth in her gaze, the terror and confusion having melted away. Alan felt that warmth invading his own soul. Yes, in some sense, everything had changed, knowing what and who he truly was. But in another sense, nothing had. Everything he'd experienced: the love, pain, triumph, and tribulation, all had been real. As Hao had said, he'd made it real. And after all, was that not the role of the senses? To make real the illusory reality of waking life, helping lost souls navigate its tunnels, before they slept forevermore, and came to know the secret, dreaming truth.

I am that which lies dreaming with you.
That which dreams does not die.
The world's magical, and so are you.

Alan knew now who the quiet, guiding voice within him was.

"Thank you, dad," he whispered.

CHAPTER 28
GATSBY

THEY GATHERED THEMSELVES, ready to continue on their journey. There was much more Alan wished to ask Master Hao, as did Petruccio, but moments after Alan had realised the true nature of the voice within him, the old man had vanished. He took with him the log and the fire, leaving the cave in shadow.

They knew he would not reappear, nor would they be able to open the secret doorway to the inner depths of Al Qaf Saba. Even Cassilda's staff would be unequal to overcome *that* magic. But they had little desire to linger. Once the mania of the revelations had calmed—Alan feeling a surreal inner peace settle into his being like a heavy dose of narcotics—their thoughts had returned again to Cali. She was likely several days ahead of them now, unless she had been held up in the desert.

Alan stood at the mouth of the cave, upon the flower-bright slopes of Al Qaf Saba. It looked for all the world as though the Emerald Mountain had been planted in the middle of a desert without end. The sky was clear, without a storm in sight. In the distance, shapes materialised in the heat-shimmer then dematerialised just as rapidly. Flickering mirages spread their colourful visages across the horizon only to melt, like snowflakes in dawn's warmth. With a start, Alan realised that these were not illusions. No, the *desert* was the illusion. Nothing could be so vast, nor so empty, save perhaps the primordial chaos preceding Creation. These shapes were the reality that lay beneath. Demhe's dreaming was coming to an end. *The peace you feel is calming the storm,* he thought. *Is this what Master Hao meant about conscious awareness?*

THE DREAMS OF DEMHE

Roland exited the cave. He gave Alan a curt nod, saying nothing, not wishing to intrude upon his moment of reflection. Alan liked that Roland respected people's boundaries, and knew the value of silence, but on this occasion, he wished to speak with someone. He had been too long locked in solipsism, with The Claw, and with fragmented parts of himself.

"How far to the lands of Blue Light?"

"The distances here aren't measured in miles," Roland said. He squinted powerful eyes. "With the desert calming as it is, perhaps the journey will be a swift one."

LeBarron exited the cave next, a bag of provisions slung over his shoulders. They had harvested what they could from the slopes of the mountain: meagre supplies for five travellers, but it would have to do.

"Those spires," LeBarron said, pointing in a direction that must have been west, though Alan had no clue how the actor had determined so. "And can you see, the light creeping through? That is Pe'kar's domain. We're close indeed, just as the mad harvester foretold."

Once more, the weight of the secret weighed heavily on Alan. Dare he tell LeBarron that he had met his precious Stranger, that he had unmasked him—albeit in a dream—and that Cassilda had sent him away forgiven, yet also utterly vanquished, a shadow of his former self? Such secrets could do no good. And even if Alan did reveal it, he would scarcely be believed.

By way of diversion from the topic, Alan approached Roland and held out the cylinder containing the tattered banner of Uboth.

"I actually think this belongs to you," Alan said. "I heard stories throughout the court of how you used it to defend Carcosa. You earned it more than I ever earned a birthright."

Roland smiled, taking the cylinder from Alan and clipping it once more to his belt.

"Birthrights are a privilege, that much is true. But they can also be a curse. I don't envy you your origins, Alan. It comes with grave responsibility."

Alan nodded.

"Let us hope I can live up to it."

Once Cassilda and Petruccio joined them, saying they were ready, the five descended the mountainside, and began their journey through what remained of Demhe. As they reached ground-level, sand crunching underneath their worn and tired feet, Alan wondered if the dream storms would sweep over them regardless. He remembered his panic as one by one he had lost sight of his companions. But after ten minutes of walking, their way still remained clear. LeBarron led them confidently towards the mirage-like image hovering over the desert he had pointed out earlier. He had described it as spires, but Alan couldn't make out such detail. They seemed more like pillars to him, or pylons. Blue light spilled from between them, then seemed to be drawn back into some unseen reservoir, as though the two towers were set into the shore of a beach, the sea water rushing up to greet them, spilling beyond the threshold, then sucked back by the tide. This gave the impression of the light winking.

"What are you laughing about?" Cassilda said. Alan hadn't realised he had been chuckling to himself. He heard playfulness in her voice, but it was forced, an attempt to plaster over a secret room—with all its fell purposes—that had been exposed by knocking through drywall.

"Gatsby," he said. "I fucking hated that book . . . But I can't help feel it's profound at the same time."

"Gatsby . . . " Cassilda said, mulling over the word. "It is a name?"

"Yes. Of one of the principle characters. A sort of tragic figure." Alan cleared his throat, pointing at the winking light in the distance, and began to quote, "'Gatsby believed in the green light, the orgastic future that year by year recedes before us. It eluded us then, but that's no matter—tomorrow we will run faster, stretch out our arms farther . . . '"

"By the Pallid Mask!" LeBarron said, interrupting what Alan had thought of as a private interaction. "You almost have the memory of a mummer, Alan."

"It's the pigment," Petruccio muttered. The dwarf had been deep in thought ever since they left the mountain. "It makes sense now. His perceptions have been altered, so he thinks he is merely parroting things he's read. But it's deeper than that. He's accessing it directly."

LeBarron frowned.

"What do you mean 'directly'?"

Petruccio paused for a long time, whilst the others—even Roland, who was pretending not to listen in—waited for his answer.

THE DREAMS OF DEMHE

"The pigment is Uboth's dream, and he is the ultimate artist, Art incarnate, we might even say. But it is more than that. For to dream, as Jung and Freud suspected, is to access a *collective* resource of human imagination. Therefore, the pigment, being this collective dreaming made flesh, knows all the archetypal forms." Petruccio's eyes darted from one to the other, finally resting on Alan. "He isn't remembering the quotes. He's speaking them organically from the dream source all poets draw from."

"An interesting theory," Cassilda said, a little archly.

Petruccio sighed.

"I suppose you are right. It is good not to become too wedded to what one thinks one knows. I shall return to pondering the many mysteries of Alan Chambers."

Once, those words might have made both Alan and Petruccio smile, but they were tinged with sadness now. Alan had denied Petruccio his deepest wish. He could tell the dwarf was fighting not to display or hold onto any resentment for that, but Alan couldn't blame him for feeling it.

"What does it mean?" Cassilda said, returning him to the moment. "The quote?" There was wonder in her voice that made Alan's heart sing. For all her power, her ancient age—something he tried not to think about, lest it intimidate him, even break his intellect—she had a strange innocence about her, something all the horrors of the world—and demons like The Stranger—had not been able to take away. In that moment, he thought she would have been a far better bearer of The Claw than he.

"Then give me to her," The Claw said. "If she has the courage to do what must be done . . . "

Alan ignored his malevolent counterpart and tried to answer her questions as best he could.

"The book is about many things, as all great works of literature are, but partly it's about the tension between past and future, between who we were and who we'd like to become. We strive after this promised land of tomorrow, but ultimately we keep being brought back to the past."

"That sounds rather bleak . . . "

"It is. Which is why I didn't like the book."

"But you said it was great. Profound, even."

Alan shrugged.

"The two are not mutually exclusive."

172

"Yes," Roland said, surprising all of them. "Look at LeBarron: I hate his guts, but I can't help but respect his shameless careerism."

They all shared a laugh at that, which is why none of them saw or heard the black, writhing shape cutting its way through the bland falseness of the desert, like wasps spilling from a gashed hive. Manifold forms dribbled onto the sand, plashed in the ichor of their own excreta. A hulking mass squeezed itself, bonelessly, through the wormhole of dreaming illusion, following the scent, not of prey, but of the one thing it desired above all.

It was upon them in seconds. If not for The Claw, screaming in Alan's ear, all might have been lost. But he wheeled, guided by his supernatural talisman, for once grateful for its cretinous voice. The beast came on—flesh, claws, bubbling eyes, orifices of profane design, faces and teeth and wombs bearing slimy, half-living fruit.

Haercus!

But he did not come for Alan, did not come directly for The Claw. There was enough intelligence left in him to realise that one threat to his being remained, and that threat had to be dealt with before he could claim his prize.

Alan launched himself, grabbing Cassilda about the waist, bearing her to the ground just as a monstrous limb swiped at her. She shrieked as she hit the ground, her staff flying from her grip, unprepared as she had been for Alan's weight.

They rose quickly, turning to face their opponent. The black staff lay at Haercus's feet. Its multiplicity of bulging eyes alighted upon the glowing artefact, and then it was scooping it up in a tangle of tentacle-like limbs. Cassilda went to step forward. Spines pushed their way through Haercus's limbs, emerging from flesh like maggots, a row of green arrowheads. With a flexing move, they shot out poisoned darts. Alan stepped in front of Cassilda and swiped them from the air with The Claw, yellow lightning incinerating whatever the metal talons missed.

"The staff!" Cassilda cried. Alan heard the desperation in her voice. And he knew that in her mind, all of Carcosa's hopes lay in that talisman, for without it, the armies of the dead slaves that currently defended the city would perish. He knew, too, that underlying such altruism was the obsession all powerful magical objects inspired in their wielders.

Alan stepped forward, intending to claim the staff back, but he was already too late. *Hope's Devourer,* a blade forged by the hand of Pe'kar—much like Alan's own Claw—descended like a lightning bolt. It cleaved the staff in twain. An explosion of magical energy rippled outward as the ruby shattered. The force lifted Alan from his feet and sent him flying across the dunes, landing with a near back-breaking thud in the sand. Stars swam across his vision. He tasted blood in his mouth. Red light played across the sky, the vestigial energies of the almighty staff erupting, unspooling, lashing, kindling new explosions of kinetic force.

But worst of all, Alan heard Cassilda's anguished scream, like a mother who had watched their child dashed upon the cruel rocks of a blustering cliff.

CHAPTER 29
SHOWDOWN

"**ON YOUR FEET!**" LeBarron said, hauling Alan upright.

Alan blinked away the lights still swarming his vision. Pain coursed through his head, shoulders, and spine. His legs felt weak beneath him.

Petruccio stood to his left, his eyes glimmering with dangerous focus. LeBarron supported Alan. Cassilda knelt before the monstrous form of Haercus, trembling, utterly mad, staring at the shattered remains of the black necromancer's staff and its deadly jewel. Nothing but dust remained of the ruby. The sand was scoured black where its disgorged magical energies had unravelled.

Roland strode towards Haercus, unclipping the cylinder containing the banner from his belt. The spear Roland had so heroically driven into Haercus's spine was still there, like the flag of some space-farer that'd conquered a hitherto unknown planet.

"Careful, Roland!" Alan called.

"You sent me to the next world, beast!" the soldier snarled. "But hell had no place for me! It waits for you!"

With a dramatic flourish worthy of LeBarron, or indeed a stage magician, Roland pulled the banner from its housing. Fell irradiance speared out in every direction, as though the banner were a gemstone, a prism, catching the sun's rays and multiplying them. Alan stared in awe at the hallowed image: The King In Yellow, enthroned, the woman bearing the Yellow Sign upon her back—perhaps the Mother to whom Hastur had alluded in Alan's brief interview with him—and a squalling, six-limbed child. Pe'kar, depicted as subservient to the true master of the black planet.

The light that shone forth from the banner could have blinded angels, yet Haercus did not recoil, did not retreat. It was true he paused, not as though the light stung him, but rather as though it had awakened a memory.

"Haercus bears the Yellow Sign," Petruccio said, desperation tinging his voice. "That will be no use here! Back away, Roland!"

The soldier cursed, throwing the banner aside and drawing his sword.

"Come then!" Roland cried. "Let us dance again."

The scorpion-tail—though in truth it was nothing so comprehensible—bearing *Hope's Devourer* whipped forward, thudding into the ground where Roland had been moments before. More limbs surged forward. Some crablike and pincered. Some lashing and tentacled. Some altogether too human. The agile warrior danced his way, cutting left and right, but wherever he cut, new growths appeared.

"We must help him," LeBarron said. "Alan, can you stand?"

Alan nodded.

Without another word, the actor drew his own scimitar and launched forward into the fray. Alan searched for Cassilda. Haercus's attention had left her now that she no longer bore the black staff. She knelt between the two shattered pieces of the wand.

"I can feel them slipping away," she wept. "Thousands of them. Slipping into nothing." She wailed. "I thought it would be a relief. It is *agony*."

Alan wanted to comfort her, to run to her, but he couldn't. Mortal danger was at hand. He'd seen enough, however, to recognise that Cassilda was not merely experiencing emotional trauma. The staff's powers had wended their way deeper into her psyche than any of them imagined, and the sudden severance had caused psychic rupture. Blood flowed down Cassilda's cheeks, weeping from her carnelian eyes.

"Alan!" Petruccio said, bringing him back to the present moment. "We charge him together?"

"Together!"

Petruccio sprinted, drawing his bright dagger. Alan was with him, holding aloft The Claw.

Haercus came to meet them, now more like many entities conjoined by some dark surgery than a single organism, pieces of him separating, scuttling towards them with chomping jaws, great gashes opening in his spine and spawning oily suckers that blindly roved toward them. Alan roared, slashing with The Claw, great waves of lightning rippling out from the weapon's path, scouring the monstrous limbs. But always whatever he destroyed regrew, not only replacing what was lost, but hydra-like dividing itself into horrifying new multiplicities.

Alan hacked, slashed, shrieked, and stomped. This was not fighting, truly, but the work of a butcher. Yet the meat he sliced apart was alive, frothing with ugly, blind life. Ribbons of flesh, cut by the five perfect talons of his deadly armament, became serpents that slithered towards him. Petruccio slashed them to pieces with his knife. But even those pieces became insects that leapt onto the dwarf, biting and stinging.

Alan ran up to Petruccio and with talons plucked the squirming little horrors from his friend and crushed them in his gauntleted fist. Petruccio nodded in thanks, already covered head to toe in gore and slime and flesh that had the qualities of too many different species.

"We can't defeat this," Alan said.

"But we can't run either," Petruccio said.

Alan heard Roland roaring as he set about him with his scimitar. The tangle of limbs about them was so thick it was like a flesh-forest; now Alan could hardly see his companions. He had entirely lost sight of LeBarron.

"We need to think of something fast," Alan said.

"I normally leave that to you!" Petruccio said. He left off speech as more violently lashing limbs surged toward them. His dagger flashed, coated—it seemed to Alan—in an aura of flame. He heard Petruccio humming faintly under his breath. The dwarf was using magic, something Alan had not truly seen him use before. *Such is the dire nature of the situation,* he thought.

"There is one thing, perhaps," Alan said. "But I need time."

Petruccio nodded instantly, and Alan felt a pang of love and humility realising how much the artist had come to trust him.

"You shall have it! Yaahh!" Petruccio let out a sharp battle cry and threw himself forward, hacking left and right, doing his best to fend the dreadful, transforming flesh from his friend.

Alan closed his eyes.

Can you hear me, Claw?

"I can always hear you, Abracadabra. I wondered when you would seek my counsel."

THE DREAMS OF DEMHE

We must defeat Haercus. Tell me how.

"And what shall you give me in return?"

Alan, though focused inward, was still dimly aware of the battle raging. He heard Petruccio's humming and intermittent shouts. The shrieking of a thousand animals as Haercus's multitude of orifices vented their frustration and hunger. He heard Roland's swordplay as he duelled *Hope's Devourer*. He heard Cassilda, still murmuring to herself, lost to the world.

Without me, you are nothing, Alan said. *Without me, you are simply an animate tool.*

"You know that is false. Though my awareness was diminished, I was fully awake as I waited out the long eons in Namtar's care . . . Yes, Abracadabra, you know of what I speak. Are not *you* also a tool, created by Uboth for the purpose of painting his grand vision? Do not be so quick to dismiss tools, for without them, even the Great Creator could not have shaped the world."

I will not betray my friends to appease your whims. I will not shed blood needlessly. Alan felt rage, his fists clenching. The battle around him seemed to mirror that anger, its intensity waxing with every precious moment Petruccio and Roland bought him. Still, the question lingered of where LeBarron had gotten to. Was he dead? Alan prayed not.

"You have no choice," The Claw said. "If you wish to kill the monster, you shall have to do as I say."

No!

"Then I will leave you to your fate, until someone stronger, someone with courage, finds me in the sands . . . " A dark laugh, like metal shrieking on whetstone. "Perhaps it shall even be my old master!"

You will not abandon me! But there was only dark silence following Alan's challenge. He called out once again, but The Claw did not answer. In fact, he could no longer feel the potent currents of energy flowing through his limbs. He could no longer feel the wreath of lighting about his fingers. The power was gone. The Claw merely inert metal at the end of his sore and aching stump.

"Alan!" Petruccio's voice, screaming.

Alan opened his eyes—and immediately felt an impact so tectonic it robbed him of the right to scream. He was lifted off his feet, but only for a moment, for the limb that had struck him, nearly shattering his ribcage entirely, was still attached, its hideous, worm's mouth suckered to his chest, its teeth imbedded deep in the skin. Up he went, then down. Slammed against the sand, pinned by the mighty worm, its lamprey teeth digging deeper and deeper. He could feel his blood flowing out of him into the limb with shocking swiftness. Haercus, draining his life essence with the thirst of a raving castaway.

He raised his right hand—The Claw—and brought it against the side of the worm, but without magical energies, without the dark sentience that powered it, it had no more effect than swinging a blunted kitchen knife into the side of thick rubber. Alan felt even his natural strength leaving him. The weight of the worm-limb alone was enough to wind him, crushing the air from his lungs, pinning him as helplessly as a mouse beneath the paw of a giant cat.

"Help . . . !" He wanted to shout, but only managed a feeble croak. Looking around, he saw Petruccio tangled in a spider's web of spongy tendrils, each ending in poisonous looking hooks that blindly found flesh. Petruccio screamed as they pulled, leveraging skin from muscle, distorting his features like some sadomasochistic ritual gone wrong. Roland was on the defensive, barely one step ahead of the awfully potent blade that had already ended his life once before.

"Alan!" He turned his head and saw Cassilda. His plight had finally awoken her from her reverie. She had drawn the dagger she kept strapped to her thigh, and slashed to and fro, trying to make her way through what seemed a tangle-wood of flesh and bone. But she would never get to him in time. The sky dimmed. Sound slipped away from him like the hush following snowfall.

And then a shadow passed over Alan. Either he was going blind, finally slipping into the next world, or else some pincer or crustaceous limb hovered overhead, about to crush his skull and spill his brains over the sands.

But it was neither.

LeBarron stood over him, though not as Alan had known the actor in times past. When he had first met LeBarron, the actor had been a chameleon, a shapeshifter in all but name, assuming the guise of a hundred different characters, including Haercus himself. After his death and resurrection, LeBarron had changed. He had perhaps become more humble, but also somehow reduced, his magnetism waning like a moon in decline. He had striven to reforge parts of his personality, to reveal the inner spirit, but it was increasingly clear LeBarron did not know who he was without a mask and a stage.

Or had not known, until now.

LeBarron looked less like a man, and more like a being of shadow. Alan had thought of LeBarron as a shadow of his former self in the negative sense, but now that shadow gained an actuation beyond absence or repression. The shadow had substance, a dark and roiling substance, like the very *prima materia* of the cosmos itself. His eyes gleamed like the twin suns. His cloak fell about him like a mantle of night. Black was the radiance that surrounded him. Black the heart that burned, visibly gleaming, at the core of his cosmic being.

And then, from that shadow, birthed flame.

The scimitar LeBarron had wielded on their countless adventures—an ordinary blade—had become not merely a torch, but fire itself, a dazzling fragment of some ember still red hot from the first moment of the universe exploding into being. LeBarron swung the blade and the worm was severed, cleaved in half, the wound soldered. Hissingly, the limb recoiled. Dreadful, drooping eyes turned upon LeBarron.

"Back you fiend!" LeBarron cried.

LeBarron stepped over Alan—who gawped, speechless and astonished—as he charged forward. Cruel tendrils surged toward the actor, but with one sweep of his blade they were incinerated, the fire blindingly bright, the heat it gave off causing perspiration to run down Alan's face.

LeBarron cut his way forward, dismembering the great beast, but unlike their efforts—where whatever was severed either regrew or birthed new horrors—his flaming sword cauterised all, stymying the wounds. Like a surgeon cutting away tumours, LeBarron plunged headlong into the writhing mass. He did not stop at fighting back the now manically assaulting limbs, but reached the gelatinous mass of Haercus's overly fecund body. He sliced, searing great slabs of festering meat from the undead carcass. His face was grimmer than a war-mask. Frightening. The dark light of his eyes fixed unblinkingly upon some invisible prize that lay behind the tumour-rot.

Mycelial appendages sprouted at LeBarron's feet. Gas spores rose from their tubular orifices. But the flame of his sword purified the air with each swing, and fungus fell before fire.

Cut, cut, cut. With each slash, LeBarron stepped deeper, tunnelling into the gross mass of Haercus's being. The monster seemed powerless to stop the warrior. Its shrieks were inhuman, the shrill panic of an insect pinned with a needle to a wall. Fire was its bane. And LeBarron wielded it without mercy.

Deep in the cavern he had now hollowed out in its disgusting flesh, something shone. At first, Alan thought his eyes must be playing tricks on him. He still felt weak with loss of blood, and it had taken him some time to extricate himself from the dead worm's slackened jaws. His chest bled profusely—and The Claw would not heal him as it normally did. But he soon realised his eyes were not deceiving him. A bright blue gemstone lay inside Haercus.

"Blue stone from the Land of Blue Light," LeBarron cried. "The work of our enemy, the Dark Master. It ends now!"

LeBarron brought his flaming sword down upon the stone. Just as the ruby had before, the stone shattered, though there was no explosion of kinetic force. Instead, a gargling sound rose up, as though every atom of the flesh were a separate being, screaming in its death throes. LeBarron fled the tunnel he'd carved, and just in time, for Haercus's impossible bulk began to collapse. Before Alan's eyes, rippling musculature turned gangrenous, then rotted, finally becoming liquid, a stinking sludge not even the endless sands were able to swallow. Everywhere he looked, Haercus was melting, his skin and eyes and mouths and teeth sloughing into nothing more than rank slime.

His mass was such that even with the rapid speed of decay, it took many minutes, while all of them watched in horror and also strange satisfaction. Eventually, only one solidity remained, a human form, curled foetally in the emulsion of liquefied tissue. For long seconds, they all stood stock-still, wondering if the human shape beneath the layer of scum would stir.

At last, it did. Gaps appeared in the thick, slaggy ooze. A single hand rose, scraping off sediment from the face of a feeble man. He looked like he had not eaten well in years. Greyness haunted his face, even though it was not overly wrinkled. Alan noted that his right hand was missing.

"My," the old man croaked. "I haven't seen with my own two eyes in . . . in such a long time."

"Haercus," Cassilda said, her eyes wide.

The old man looked at Cassilda. Then his eyes turned and

regarded LeBarron. Some of the shadowy aura had faded now, and LeBarron looked once again like a man, albeit devilishly handsome. His blade no longer wreathed with flames, but its metal was white hot, evidence that the power had been no mere illusion. Alan's brain turned over what he had just seen. Was LeBarron secretly a magic-user too? Or had Cassilda or someone else empowered him?

"I am unworthy of that name," the old man said. His eyes shifted to LeBarron. "Thou art Haercus now. Thou playest the part better than I did."

LeBarron bowed.

"Pe'kar shall pay for what he did!" Roland said, slamming his fist to his chest, the gesture of a warrior's salute.

The old man shook his head.

"Pe'kar? Oh, yes, he played his part too. But I failed—became unworthy—long before that." The old man pierced Alan with a gaze that held many meanings. Sadness, jealousy, hope, despair, all seemed to war within those ancient, tired eyes. "The Claw . . . I could no longer resist it. Could no longer bear it. I sense thou knowest of what I speak." Alan nodded, but the old man was not done. "O, even now I long for it." Tears fell down his eyes, thick as blood. His voice quivered. "Even now, after all it has taken, after all I did . . . " The old man breathed deep, let out a sigh, closing his eyes. "'Twere better that Claw was never made!"

"It was Pe'kar who made The Claw," Alan said, sadly. "The blame once again lies at his feet."

"I know that, boy!" the old man snapped, and something of his hawk-like fierceness returned, if only for a moment. "But it is not the hand that makes a tool who bears responsibility for it, but the hand who wields it!"

"You can find healing in Carcosa," Cassilda said. "Let us . . . "

"No, no," the old man said. "I have only a few moments more. I can feel it. A warrior knows. And I have no great desire to live on, not after . . . " He could not finish, screwing his eyes shut again. "Warrior . . . " He addressed LeBarron. "Take my sword. *Hope's Devourer*. If anyone has earned it, it is thee. Thou art Haercus now . . . "

With that, the man who had once been the saviour of Carcosa seemed to give in to some great internal gravity, invisible and ineffable as the laws of a black hole. Collapsing backward and inward, his whole frame surrendering, he became as grains of sand, his entire being scattered and unmade. There was a moment—the briefest flash—where Alan glimpsed his face. A smile had begun to spread over his features, a joyful radiance. Was it freedom, at last, from the psychic talons of The Claw? Freedom, at last, from the woes of addiction? Alan wished he could have asked, but the old man was no more, nothing left of him except dust, which even now was being stirred by the winds into the very sands of dreaming itself.

CHAPTER 30
THE LAND OF BLUE LIGHT

A S PE'KAR PROPHESIED, the dreaming died, and Cali was left with the starkness of a road leading out of perdition and into stranger worlds still. For moments, she held her breath, scarcely believing it was possible she had finally emerged from the labyrinth of Demhe's illusions. But the more seconds drifted by, the more she believed truly that she had risen living from the jaws of madness.

The final evidence that she stood once more upon solid ground was the presence of Satan. It was strange to be so overjoyed by the sight of such a repulsive creature. Its brutish head, sporting murderous, feline eyes, lowered as it slunk slowly toward her, a strangely affectionate greeting.

"It seems you bested the dreams before I did," Cali said, slightly unnerved by its intelligence and power. But then, gorgonopsids were Pe'kar's creatures, and the Demon King clearly had ways of traversing the dreamscape freely. *There must be a cost. The energy such a projection would require . . .* She knew the Demon King was powerful, but he was not omnipotent. Like her father, the King In Yellow, Pe'kar had limits—and secrets. Secrets which he had promised to reveal in exchange for the location of the oneiric pigment. She did not know its location, of course, but she knew of the secret temple beneath Al Qaf Saba, a temple that had evaded even Pe'kar's knowledge. He would find his answer there.

Cali reached out and placed a hand upon Satan's head, stroking the beast with great respect and sensitivity. Her smile was a rictus of hidden satisfaction. She would never reveal the temple's location to Pe'kar. He would die before she divulged that secret. If she could make him reveal the source of his divine power before she killed him, the gnosis of the serpent, then so be it. But if not, she would simply take by force whatever she could, and there would be a new Demon King . . .

"Not a Dark Lord, but a Queen," she murmured. Once again, she thought of Alan Chambers, forever ready with quotes and witticisms from another world. As much as she hated him, she missed him in that moment, wished he could be there to see how far she had come, how much she had learned, and the scope of her dizzying ambitions. She was grateful, in the end, for all he had done to her: for every deep scar he'd left upon her body. For he had taught her so much, both wittingly and unwittingly. She saw that. Without him, her plans would have failed. But now, she would succeed beyond her wildest dreams.

Satan knelt, and Cali mounted him. They rode hard down the road that had been revealed to them. In the distant west, blue light shone forth from a rend in reality, like a mouth spilling the secrets of the cosmos, the guttering foam of a madman's dying words.

Brighter and brighter the light shone. Blue, turquoise, azure, jade, a reality constructed of diaphanous gemstones, interlinked with the gluey immutability of cells. Faster and faster, she urged on her tireless steed. The gorgonopsid galloped like a cheetah, draconian scales shifting beneath her legs as the beast's rippling musculature carried her towards her ultimate goal.

Proud spires loomed. Two dark columns, so titanic as to pierce the heavens. They seemed made of dirtied stars. And beyond them, through the portal, sprawled the land of Blue Light, Pe'kar's domain. Even Cali, who had spent long ages here at one point in her life, drew in a sharp breath of awe as she passed between those daunting pylons, and saw before her the full vista of the glamorous and fatal land. Ziggurats rose in crooked alignments, aping constellations of occult power. Effigies the size of mountains stared deathlessly at the roiling skies. The ground itself was alive, with flowers raising horridly human faces to the twin suns—sunlight tinted aquamarine by the warped atmosphere of the forbidden lands. Graveyards stretched to the horizon, which was no natural vision, but rather the minarets and spires of a darkling citadel, so massive as to dwarf even the chthonic immensity of Carcosa, and which the searching light, however ardently it strived, could never touch.

It was with a shocking and powerful surge of emotion, enough to pull tears from her glittering eyes, that she realised this—this terrible and mysterious land—was her true home.

And where she would claim her everlasting throne.

EPILOGUE

THE OTHERS SLEPT fitfully by the campfire, but LeBarron had experienced enough of dreaming to last a lifetime. The time had come to wake up.

The dark called to him, and he answered. The dark was, after all, the natural home of any true actor: the shadows of the wings, where mummers exited and entered; the secret compartments that lay beneath any good stage, accessible by a magician's trapdoor; and the hidden faces that dwelt on the dark side of the soul.

He walked a little way from the bright yellow fire. Even in the depths of night, the roiling conundrum that demarcated the land of Blue Light was easily visible, shining like a lighthouse beacon. Only, unlike a lighthouse, which was designed to guide ships safely to their harbours, the land of Blue Light was a siren-light, a light designed to lure souls onto the rocks of insanity. Only those who were already mad could survive long in Pe'kar's domain. Thankfully, LeBarron had long ago left the rags of sanity behind, discarding them in favour of the sacred emptiness that made him the truest servant of The Stranger.

Soon, he found a withered tree. The desert was barren, but as they drew closer to the lands of Blue Light, life was beginning to bloom again, albeit strange life. The starlight—and the western flashes of green, blue, and colours eye-piercingly in-between—revealed gnarled faces that stared blindly out from the tree's mottled trunk.

He sat beneath the tree, cross-legged. On his lap, he laid what had once been called *Hope's Devourer,* but which he had renamed *Hope Reborn.*

"A little corny," Petruccio had said, when LeBarron first announced the name.

"The best stories are," LeBarron had replied.

THE DREAMS OF DEMHE

The weapon was a marvel: with a serrated nearside and an edge so sharp it seemed to hum, shining with a polish of venom straight from the mouth of a god. He admired it for a long while, singing softly beneath his breath. Then, he raised his hand, palm face-up, closing his eyes and visualising flame.

He felt the same quickening in his blood that he had felt as he stepped into the role of the shadow warrior, as he kindled his sword and donned the cloak of the abyss, as he dismantled Haercus, piece by bloody piece, burning away the tumorous excrement of his being, and revealing the man beneath. That had been a powerful dream. A dream of prophecy. He only wanted a small dream now. Just a little one to let him know he still had the gift.

He opened his eyes and saw, burning in his palm yet not wounding his flesh, a tiny fire, like a flickering candlelight. He smiled, and in the light shining from below, his face was unmistakeably devilish, his grin too gleaming, his eyes too deep and dark. With a concentration of will he thought about changing the colour of the fire, and before his eyes it flashed through red, orange, yellow, green, blue, indigo, and then deep purple.

"Are there limits to you?" LeBarron whispered. "Or can I . . . "

The purple flame expanded, turned white. His unconscious knew the shape he was going to form before his conscious mind did, but as it began to emerge, he smiled in pleasure and recognition. The flames began to harden, as though each point of fire were sucked in on itself, crystallised. The transubstantiation of energy into matter. The hardening of dream into reality.

He held now a beautiful, porcelain mask. The empty sockets of its eyes stared at LeBarron with intense scrutiny. Its beautiful lips—full and feminine—were pouted as if to kiss.

And kiss them he did.

Then he turned the mask around and placed it on his face.

He could be anyone, or anything.

Of course, the others assumed he was dimwitted, just a pretty face with a witty line or two but no deep intellectual aspirations. But how wrong they were. LeBarron was the only one who had realised the secret implication of Master Hao's revelation. He grinned behind his mask, a mask that was already morphing and changing, becoming a new face, a familiar face . . . Yes, LeBarron had been rather quick on the uptake, unlike the others.

If Alan's blood was magical, and that same blood now ran through LeBarron's veins as a result of the blood transfusion that had taken place in Yhtill, then he, too, held the power of the pigment. The power to reshape reality. The power to change himself into a living dream . . . Alan hadn't mastered the art yet. He was too caught up in his battle with The Claw—and with his own angst.

LeBarron had lost something great in visiting the underworld, but had found something greater in the desert. He was no longer a performer, a mere master of mimicry. Now, he could *become* the subject. In essence, he could choose his own destiny. And perhaps he did not wish to play a minor role. Perhaps he wished to play the role of the hero.

After all, who was more fitting for the part?

THE STORY WILL CONTINUE IN
BOOK FOUR:
THE COURT OF PE'KAR · · ·

THE COURT OF PE'KAR

The Fourth Book of Lost Carcosa

CHAPTER ONE
THE CHILDREN

THE SHADOW OF Pe'kar's land fell upon Alan like a great and ruinous tower. It was, according to Petruccio, night in the lands of Blue Light, though Alan found it nearly impossible to tell what was day and what was night, for the skies were forever scarred by grey, obstreperous cloud.

He knew, though the knowledge was wordless, that a terrible destiny awaited him here. The gut instinct was so powerful that he almost considered turning back. Cali could wait. She and Pe'kar would come again, and Alan and the others would be ready to defend Carcosa when they did. Why pursue her into this profane realm, where nothing seemed right, where the sky itself seemed to foam at the mouth with the same mad rage as the dying Judas.

But then he thought of all the lives lost: Eric The Courtier, the soldiers and civilians of Carcosa, the King In Yellow Himself. He thought of everything he and the others had been through to get to this point.

Cassilda had lost not only her father but also the Black Staff, her means of defending her city—and let go of her desire for revenge upon The Stranger. He couldn't imagine what that cost her.

Petruccio had risked everything to obtain knowledge of the pigment, only for that knowledge to become a wound.

LeBarron and Roland had both given their lives. Though Cassilda had brought them back, Alan knew both had lost pieces of themselves: memories, abilities, perhaps even pieces of the soul. Death left its mark on that which She could not keep.

He thought of how Cali had escaped him in Namtar's Temple, how she had also escaped the Screaming Pit. He'd no doubt she had crossed the desert successfully. On the border of Pe'kar, Roland had descried the tracks of a large gorgonopsid. It had to be her. She was resourceful beyond sanity.

If they let her go now, all was lost. She would return to Carcosa at the head of Pe'kar's legions. And this time, the city would not be able to turn her back. Alan might slay a thousand Pe'karians. Ten thousand. But it would not be enough. Cali would win. They could not allow her to obtain whatever power or influence she sought in the lands of Blue Light. They had to stop her.

Alan looked down at The Claw. It hung inert, like a dull slab of iron affixed to his arm. He could not fight the Pe'karians as he had done when the second legion lay siege to the city. Not anymore. The Claw continued to ignore him, withholding its power. But Alan knew it was more sinister than that. He sensed beneath the inactivity The Claw's hatred, mixed with an ageless cunning. The Claw waited for Alan to lower his guard, and then it would betray him. He half expected to wake up during the night with its terrible talons about his throat. He had to be careful.

"Alan . . . "

Cassilda took his hand. She looked tired—in a way he had never seen her before. He wanted to protect her, to comfort her, but he knew the only way to do that was to find and finally kill Cali.

"I can't believe we're here," he said. Overheard, the sky thundered. In the distance, strange flowers winked and shone like fallen stars. Sometimes he felt like the world had turned upside down once they passed through the pylons demarcating the lands of Blue Light. "So many whispers and legends. But we're here at last."

Cassilda nodded. "I hoped to live my life never having trodden these lands."

With a pang of deep sadness, Alan realised that only events as drastic as the capture of her mother, and the death of her father, could have compelled her here. When he had first met Cassilda, she had only just been emerging from her chrysalis, braving the world after years—no, eons—hiding away in the palace. How far she had come—it made Alan's chest swell with pride. But also, he feared a precipitous fall. Though it remained largely unspoken between them, Alan was aware Cassilda's mother dwelt in captivity somewhere in the lands of Blue Light. Roland had spoken of how the Pe'karians had paraded Camilla before the walls of Carcosa. Of course, that might have been trickery and illusion, but the soldier seemed to think not. Pe'kar had Cassilda's mother still, probably locked away in one of his dungeons, which by all accounts and the example of Haercus was a fate worse than death . . . Alan dreaded that encounter, if it ever came.

"What is that sound?" Roland said. He had a soldier's ear for danger.

Shrill and pealing, the stark cry reached their ears over the lugubrious wastes. It did not come from the West, and that unsettling horizon-line, where some ancient city sprawled like a vast monster arisen from the depths of the earth. Nor did it come from the South, where fields of demented flowers waved and sang in sibilance—for miles on end. It came from the North, where a black ziggurat reared, its stone volcanic, dark figures crawling across its steps.

"Was that . . . children?" Cassilda whispered.

The cry came again, and Alan's chest tightened. Yes, it was not the cry of a man or woman or even a beast, but children. The noise was unmistakeable, hardwired into the human brain; even those who'd never had kids of their own knew the sound and responded to it with instinct.

All of them were moving in the direction of the screams before they knew what they were doing consciously. LeBarron had drawn his sword, a dark look in his eye. He seemed to be mantled in shadow, the ghostly apparitions created by the land of Blue Light's strange atmosphere clinging to him. Yet another change had come over LeBarron in recent weeks. Alan wasn't sure exactly when it had happened, but he'd noticed it during the fight with Haercus. LeBarron had become something more, not just more than his former self, but perhaps more than a man. A god-being, armed with a sword of fire. How had he done that? From where did he draw such power? Alan did not know. Ever since Alan had obtained The Claw, he had been the protector of the group, able to wield devastating force upon their enemies, but now he felt helpless. As much as he had cursed and loathed The Claw—and its dismal promptings—now he longed to taste its power again. Perhaps this was The Claw's intent: to make Alan miss it.

Petruccio had his jewelled dagger in hand. Roland a blade. Cassilda lacked her necromantic staff, but she could still wield potent magic. Only if she were to lose her vocal chords would she be powerless. And even then, Alan doubted that the magical music she could produce derived its efficacy purely from sound. Vibration, perhaps. Or the resonating power of intent.

If Carcosa truly makes its inhabitants immortal, then you have many lifetimes to study magic here, once this is over. Then Alan laughed, correcting himself. You fool, you are already immortal, and always have been, for you are the oneiric pigment.

He still did not know what that meant. He had found no secret reserves of power within himself. The dreaming of Demhe's desert had died down once he gained conscious awareness of his identity, but that seemed about as far as Alan's magic extended. He knew it was dangerous to wait for an awakening, to assume that a point was coming in the future where enlightenment struck, a lightning bolt from heaven, and suddenly his inner strength became known to him. You had to go out and seize it. But at the same time, it was pointless stumbling around in the dark. He did not know himself, that was the truth. Much of it wasn't his fault, he had been brainwashed and encouraged to forget. Encouraged to dream . . . Yes, his fog of unknowing was the dream—and perhaps he was even now unconsciously using his oneiric magic to dream that falsehood into being?

He was tying himself in knots. Better to focus on what was at hand and do what he could. The children's voices guided them towards the black pyramid in the distance. It occurred to Alan this could well be a trick, a ploy to lure them in.

"Be careful," Alan said. "This could be an illusion or trick."

LeBarron, to Alan's surprise, laughed.

"What's funny?"

"You're learning the ways of Pe'kar far quicker than I did. Still, as a mummer, one who used to practice deception for a living, the cries sound real enough . . . "

All too soon, LeBarron's words proved prophetic, for they stumbled upon a scene that seemed drawn from a warped, Dickensian nightmare.

Children in filthy rags shuffled along a dark road, towards the ziggurat, their helpless faces either downcast or contorted in agony. The source of their pain was evident: not only the harsh and biting manacles about their ankles, throats, and wrists, which chafed to bleeding, but also the lashes of their tormentors, great hulking demons gifted with the strange physiology of Pe'kar. The crack of their thonged whips was lightning. Their faces showed expressions neither of glee nor remorse, only a terrible neutrality, like a drone office-worker bored out of their mind by the repetitious nature of their task. Could any living being become so desensitised to suffering? Alan wondered. It was a mute question, he saw it before his eyes.

"I count four," Roland said. "We are a match for them."

But there was hesitation in his voice. Unlike Pe'karian soldiers, these were true demons, or closer at least. The loomed seven and eight feet tall, their limbs overlong, with the strength and dexterity of an orangutang. Alan remembered fighting Tal'agron upon the back of the Siege Ender. There, Alan had been able to unleash near enough The Claw's full potency, and had slain both the demon and the antediluvian beast upon which they fought. Here, he would not be so lucky.

"None can survive," Petruccio said, breathlessly. "Or Pe'kar will know of our arrival."

"I suspect he already knows," Roland said.

"Enough talk," LeBarron spat. The eagerness in his eyes and voice was a flame. "On my lead, we take them!"

Without waiting for response, he leapt forward, brandishing *Hope Reborn* as though it was a lamp. And indeed, before Alan's astonished eyes light shone forth from the weapon, and the demons recoiled, blinded. *Where is he drawing such power from?* Alan thought again, jealousy twisting his heart. LeBarron always seemed greater than he. More of a man. More of a warrior. And now, more magical too.

But the demons did not stagger long, recovering themselves, and drawing Pe'karian daggers, no doubt lathered with the dreadful toxin of their master: a single kiss was death. LeBarron hesitated for a moment. Perhaps he remembered that it was

Pe'kar's bile that had undone him before. He'd been careless, overconfident then. But he seemed to find his courage, for he lunged forward again, slashing with the meteoric and magically forged weapon gifted to him by Haercus. As he did so, his blade became flame, which spread out in a fan before him. The demons hissed as it scoured their flesh, but still they came on.

Roland uttered a battle cry and threw himself forward, his humbler scimitar flashing to intercept a downward stroke. Now the battle was well and truly commenced. Cassilda raised her hands, then shrieked, but the sound was strangely faint, concentrated to a sharp point, an almost visible shimmer like an etheric javelin. This, she threw. One of the demons was launched off his feet, travelling far away from his companions and landing in the dirt, his chest caved inward, blood running over the dark earth beneath. He did not rise.

Petruccio drove his dagger into the hamstring of a demon attacking Roland. It cursed and wheeled, swinging its dagger, only narrowly cutting above the dwarf's head. Petruccio grinned mischievously. His height had saved him. He drove the dagger forward again, this time into the demon's groin. Before the howl of agony had even left the demon's lips, Roland took its head off with a two-handed blow that could have shattered an anvil. LeBarron fought with two demons, their whips and daggers flashing. But somehow, though the whips were many headed, and though their daggers moved with inhuman speed, LeBarron was always one step ahead, seeming to phase in and out of existence, to flicker like the shadows cast by a burning candlewick.

And then with two bright explosions of fire, scarring the eye, both demons fell, bearing wounds issuing hissing smoke, already beginning to cauterise.

LeBarron stood over the two corpses, a triumphant madness upon his face.

"O I love this skin," he whispered.

"LeBarron."

He turned to face Alan. When their eyes met, Alan saw someone else looking back at him from the braggadocios friend he'd known. He saw a gleaming shadow-man, a demigod whose mind he did not know.

"You risked us all."

"I risked nothing," he said. "If Haercus is no match for me, then these were as rodents. He entrusted his blade to me." The sword seemed to wink felly, its serrated to chatter with laughter. "I am the bearer of Hope Reborn."

"Pride cometh before the fall," Cassilda said, moving up beside Alan.

"Pride?" LeBarron sneered. "False modesty is the greater sin." The actor's expression softened. "I have you to thank, Alan. In so many ways. You told me to be me; it took me a while to figure out what that meant. But I have found myself. Truly and surely." He bowed, and though Alan looked for irreverence and mockery, he didn't find any. He finally chuckled.

"What's funny?" LeBarron said, aping Alan's intonation when he had asked not long before.

"We went into Al Qaf Saba to find out who *I* was. But it seems we found out who you were instead."

LeBarron grinned.

"Yes. Isn't that the way of any good play? Subvert your audience's expectations."

"When you are done posturing," Petruccio said. "What shall we do with them?" He pointed to the children, who were frozen in terror. They could hardly flee at any pace, manacled as they were. Yet, they clearly feared their wouldbe liberators just as much as their previous tormentors.

"These are Carcosan children," Cassilda said.

"How else might Pe'kar's eunuchs maintain their ranks?" LeBarron replied, darkly.

"Surely the officials of Carcosa would notice this many children being taken?" Alan could not disguise his horror.

Cassilda bit her lip, her eyes conveying a harrowing guilt.

"The city numbers in the millions, Alan. The billions, even. The number changes day by day. And yet the city itself *never* changes . . . This is not your world, Alan, where people are counted in census. This is a world with rather more chaos in it."

Alan turned away from her, sick to his stomach. Pe'kar's ways were evil, of that there was no doubt. But how was Carcosa any better in its negligence? One other thing she'd said bothered him. *This is not your world, Alan.* But according to Master Hao, it *was* his world; he had been born in Al Qaf Saba, in Demhe. Was this the truth he had been avoiding ever since the cave, then? That he didn't really belong anywhere?

THE COURT OF PE'KAR

"What should we do with them?" Petruccio asked again.

"Free them, of course," Cassilda said.

But when they had destroyed the manacles, which in the end could only be undone with Cassilda's magic, the children stood, whimpering and afraid, not knowing where to go, nor what to do.

Join Blood Bound Books
Newsletter for updates and
receive 20% off your next order at
www.BloodBoundBooks.com

ACKNOWLEDGEMENTS

I would like to thank the incredible author Steve Stred from the bottom of my heart. His amazing reviews of books 1 and 2 gave me the courage to keep going, and to keep believing in this series. Steve has been a constant companion on the writing road, and someone whom I constantly look up to. His grace, generosity of spirit, and work ethic set him apart.

I would also like to thank S. C. Mendes, Joe Spagnola, and the rest of the Blood Bound squad for their continual belief in and dedication to Lost Carcosa.

A special mention goes out to Murray Samuelson at Monster Library for his phenomenally insightful reviews, and also for introducing me to the Averoigne Chronicles of Clark Ashton Smith.

And lastly, I would like to thank the writers of the Let's Get Published mastermind for their continual support of my writing and this series.

ABOUT THE AUTHOR

Joseph Sale writes dark fantasy and epic poetry. He has authored more than ten novels. He grew up in the Lovecraftian seaside town of Bournemouth.

His short fiction has appeared in *Tales from the Shadow Booth*, edited by Dan Coxon, as well as in *Idle Ink, Silver Blade, Fiction Vortex, Nonbinary Review, Edgar Allan Poet* and *Storgy Magazine*. His stories have also appeared in anthologies such as *Blood Bank* (Blood Bound Books), *Lost Voices* (The Writing Collective), *Technological Horror* (Dark Hall Press), *Burnt Fur* (Blood Bound Books) and *Exit Earth* (Storgy) alongside writers such as Richard Thomas and Neil Gaiman. In 2017 he was nominated for The Guardian's 'Not The Booker' prize.

You can chat with him on Twitter @josephwordsmith, or, if you want to go deeper down the rabbit hole, you can sign up to his newsletter for a free eBook novella: http://themindflayer.com

www.ingramcontent.com/pod-product-compliance
Lightning Source LLC
Chambersburg PA
CBHW032123170626
46808CB00006B/2083